When It Truly Matters

Sheri Abild

Published by Sunny Love Stories LLC

ISBN: 978-1-960181-04-6 (paperback)

ISBN: 978-1-960181-05-3 (e-book)

Dedication

♥

This second story in the Perky Sisters Series
is dedicated to all of the parents and
grandparents who are raising their boys
to be polite and respectful men.

You have my unending gratitude.
The world needs more influences like you.

Chapter 1

♥

"Oh my God, Abbie," my sister breathed. "Look at him."

We stood in stunned silence as we watched four men approaching us. An older gentleman led the way while three additional men walked abreast a few steps behind. A couple inches taller than the other three, with thick, gray hair and silver glasses, his face was stone cold and devoid of emotion. Dressed in a meticulously tailored charcoal-gray suit, white shirt, and light-blue tie, silver cufflinks glistened at his wrists.

My heart raced faster as they advanced, my eyes glued to the man obviously in control. Madison told us he owns every room he walks into, and she wasn't kidding. Shrouded in a commanding presence, if our dad were here, I know he'd be standing at attention, saluting this man.

Suddenly, as he got closer, I noticed something that calmed my nerves, and I felt a wave of fondness for this man. A simple gold band on his left hand caught my eye as his arms swung back and forth with every stride. Even though his wife has been deceased for twenty years, he still wears his wedding ring—a symbol of his unending devotion to the woman he loves.

As he made his way through the room, every employee sat silently at their desks—so quiet you could hear a pin drop. Still unsure which version of him I was about to see, my nerves picked back up as he got closer, his imposing force emanating throughout the room. Finally, he arrived right in front of Sarah and me, stopping a foot before us.

As he now stood right in front of me, I got a true sense of his larger-than-life presence. My eyes followed what seemed like the trunk of a massive tree, spanning broad shoulders, and finally stopped at his face. He looked back and forth between the two of us, his piercing blue eyes evaluating my sister and me. And while his eyes are the same shade of blue as Archie's, that's all they have in common. Where Archie's eyes have a kindness, a gentleness to them, his grandfather's eyes have a way of keeping you in your place, making you know right off that he's the one in charge.

I glanced at my boyfriend, now standing to his grandfather's left—with Archie next to him and John to his father's right. Neil's calm, gentle smile eased the tension holding me in my tracks, and I exhaled my nervousness. Then I looked at Archie. His ever-present bright smile illuminated his entire face, making me laugh slightly on the inside. Next, my eyes traveled to John, who looked as calm as ever, and I was so grateful all three of them were here for this. Finally, my gaze returned to the man towering in front of me to see his focus was now on my sister.

"You must be Sarah." He extended his hand to her. "Cornelius Rutherford." Yikes! As if their voices couldn't get any deeper, this Rutherford had the deepest voice out of all of them.

"It's so nice to meet you finally, Mr. Rutherford," my sister said as she shook his hand. "Abbie and I are so grateful for all of the decorating jobs you've given us."

"Thank you for agreeing to decorate the office for me." He pulled his eyes from her long enough to look around, then his focus returned to her. "The two of you continue to impress me with your diverse decorating skills. This place looks professional, while the resort looks inviting."

I looked at my sister to see her beaming with pride. "Thank you, Mr. Rutherford. And thank you for trusting us to pick everything out. It means a lot to Abbie and me that you have so much faith in us."

"You're welcome, Sarah," he acknowledged her, his facial expression barely changing. "You and your sister have proven your character, and something like that does not go unnoticed with me."

Then, his focus switched to me. He silently studied my face for what I'm sure was just a few seconds, but it felt like an eternity. The intensity in his eyes made my nerves pick up again, and my gaze switched to my boyfriend. His calm smile was still on his face, once again putting me at ease. I took a deep, confident breath and returned my focus to the man in front of me.

"It's a pleasure to meet you, Abbie," he said, extending his hand to me. "Cornelius Rutherford."

"It's wonderful to meet you too, Mr. Rutherford," I replied graciously. "Like my sister said, we are truly honored that you put so much of your trust in us."

His face softened slightly as he looked at me. "The last time this place was decorated was fifty years ago. I've known for several years now that the décor should be updated, but I needed the right people to entrust with the job." He looked back and forth between the two of us. "So, thank you, ladies, for agreeing to help me."

Sarah and I smiled proudly at each other. We looked at him as she replied, "You're welcome, Mr. Rutherford. We're happy to help."

Then his focus zeroed in on me, his blue eyes sharp with patriarchal authority. "And I trust my grandson has been treating you well?"

I smiled at Neil, then looked at his grandfather and answered, "I promise you, Mr. Rutherford, Neil has been a perfect gentleman to me this entire time. All while we were decorating the resort and especially since we've been dating."

Mr. Rutherford's focus switched to his grandson. Feeling his authoritative glare, Neil's eyes moved to his grandfather, his expression becoming serious.

"And what about when you met Abbie's parents?" the older Rutherford asked. "Did you look her father in the eye and address him formally?"

"Yes, Grandpa," he answered, looking his grandfather square in the eye.

"And you showed him the utmost respect as you told him about your intentions with his daughter?"

"Yes, Grandpa," he repeated.

Mr. Rutherford's focus stayed on his grandson for a moment; then, his eyes switched to me. "What did your parents think of Neil?"

A smile spread across my face as I thought about my parents instantly welcoming my boyfriend. I glanced at Neil, then looked at his grandfather and answered, "Both of my parents love him, sir."

"I was there, Mr. Rutherford," my sister jumped in, making his attention turn to her. "When Abbie first introduced Neil to our parents, they were stunned. They cannot get over how polite and respectful he is."

As my sister spoke to him, I noticed how easy it seemed for her to look him in the eye. His focus stayed on her for an additional moment before returning to me.

"I guarantee you, Mr. Rutherford, your grandson is the best boyfriend I have ever had. I haven't exactly dated the nicest guys in the past, and Neil is nothing like any of them."

His facial expression changed slightly. "How do you mean?"

"Oh, you know...," I said, looking away nervously. After a moment, I forced myself to look at him. His blue eyes were staring intently at me—waiting for an answer. "The typical things a lot of guys do." His eyes continued to bore through me, and after a second, I glanced away again. *It is impossible to maintain eye contact with this man,* I thought, still feeling his eyes on me.

"I'll tell you, Mr. Rutherford," my sister very willingly offered to help.

A feeling of dread instantly came over me. Considering the guys I've dated mixed with my sister's complete lack of a filter, I can only imagine what she's going to tell him. I barely glanced at Mr. Rutherford to see him still intently focused on me. His attention was pulled to my sister as she started speaking.

"Abbie's been dating jerks since high school, starting with the first guy she brought home to meet our parents. He made a memorable first impression when he told them that his favorite TV show was 'I Dream of Jeannie' because Barbara Eden called Larry Hagman '*Master.*' Ugh." She rolled her eyes. "He was only a teenager and already a misogynist."

I glanced at Neil and shrugged. At least she's starting with one of the tamer ones.

"But her taste in men didn't get any better for years, Mr. Rutherford," my sister continued. "There was this one guy she dated about a year after we moved to Milford. His apartment was an hour away from his work, and where we live was only a half hour. So, he stayed with Abbie during the week but was nowhere to be seen on the weekends—until Sunday night."

My sister glared at me. "I told you he was just using you for a place to stay." Her focus returned to the man in front of us, and she continued, "My sister is way too trusting, and I guess she was hoping it wasn't true. We had just moved into separate apartments, and I had to go back to my place. I couldn't stand to watch him take advantage of her like that. And then what do you know?" She looked at me with raised eyebrows and crossed her arms. "As soon as he found an apartment five minutes from his work, he dumped you like a hot potato."

The entire time my sister was talking, I looked at either her or the floor. I glanced at Neil again to see an expression of sadness on his face, hurt that someone had treated me so horribly. Then I looked from Archie to John and noticed their feelings matched Neil's. Finally, I barely glanced at his grandfather to see his expression was totally different. Where the other three seemed compassionate, his face was full of anger. I looked at my boyfriend again with an even smaller, hopeless shrug. Everyone's eyes switched to my sister as she resumed speaking.

"But the worst guy, Mr. Rutherford, was the jerk she dated her senior year of college."

Uh-oh. My heart sped up as panic instantly flooded me. I know who she's talking about. "Sarah," I whispered, discreetly tapping her to get her attention before she could elaborate.

She apparently didn't get the hint because she continued, "Mr. Rutherford, I hated that guy, and I never even met him."

"Sarah," I whispered a little louder, glancing between all four men—who were now focused on me.

"And our parents never met him either. When Abbie told me that he refused to meet our mom and dad, that's when I knew he was just using my sister for—"

"Sarah!" I yelled at her, my eyes bulging as I glared daggers at her.

Now realizing exactly what she was saying—and how it made me feel—her expression completely changed. The anger that was on her face as she talked about my past relationships suddenly turned to remorse.

"I'm sorry, Abbie," she said quietly, her tone full of heartbreak.

I closed my eyes and inhaled sharply, trying my hardest to fight back the tears stinging my eyes. I cannot believe my sister. To tell Neil's grandfather that I was used for a place to stay was bad enough. But to tell him that a man used me for sex? I wanted to crawl under one of the desks and cry.

Suddenly, I felt a hand squeeze mine. "I really am sorry, Abbie," my sister gently whispered, and I knew she genuinely meant it.

I squeezed her hand in return, our secret, unspoken language of apology and forgiveness. "It's okay, Sarah," I whispered, still fighting back the tears. "It's all true."

And that's what bothers me the most. It's not that Neil's grandfather—and all their employees, for that matter—know I was taken advantage of by several men. It's the fact that it happened. I have let so many men use me and mistreat me, giving all of them the benefit of the doubt.

I felt a gentle hand slide around my shoulder, and I opened my eyes to see my sweet boyfriend standing by my side. His expression was so soft, so caring as he looked at me. As he lovingly wiped away the tears that had managed to escape, I realized all those other guys no longer mattered. I had found a truly great man, and the only thing I cared about was him and our future. I kissed his hand and held it as I turned to his grandfather.

"So, as you just heard, Mr. Rutherford, I have not dated the nicest guys. But I assure you, sir, your grandson is nothing like any of them. He is so kind and so patient, and he sees my value—as a person and especially as a woman." I smiled at my boyfriend, then turned to his grandfather. "And I want to thank you, Mr. Rutherford."

For the first time, his facial expression changed significantly. His stone-cold face switched to an expression of stunned gratitude. He blinked at me several times, then looked from his grandson to his son. When his focus finally returned to me, he said with genuine appreciation,

"Thank you, Abbie." As he continued to study my face, he inquired, "May I ask what you're thanking me for specifically?"

I smiled at my boyfriend again, then focused on the man in front of me. "Neil says that your strict discipline is the reason why he treats me so well. But it's more than just that." A warmth spread through me as I thought about the second picture in John and Helen's hallway. "He said the example you set for him shaped him into the man he is today, and you set a perfect example for him as a man and especially as a husband."

I smiled at my boyfriend again, my gratitude deepening. Then I looked at the person responsible for this amazing man and continued, "So thank you, Mr. Rutherford. It's because of you, John, and Helen that my boyfriend is so good to me, and I need you to know how grateful I am."

He silently blinked at me several more times, still processing everything. His face softened as pride mixed with gratitude took over his features. "Thank you, Abbie. There is nothing that pleases me more than to hear people talk nicely about my boys—especially a young lady who is dating one of them. And to have you thank me for the way Neil treats you..." His face softened even further. "That means more to me than you know."

He was silent for a moment, looking back and forth between Neil and me. Then, a surprising thing happened. His sharp blue eyes relaxed, and his entire face lit up into a bright smile. He pulled his focus from us and looked at his son.

"John?"

"Yes, Dad?" John's focus switched to his father, and his eyes brightened at seeing the unusual expression.

"Do you remember the first time you brought Helen home to meet your mother and me?"

"I still remember the first time I saw Helen." A peaceful look came over his face as he closed his eyes and sighed contentedly. He opened his eyes and met his father's, then turned his attention to the rest of us.

"It was six months after we had graduated college, and I was at a fundraising event with a friend. I noticed Helen immediately. She was wearing a black dress and heels, and she looked so elegant in her pearls." He stopped for a moment and laughed gently. "It took me two hours to get up the courage to go over and speak to her."

He looked at his father. "I had already taken the lead on several tough negotiations, which all seemed like a breeze at that moment. Facing business owners who weren't ready to budge was a walk in the park compared to approaching such a pretty lady." He laughed again and shook his head as his focus traveled around through all of us.

"I finally got the kick in the pants that I needed when my friend said, 'I'm giving you five more minutes, Rutherford. Then I'm going to go talk to her myself.'" He shook his head again with an amused expression.

"Four-and-a-half minutes later, I was sweating bullets as I walked across that room." His eyes had a far-off look to them as he relived the memory. "And I knew, as soon as I spoke to her, that Helen was the girl for me."

His focus returned to his father as he concluded, "And I couldn't wait to bring her home and introduce her to you and Mom."

Mr. Rutherford smiled at his son. "I remember meeting Helen. She was so poised and beautiful and even more lovely than you had described her. She was the third girlfriend you brought home to meet your mother and me, and I instantly knew she was different." His focus switched to Neil and me, and he smiled at us for a long moment, then looked at his son again. "And do you remember what I told Helen to call me?"

John glanced at Neil, then turned back to his father. "You told her to call you Dad."

"That's right," Mr. Rutherford confirmed. His face softened even more as he continued, "Your mother was so warm and welcoming to the other two girls you dated, telling each one to call her Mom. But I knew there would only be one young lady I would ever tell to call me Dad. And that would be the young lady I knew you would marry. And I knew the moment I saw you and Helen together that I was looking at my future daughter-in-law. There was something special in the way you looked at her. And even your voice sounded different as you talked about her."

Mr. Rutherford's attention returned to Neil and me, his eyes full of love and acceptance as he looked at us together. His face softened even further as he said, "And I heard that same tone in Neil's voice when he called me a few months ago and told me that a pretty girl named Abbie had spilled her coffee all over him, and he wanted to give her the decorating job at the resort. And now, seeing you together, I can see how much the two of you mean to each other." His focus switched to just me, his face brightening as he continued, "And that is why, Abbie, I want you to call me Grandpa."

"Aww," one of the female employees voiced her admiration. I looked over just in time to see one of her co-workers yank her arm and pull her down below her cubby. I just now realized that every employee's focus was on us—their bright faces barely visible above their cubicles.

I turned to my boyfriend to see that his expression matched mine. There was a hint of amusement in his eyes from his employee's reaction, but we agreed with her sentiment. I felt so special, so accepted to hear his grandfather say this, and I knew Neil felt it, too. We turned to the man in front of us as Neil said, "Thank you, Grandpa."

My focus switched from Grandpa to John, his face beaming with pride as he looked at his son. Curious to see someone else's reaction, my eyes moved to Archie. His ever-present smile brightened his entire face, and I knew he couldn't be happier for his brother and me. Then, my focus returned to the man in front of me.

"Thank you, Grandpa," I repeated my boyfriend's words. I felt honored as I looked at this man—my fondness for him deepening. I'm guessing this is the first time this has ever happened—and I couldn't believe it. I was wondering which version of him I would get to see, and it turns out I got my very own version. The grandfatherly version. And the longer I looked at him, the more reality sank in. He sees the same thing in Neil and me that he saw with John and Helen all those years ago. And he heard the same tone in Neil's voice the first morning we met. I pulled my focus from him to smile at my boyfriend—his eyes full of dreams for the future. Then I turned back to Grandpa as I heard his voice.

"You're welcome, Abbie." He smiled affectionately at me. "Hearing you call me Grandpa feels very natural. And honestly, I see no other option. Just like Helen all those years ago, it would not feel right to have you call me Mr. Rutherford. And the only person who has ever called me Cornelius was my late wife, Eleanor. Even my parents and sister never call me by my real name. I am eighty-three years old, and to this day, my sister still calls me Junior."

This got a laugh out of my sister, which she abruptly cut off. "I'm sorry, Mr. Rutherford."

He smiled gently at her. "That's quite all right, Sarah. In fact, I think the two of you would really like my sister." He thought for a second, then added, "But then again, everybody who meets my sister falls instantly in love with her."

His focus switched to his grandsons. "Why don't you boys bring Abbie and Sarah by my place this weekend so they can meet your Aunt Dottie for themselves."

"Yes, Grandpa," they answered as they smiled at each other.

Grandpa gazed around the room, observing the work we've done so far. His focus settled on a window we hadn't gotten to yet—the old, outdated curtains happily soaking up the late-morning sunshine. His eyes lingered there for a moment, an expression of nostalgia mixed with longing taking over his features.

Finally, he looked at Sarah and me, his blue eyes easing to a look of peace, and he was quiet for a few more seconds. When he spoke, his voice was gentle. "And if you ladies would be so kind to help me, I have one more, very special decorating project for you."

Sarah and I smiled at each other. Another decorating project? We looked at him, and she answered, "Of course, Mr. Rutherford. We would be happy to help you."

"Thank you," he answered, the gentleness still on his face as he looked at us.

After a moment, his focus switched—along with his facial expression. His strict, patriarchal, man-in-control presence that he walked in here with returned as he looked at his son and grandsons. Every employee immediately sensed the change in mood and quickly scattered back to their seats, no one saying a word.

"Right now, you three, it's back to work. We have a lot to go over regarding the Sutherland acquisition, and I want all of you in the conference room in twenty minutes."

"Yes, Dad. Yes, Grandpa," they all answered.

Then Grandpa's attention zeroed in on his younger grandson. "Archie."

His ever-present smile disappeared as he regarded his grandfather seriously. "Yes, Grandpa?"

"Now that your brother has a steady girlfriend, I want him out of here early from now on. Just like how I insisted your father was home for supper every night while you boys were growing up. So, I'm putting you in charge of this project." His expression became even more commanding as he firmly stated, "I trust you can handle it?"

A proud smile spread across Archie's face as he stood up straighter and answered confidently, "Yes, Grandpa."

"Good. That's what I thought." He continued to look at his grandson until Archie glanced away. Then he turned to his son. "But first, John, you're coming with me to my office. The two of us have a very important phone call to make."

"Yes, Dad," he answered.

He turned to his grandsons and stated authoritatively, "I expect to see you boys in that conference room, ready to go, by the time your father and I get there."

"Yes, Grandpa," they answered.

John smiled proudly at his sons, then put his arm around his father's shoulders as the two men turned and exited the room.

As soon as they were gone, excited chatter erupted amongst the employees. They all smiled at us over their cubicles, so happy for us and everything that had just happened.

"Congratulations, Abbie," Archie beamed at me. "You just won over Cornelius Rutherford in a matter of a few minutes. That's a new record!"

I looked at my boyfriend's glowing face. "So, he's never done anything like that before?" I asked him.

Neil ran his fingers through my hair. "You're the first girl either one of us has ever dated that he's spoken to like that. Or smiled at, for that matter."

"See, Abs," my sister said. "I knew all the Rutherfords would love you."

I smiled at her. "Thanks, Sarah."

She glanced away briefly, still remorseful for spilling the beans about my dating history. Then she looked at me with a slight smile and apologized, "And I really am sorry about embarrassing you like that."

I pulled her in for a hug. "It's okay, Sarah. All you did was tell the truth." I gave her a final squeeze, then let her go with a smile. I redirected that smile at my boyfriend. "Besides, none of those guys mean anything to me anymore."

Neil's face softened to a caring expression. "I'm sorry about all those guys, Abbie."

Looking at my boyfriend's sweet face, I realized how fortunate I truly am. "Thank you," I said, taking his hand and intertwining our fingers. "But I guess, in some ways, I'm maybe a little grateful for them. After being mistreated by so many guys, they make me genuinely appreciate a great man even more. They remind me to never take a wonderful man for granted."

He smiled fondly at me. "And that's one more thing I love about you, Abbie Perkins. You continue to amaze me with your positivity and gratitude." His smile softened even more as he gazed at me. "And I appreciate you too." I was lost in my boyfriend's gorgeous brown eyes when my sister's voice pulled me back to reality.

"And congratulations to you too, Archie." She looked at him with a beaming smile. "Your grandfather is putting you in charge of this new project. That must feel great."

"Thanks, Sarah," he accepted her praise. His smile grew brighter as he looked at his brother and me. "But you heard Grandpa. He wants Neil out of here early every night so he can spend more time with Abbie."

"That's just an excuse, Archie," Neil said as he smiled proudly at his brother.

Archie's bright smile turned to a look of confusion. "What do you mean?"

"Grandpa has wanted to put you in charge of a project for the last six years. He's just been waiting to see some sort of maturity out of you to know you're responsible enough to handle it. That's really why I told him you had cleaned your car and apartment. I hoped that would give him the proof he needed to trust you to take the lead on an important deal." He smiled at his brother. "And it worked."

Archie's bright smile returned as he looked at Sarah and me. "My brother always knows the right things to say. Especially when it comes to Grandpa." He looked at his best friend. "So, thanks, Neil."

"You're welcome, Arch."

Archie's smile glowed even brighter as he turned to Sarah and me. "Wait until you meet Aunt Dottie this weekend. You are going to adore her!"

Neil smiled at me. "And I know she's excited to meet you. I've told her all about how sweet and beautiful you are." He held my gaze for another moment, his smile softening. "Then all the important people in my life will officially know how remarkable my girlfriend is."

"And we'll get to see what Grandpa wants Abbie and Sarah's help with," Archie commented to his brother.

"Now I'm really intrigued!" my sister said with an excited smile.

"Me too," I agreed. I smiled at my boyfriend as I took his hands. "And it was wonderful meeting your grandfather." A wave of love flooded me as I thought about him telling me to call him Grandpa. My smile brightened even more as I realized, "And he's my grandfather now, too. And I love how that feels."

"I love it, too," my boyfriend whispered in my ear as he kissed me on the cheek. He smiled at me affectionately for a long moment. Then his eyes moved to the clock on the wall. "We should get going now." He grinned at his brother. "We can't have the man in charge showing up late to his first meeting."

Archie laughed. "Good point." He smiled at my sister. "I'll see you later, Sarah."

"See you this weekend, Archie," she replied, her expression matching his.

"And I'll see you tonight," Neil said with a playful wink.

"I'm looking forward to it," I happily confirmed.

Sarah and I watched as the two brothers left the room. Then we turned around to discover that we had been swarmed by excited employees. None of them could believe the change in their boss. They were all elated to see a softer, gentler side of the stoic disciplinarian. It was quite some time before my sister and I returned to our decorating—everyone congratulating me on being welcomed by the family patriarch. Once again, I felt perfect after meeting another member of Neil's family who so willingly accepted me with open arms. I can only imagine what meeting his sister will be like...

Chapter 2

♥

"I CAN'T WAIT TO show Aunt Dottie a funny video I found online this morning," Archie said excitedly as his brother pulled into a driveway on Saturday morning.

Neil drove up to the three-car garage and parked between a large van and a Cadillac. No sooner had he turned off the engine, and his brother unbuckled his seatbelt and jumped out of the seat behind him. The three of us got out of the car as Archie ran toward the front door.

"Aunt Dottie is Archie's favorite person, if you couldn't tell," Neil commented with a laugh.

As Archie got to the door, it opened. "Hi, Grandpa," he said as he ran past his grandfather.

"She's in the library," he said, watching the flash of excitement run past him.

"Oh my God, Abbie," Sarah breathed as she looked at his house. "Can you believe this place?"

"I know," I agreed, looking at the magnificent home before me. "And I thought John and Helen's house was incredible."

We stared wide-eyed at the Tudor-style home that seemed to go on forever. The two-story house rose to a steep roofline with three front-facing gables and two prominent chimneys. Several large groupings of tall, narrow windows with diamond-shaped panes decorated the house, with a large wooden front door off to the left. As I walked closer, I marveled at the intricate stonework, accented with half-timber framing—the dark beams contrasting beautifully with the white stucco. The sprawling grounds surrounding the home were perfectly manicured with trees and shrubs. Chrysanthemum bushes full of yellow and orange blossoms added a cheerful pop of color to the crisp autumn air. Neil intertwined his fingers with mine and led me up the ramp to the man waiting for us in the doorway.

Dressed in dark-blue pants, a light-blue button-down shirt, and a navy-blue cardigan, he greeted us as we approached the threshold. "Abbie, Sarah, thank you for coming this morning."

"Thanks for inviting us, Mr. Rutherford," my sister replied with a cheerful smile.

We stepped inside, and I looked sideways at my sister as we surveyed his home. An open staircase with a mahogany railing led to the second floor while an exquisite chandelier sparkled against the towering ceiling. The ivory walls, mixed with the morning sunshine, brightened up the entryway. The entire space was finished with mahogany crown molding—the dark accent perfectly complementing the light-colored walls. I must admit, his home isn't what I expected. After listening to Neil talk about his grandfather's love of mahogany paneling, I was expecting to see it everywhere. As my eyes traveled around through antique side tables and walnut flooring, they stopped when a picture caught my attention.

I went over to get a closer look and realized it was his wedding picture. My heart flooded with love as I marveled at the image of a happy young couple gazing lovingly at each other. Taken several decades ago, Grandpa was dressed in a light-gray suit, his hair the same shade of brown as Archie's. His entire face was lit up as he looked at his beautiful bride, whose hands he held clutched to his chest. Slender and petite, and at least a foot shorter than him, she was dressed in a simple white gown with her hair in a ponytail. Her only accessory was a dainty gold bracelet on her left wrist designed with open hearts alternating with diamonds. Her face glowed with happiness as she gazed at her new husband. Even with just their side profiles visible, the love between them was obvious as they looked at each other and held one another's hands. Lost in my own little world, my sister's voice next to me pulled me back to reality.

"Mr. Rutherford, your wife is so pretty."

"Thank you, Sarah," he replied.

I felt an arm slide around my shoulders and realized everybody was standing in front of the picture with me. I turned to see my boyfriend smiling at me; his face lit up with the same happiness as his grandparents.

"And you look so young and happy," my sister continued. She was still focused on the picture, intently studying his face.

"This was the happiest day of my life," he replied, his face soft as he gazed fondly at the image of his wife.

"You weren't kidding, Abbie." Sarah's attention switched to Grandpa as she observed, "You look like a completely different man, Mr. Rutherford, when you're looking at your wife."

His focus switched from the picture to my sister as he said, "You're not the first person to say that, Sarah. My sister was the first one to see me looking at a pretty young waitress in a diner on Easter Sunday fifty-three years ago." He looked at the picture again, his face so full of love. "Dottie was shocked when she saw me looking at Eleanor—she didn't even recognize me." As he continued admiring the picture, his expression switched to longing for the woman he lost. Eventually, he turned to Sarah and me. "So, would you girls like to meet my sister?"

The two of us smiled at each other as she answered, "We would love to."

Neil took my hand, and we followed his grandfather through a large, sun-filled room arranged with antique furniture and lighting. The walnut floors extended into the room, with matching beams on the ceiling. I marveled at the old-world charm of his home, especially the fireplace. Decorated with an ornate walnut mantle, the slate hearth had some ashes on it, suggesting it was recently used. My heart swelled with love for the couple who made this house their home when I noticed another picture from their wedding day hanging above the fireplace. In a more candid shot, a carefree young bride was laughing as her new husband smiled fondly at her. I envisioned the two of them spending many romantic evenings in here together, enjoying the intimacy of a crackling fire.

We stepped into the next room, set up with four oversized, dark-brown leather chairs. Even bigger than the previous room, walnut flooring continued into this space, and a large, dark-blue oriental rug sat in the middle. Floral wallpaper decorated the walls, and the sunshine streaming in through the windows brightened the entire room. Two large bookcases lined the wall across from the windows, full of leatherbound books. A closed door framed with intricately carved walnut separated the two bookcases.

Sitting in one of the chairs, a brunette in her mid-thirties, dressed in jeans and a dark-purple sweater, was engrossed in a book. My focus shifted, and a smile spread across my face as I watched two people laughing at a video. Archie stood behind an older lady in a wheelchair, leaning down so his face was right next to hers. A dark-blue dress looked beautiful on the lady's slim frame, and her wavy, shoulder-length gray hair was accessorized with a silver barrette. Her brown eyes danced with amusement behind her tortoiseshell glasses, and my smile grew as I watched them together. She lifted her left hand to touch Archie's phone, and her bright-pink fingernails caught my attention. In just these first few moments of observation, she seemed nothing like her brother.

Sensing us there, Archie stood up quickly, putting his phone away as he noticed his grandfather. The lady's expression instantly changed—her laughter stopping as she glared at her brother, her expression clearly telling him to be nice. Then her focus shifted, and her entire face brightened when she noticed Sarah and me.

Grandpa led us over to her and said, "Abbie, Sarah, I would like you to meet my sister, Mrs. Dorothy Buchanan."

I extended my hand to her with a friendly smile. "It's nice to meet you, Mrs. Buchanan."

Her smile vanished as she looked at my hand with disapproval. Her focus traveled back up to my face, and she stated with mock sternness, "Put that hand away and save that formal nonsense for my old coot of a brother!" Her smile returned as she declared, "Both of you are to call me Aunt Dottie." She lifted her left arm and said, "Now get over here and give your new auntie a hug and a kiss."

My smile matched hers as I leaned down and hugged her, giving her a kiss on the cheek. After my sister did the same, she grinned at me and said, "I love her already, Abbie. She's so sassy."

"Lydia, honey, come here," Aunt Dottie said to the girl sitting in the chair reading. Setting her book down, she came over to us. Aunt Dottie took her hand and said, "Abbie, Sarah, I want you to meet my friend, Lydia."

"Hi, Abbie. Hi, Sarah," she said as she hugged us. "It's nice to meet you."

"You too," I replied.

Aunt Dottie's focus switched to my boyfriend. "Hi, Sugar," she greeted him with a loving smile.

"Hi, Aunt Dottie," Neil said, giving her a hug and kiss.

Her eyes returned to me as she covered her heart and declared, "Your girlfriend is even prettier than you described her."

Neil smiled at me as he took my hand. "It's hard to describe someone this pretty."

"Aww, Junior," Aunt Dottie gushed. "Aren't these two adorable?"

"Yes, they are, Dottie," Grandpa agreed as he watched us together. Then his eyes switched to Sarah and me. "So, as you know, I invited you here today so you could meet my sister. And I also told you girls I have a project I would like your help with." He smiled at his sister. "What do you think about Abbie and Sarah decorating your room?"

"Oh, Junior!" she exclaimed. "That sounds lovely. And they can do Lydia's room, too."

Lydia's brown eyes were huge as she looked at Grandpa, unsure what to say. "Oh, Mr. Rutherford, you don't have to—"

"Yes, he does!" Aunt Dottie cut her off. She glared at her brother. "Lydia's room has barely anything in it, and she's lived here for almost four years."

"It's okay, Lydia," Grandpa reassured her. "Abbie and Sarah can spruce up your room as well."

Her face lit up with a smile as she replied, "Thank you, Mr. Rutherford." Turning to her friend, she said, "This is so exciting, isn't it, Dottie?"

"Yes," she replied, the enthusiasm returning to her voice. "It will feel like we're having a fun slumber party in a whole new place." She beamed at her brother. "So, thank you, Junior."

His face softened as he smiled at his sister. "You're welcome, Dottie." Then Grandpa looked at Sarah and me like he wanted to say something else but hesitated momentarily. When he spoke, his voice was gentler, with a hint of emotion to it. "And I have another favor I would like to ask the two of you as well."

Sarah took my hand as we smiled at each other. Turning back to him, she replied with the same gentleness, "We'd be happy to help you, Mr. Rutherford. Whatever it is."

He looked at his sister. "This place hasn't been decorated for Christmas in twenty years, Dottie."

She reached out for her brother's hand. "I miss her too, Junior."

His focus returned to us as he said, "Christmas was my wife's favorite time of year. We even got married two weeks before the holiday."

"Eleanor was such a beautiful bride, Junior."

"Yes, she was, Dottie," he agreed quietly. He paused for a second, his eyes full of memories. "When Eleanor and I returned from our honeymoon, I carried her over the threshold to my apartment, ready to make my home our home."

I felt Neil squeeze my hand, and I turned to see him smiling fondly at me. A wave of happiness flooded me as I remembered him saying the same thing at his house. I returned his smile; then my focus switched to Grandpa as he resumed speaking.

"I asked her if she wanted to go to her parents' house to get her belongings, and she said, 'We'll get to that, Cornelius. Right now, I want to go and get a Christmas tree.'" He paused again, his face softening with the memory. "So, we went out and cut down a tree and picked up a few decorations. Then we went home, and she transformed my sparse apartment into a magical wonderland fit for newlyweds."

"That's so sweet, Mr. Rutherford," my typically unromantic sister gushed.

"Thank you, Sarah," he acknowledged her kindly. "And then the following summer, we bought our home, and Eleanor wanted two Christmas trees—one for the front room and one for the parlor. And that's what we did every year for the next thirty-two years."

He paused again, looking off into the distance. "And then I lost my wife. And I took all of her decorations and stored them away. I've wanted to decorate for the past twenty years, but I just couldn't." His eyes were full of sorrow as he finally looked at us. "And that's why I need your help."

Sarah and I looked at each other, and I noticed a few tears had formed in her eyes, as did mine. She squeezed my hand and gently replied, "Thank you, Mr. Rutherford, for trusting us with this special project. Abbie and I would be honored to decorate your home for you."

"Oh, Junior," Aunt Dottie breathed. "I'm so proud of you."

"Thank you, Dottie," he said as he brushed the tears from his sister's cheeks. Then he looked at Sarah and me with heartfelt gratitude. "And thank you, Sarah. Thank you, Abbie. Just like at the office, I knew I had to find the right people to decorate my home."

Aunt Dottie's eyes were full of admiration as she smiled at us. "My brother must think the two of you are quite special to let you decorate his home and the office." Her smile switched to her brother. "Only one other person ever decorated the office, Junior."

"I know, Dottie," he said with a reminiscent look in his eyes. He turned to us and explained, "While our father and Mr. Davenport ran the business, it was mostly men who worked there. And decorating was something that none of us cared about."

"But then Junior met a cute little brunette who cared," Aunt Dottie gushed as her smile glowed brighter. "Eleanor used to bring Johnny by the office all the time for picnic lunches in the hallway, and she said the place needed some cheering up."

"Oh, Grandpa," I rejoiced, my heart filling with love as I pictured a cute young family enjoying themselves on a picnic blanket. "That sounds so sweet." As I said this, Aunt Dottie looked at her brother with raised eyebrows.

Grandpa smiled softly at me. "Thank you, Abbie. Some of my fondest memories are of the three of us enjoying a simple lunchtime in the hallway. And then in the evenings, either Dottie or my mother watched John while I helped Eleanor hang curtains and arrange furniture."

I smiled at Neil. "Just like how you help me with the room in your house."

"And I'm enjoying every minute of it," he replied, his smile mirroring mine.

Grandpa's face was full of love as he smiled fondly at us, and then his focus switched to his sister. "So, would you like to take Abbie and Sarah to your room and tell them what you want for decorating?"

She smiled at us. "That's okay. I trust these two. Besides, I love a surprise."

"At least tell us your favorite color," my sister requested.

"Yellow," she replied brightly. Then she turned to Archie. "Right now, you and I are heading to the parlor. Lydia just rewound the tape of Arsenic and Old Lace."

Neil grinned at me. "Grandpa and Aunt Dottie are the only two people we know who still own a VCR."

"One of my favorites!" Archie exclaimed as he excitedly spun Aunt Dottie's wheelchair around in a circle.

"Hey!" an angry voice yelled. "You be careful with her!"

Archie stopped in his tracks, his eyes huge with panic as he looked at his grandfather. Aunt Dottie, on the other hand, was glaring at her brother. "Junior! You be nice to the boy! Archie is always careful with me. He slightly bumped me into a wall by mistake only once. And he felt so bad he apologized for an entire month."

Grandpa inhaled sharply as he glared at his grandson, his face reddening with anger.

"Uh-oh," Aunt Dottie panicked, reaching back and grabbing his arm. "Run, Archie. Run now!"

He spun the wheelchair around, and they raced out of the room, laughing as they went. We all watched with amusement until a gruff voice redirected our attention.

"Lydia."

"Yes, Mr. Rutherford?"

"Take Abbie and Sarah to your room and tell them what you would like for decorating. Then I want you in that parlor, supervising those two."

"Yes, Mr. Rutherford," she answered, trying to suppress a grin.

Then he pulled out his wallet and handed a credit card to Neil. "Your grandmother's decorations are in the carriage house. I'll be in my study if you need me."

"Yes, Grandpa," he replied.

After he was gone, my sister and I excitedly hugged each other. "Oh my God, Abbie," she said, wrapping her arms tighter around me. "He's letting us decorate his home with his wife's decorations."

"I know," I breathed, my heart flooding with love and happiness. "I can't believe it." When she let me go, I turned to see my boyfriend's beaming face.

"Congratulations," he praised, pulling me in for a hug and kissing the top of my head. "You two keep winning over Cornelius Rutherford in ways we've never seen before."

"Let's get my bags of supplies, and we'll start with your room," Sarah suggested, smiling at Lydia.

"Sure," she agreed, her eyes brightening.

A minute later, we walked into a small bedroom with a twin bed, a dresser, and a small closet. A large window framed with ivory drapes faced the side yard, and I smiled as I watched several birds happily fluttering from tree to tree.

"So, what can we do for you?" my sister asked with a bright smile.

She glanced at Neil and shrugged.

"It's okay, Lydia."

"Really, Neil, anything is fine."

I could feel her hesitance, so to take the pressure off, I said, "Why don't we start with a few measurements, Sarah?"

Taking out her tape measure, she gave one end to Neil and handed me her pen and notepad. As she got started, she asked Lydia, "So, how did you end up here?"

"I was working at the hospital the day Dottie had her stroke. Every one of us nurses fell instantly in love with her, all wanting to be the one to take care of her." She looked at Neil. "Then a certain somebody showed up."

"The mood instantly changed as soon as Grandpa walked into her room," Neil recounted. "The nurses went from cheerful and smiling to scrambling to get out of her room. And it only got worse from there. Like I told you, Grandpa was furious when he found out that her kids wanted to put her in a home. When he returned to the hospital, Archie and I knew, just from looking at him, that he already had a plan. So later that night, the five of us came back here, and Grandpa told us he was going to hire a nurse and move Aunt Dottie in here with him. Then he went back to the hospital as the four of us got to work here."

"I remember when your grandfather came back," Lydia said. "My shift had ended, but I already loved Dottie so much that I stuck around to do her nails. He sat in a chair in the corner and took out some paperwork. When I left an hour later, he was still there. He stayed in her room every night while she was in the hospital."

"What a sweet brother," my sister gushed.

"He certainly was," Lydia agreed. "One night, he had fallen asleep in his chair, and I accidentally woke him up when I covered him with a blanket. I felt bad and instantly apologized, but he told me it was okay. I asked him if he wanted a cot to sleep on, and he looked over at Dottie and asked if she was comfortable." Lydia grinned at Neil. "She was sound asleep, snoring, so I told him she looked good to me."

She paused for a second, remembering back. "For the five days Dottie was with us, all of us nurses would argue over who got to take care of her. Jokingly, of course," she added. "Except for when her brother was there. Then, I was the only one who would go into her room willingly. He watched us like a hawk, making sure we took the very best care of his sister. The rest of the nurses were intimidated by him, but I just saw him as a caring brother."

"And that's why he hired you, Lydia," Neil confirmed with a smile.

She laughed. "I remember that day. We were all happy Dottie was healthy enough to be released, but we were going to miss her. As I was giving her what must have been my fiftieth hug, your grandfather asked her if she liked me. And she said, 'Oh yes, Junior. I love Lydia.'"

This time, it was Neil's turn to laugh. "And that's when he said, 'Good. Because you're both coming home with me.'" He shook his head as he laughed again. "That look on your face was priceless, Lydia."

"I'm sure it was," she agreed, still laughing. "I just stared at your grandfather, not sure what was even happening. Then he said, 'Young lady, whatever this hospital is paying you, I will triple it to be my sister's live-in caregiver.' And I just stood there and stared at him. Dottie finally broke me out of my trance as she took my hand and said, 'Please say yes, Lydia.'"

"You were like a deer in the headlights as you looked from Grandpa to Aunt Dottie, then to the rest of us," Neil recalled. "Finally, my dad said, 'This is where you say, 'Yes, Mr. Rutherford.'"

She shook her head and shrugged. "So, I went out to the nurse's station and handed in my resignation."

"Wow! That quickly?" my sister asked.

Neil grinned at us. "*Nobody* says no to Cornelius Rutherford."

"Besides, I had just gone through a bad breakup, and I was sleeping on a friend's couch," Lydia continued. "I'm originally from Nebraska, so my family isn't around, but all my friends from the hospital already felt like family to me." She smiled at Neil. "And now I have your family, too. Your family invites me to every function you go to, and I don't think it's just so I can be there to take care of Dottie."

He shook his head. "It's because you really are a member of this family, Lydia."

"Thanks, Neil," she replied with a smile. "And I've always felt very welcome here. The day after we moved in, your grandfather was going to tell me his list of expectations. But Dottie glared at him and said, 'Junior! Leave the girl alone. She just got here, and I don't want you scaring her off!'"

"She said that?" I asked, laughing.

Lydia nodded as we all shared a laugh. "So, he went to his study, and I sat with Dottie in the parlor. While she was taking her afternoon nap, I went by his study to talk to him. He is my boss, after all. And every one of his expectations was reasonable. He just wanted his sister to get the very best care."

"And you do that for her, Lydia," Neil confirmed.

"Thanks, Neil. And so does your grandfather. He was so patient with her when we moved in here. She cried all the time at first. I think it was a combination of sadness from her children mixed with the frustration of learning how to do everything left-handed." A look of affection came over her face as she said, "Your grandfather brushed her teeth for her every day for the first month."

"Aww," my sister and I both gushed at the same time.

"And there's a lot of times I leave them alone in the parlor together. I come in here to read, or I go to the kitchen." She laughed and added, "And sometimes he'll give me twenty bucks and tell me to go see a movie. Or a *picture show,* as he calls it."

After we shared another good laugh, her expression got more serious as she looked at Neil. "I feel bad taking so much of your grandfather's money. Most of the time, it doesn't even feel like I'm working. Most of the time, it feels like I'm just hanging out with a friend."

"Aunt Dottie has that effect on people," Neil agreed with a warm smile.

"And she even introduces me to everyone that way. Not as her nurse or her caregiver but as her friend. And every one of my friends loves her." She laughed as she remembered, "Last summer, one of my friends from the hospital got married. The invitation showed up here addressed to Mrs. Dorothy Buchanan, and there was a note tucked inside that said, 'And you can bring Lydia too.'" She smiled as she said, "Dottie's become my favorite plus-one."

Neil grinned at Sarah and me. "And Aunt Dottie has gotten Lydia several dates, too."

Sarah put down her tape measure and looked at her with bright eyes. "Now, this I have to hear!"

Lydia's smile broadened as she explained, "Every time Dottie and I go anywhere, she makes instant friends with everyone she meets. And every time she meets an attractive guy around my age, she flirts with him."

"I can picture that," my sister said as we all laughed.

"And she says the same thing to all of them, 'I lost my husband ten years ago, and he wouldn't want me to be alone. So, I'm available if you want to take me out to dinner.'"

"She does that?" I asked, my eyes huge with amazement.

Her laughter increased as she continued, "Oh, it gets better. Her flirtation always gets her a good-natured laugh from every guy she does it to. That's when she takes my hand and says, 'But if I'm not your type, my friend Lydia here is single.'"

"So, what does the guy do?" my sister asked, loving this story.

"He takes me out on a date," Lydia answered simply. She shook her head and laughed again. "Every time, before I leave the house, Dottie always tells me the same thing, 'If your date is going really well, make sure to go back to his place. That way, the old coot doesn't read him the riot act!'"

My jaw dropped, and I looked at Sarah wide-eyed. "She says that?" I asked.

"Yes, she does," she confirmed humorously. Her face softened to an affectionate smile as she continued, "But then she always takes my hand and says, 'But if he gets fresh with you and it makes you uncomfortable, you get in your car, and you come straight home. And if he won't let you leave, you call back to the house, and I'll send Junior down to straighten him out!'"

"So...have you had to do that?" my sister asked.

She shook her head. "No. Dottie seems to have radar for nice guys. Most of them I only go out with once or twice, for dinner or coffee. But it's still nice to get out for a little bit." She looked at Neil. "I guess I haven't pursued anything too serious because I can't picture myself leaving here."

He smiled gently at her. "We all love how dedicated you are to Aunt Dottie." He looked at Sarah and me. "Grandpa knew right off that Lydia was the right choice."

"Do her kids come to visit her much?" Sarah asked.

Neil shook his head, his expression turning to one of sadness. "No, they rarely come by."

"I think they're still kind of ashamed," Lydia speculated. "Your grandfather will either leave the house or stay in his study, but I think they're still too afraid to face him." Her face brightened as she continued, "But the four of you come to visit her all the time, especially Archie."

Neil's smile returned as he said, "His face lights up every time he gets a text from you. And he races over here to hang out with her."

She laughed as she said, "And supervising those two has become a big part of my job." She checked the time on her phone. "So, if you guys are done with me..."

"You still haven't told us what you want," my sister said.

She glanced at Neil again, then smiled shyly at us. "Really, anything is fine."

"Lydia," Neil said, his voice firm yet reassuring. "It's okay. Whatever you want."

"Okay," she relented after a moment. Gazing around, she said, "I guess a lot of bright, cheerful colors would be fun, and I'm a big fan of animal prints." Then she quickly added, "But honestly, I know anything you do will be amazing."

"So...bright, cheerful, and animal prints," my sister confirmed as she counted off each suggestion on her fingers. "We can do that!"

"Thanks," she said, her face brightening. "I can't wait to see what you do for Dottie and me." Then she turned and left.

Once it was just the three of us, we finished our measurements in Lydia's bedroom, then did the same for Aunt Dottie's. A bit larger than Lydia's room, I smiled when I noticed a yellow patchwork quilt designed in a star pattern folded neatly at the foot of a full-sized bed. Both rooms were painted the same shade of ivory, and two smaller windows surrounded by faded blue drapes let in the same amount of bright sunshine.

As we finished, my sister asked, "Where is the closest bathroom, Neil?"

"The last door on the right," he answered casually. Then he looked at her and stated firmly, "And do not *ever* open the last door on the left. That's Grandpa's study. Just like his office, no one goes in there unless they absolutely have to."

Sarah grinned at my boyfriend. "Don't tempt me, Neil." Her eyes brightened as they moved to me. "You know I want to open that door, Abbie."

"Yes, Sarah, I know you do," I said as we laughed.

Neil and I gathered my sister's supplies, and then he picked up the bags and said, "I'm going to bring these out to the car. I'll be right back."

Now that I had a moment to myself, I checked out the photos around Aunt Dottie's room. On the wall hung a large family portrait encased in an old-fashioned walnut frame. Appearing to be in her late-twenties, Aunt Dottie's long brown hair was pulled up. A young toddler sat on her lap, with a boy and a girl, each about five or six, sitting between her and her husband. A dark-haired gentleman, he had a very kind look to him, his face beaming with pride as he posed with his family. Surrounding the family photo were several school pictures of young children, and I guessed them to be her grandchildren.

My focus moved to the frames on her dresser, and my heart swelled with love as I picked up her wedding picture. Looking so handsome in a black suit, her tall husband smiled brightly as he stood hand-in-hand with his beautiful young bride. Holding a simple bouquet of carnations, a long veil cascaded down Aunt Dottie's hair. Dressed in a long-sleeved white gown, her face was glowing with happiness. As I continued to admire the picture, I noticed she was wearing a mismatched bracelet and necklace—the design of the necklace feeling somehow familiar.

I carefully set down the frame and laughed as my eyes landed on the second picture. Taken probably seventy-five years ago, it was a family portrait of Grandpa,

Aunt Dottie, and their parents. Their father was dressed in a blue suit paired with a white shirt and gold tie, and he looked just like Neil with the same shade of dark-brown hair and eyes. Sitting next to him in a purple dress, his wife's long brown hair flowed beautifully over her shoulders, and her hazel eyes had a gentle kindness to them. A very young Dottie, wearing a pink dress, sat on her father's lap, and my heart filled with love for the cute little girl with her hair in pigtails. All three of them were smiling—unlike the fourth person in the picture. Standing next to his mother, a young boy dressed in a black suit, white shirt, and red tie had a very serious expression on his face. His short brown hair was neatly combed, and his blue eyes looked as intense then as they do now. Looking like he had just stepped from a business meeting, all he was missing was a briefcase. Even at a young age, he looked destined to be in charge of a business.

I was pulled back to reality when I heard a deep voice behind me. "Your sister isn't back yet?"

I turned around to see Neil standing in the doorway. "No," I answered. A mischievous smile spread across my face as I suggested, "Let's go look for her and make sure she hasn't opened the forbidden door."

He laughed and took my hand, leading me down the hall. We hadn't gotten very far when we saw her standing just outside one of the rooms, intently focused on what was happening inside.

"What are you doing, Sarah?" I asked, only to be met with her motioning for us to be quiet.

We stepped up next to her, and I gazed into a large, sunlit room with a long, ivory, vintage sofa and four matching chairs. In the middle was an antique walnut coffee table with intricately carved legs. Three large windows lined the wall facing the backyard, where more birds fluttered around happily. The room's focal point was another grand fireplace with a stunning mahogany mantle. My heart melted as my attention was drawn to the picture above it. A beautiful young mother held a newborn baby in her arms, her face beaming as she looked at the camera. Her husband, on the other hand, was smiling at the baby, his face radiant with fatherly pride.

After a moment, my focus returned to the furniture, and Lydia was sitting in one of the chairs, reading a book. A huge smile spread across my face as I noticed who was on the sofa. Aunt Dottie sat to the far-right side, and Archie was lying on his back with his head on a pillow next to her, his long legs extending over the armrest, crossed at his ankles. Having obviously watched the classic Cary Grant movie several times before, they laughed as they repeated their favorite lines.

"This was my grandmother's favorite room," Neil said quietly so he wouldn't disturb them. "She did all of her entertaining in here." He pointed to a closed door next to the fireplace. "That door leads to the kitchen. My grandfather put it in, along with the one leading into the library, so my grandmother could have access from anywhere." He looked around fondly, his face glowing with memories.

"Archie looks comfortable," I commented as I grinned at my boyfriend.

His expression matched mine as he remembered, "Growing up, Aunt Dottie told us we would never be too big to sit on her lap. But somebody else didn't agree. Archie had a big growth spurt when we were teenagers." He shook his head with a gentle laugh. "He was taller than me for two years, but then I caught back up to him. Anyways, one day, Grandpa saw Archie sitting on her lap and yelled at him, 'Get off of her! You are six-foot-two and fifty pounds heavier than her.'" He laughed again. "So, then Aunt Dottie glared at Grandpa and shouted, 'Don't yell at him, Junior! Archie's not going to break me!'"

"So, she's always been sassy," my sister beamed with an admiring smile.

"Yes, she has," Neil confirmed humorously. "So that's when they came to an agreement. Archie could lie down with his head on her lap. And then, after her stroke, they revised it to laying on a pillow next to her left side only. That seemed to make everyone happy."

"Have they always been close?" my sister asked, watching the two of them affectionately.

"Yeah. Aunt Dottie has always been very approachable. She told us from a young age that we could talk to her about anything, even *boy stuff,* as she called it," he said with a laugh. "And Archie especially sees her as a confidante. The two of us talk about everything, but as far as adults in our life, it's always been Aunt Dottie that he's gone to."

As I watched them together, I realized Archie was dressed very casually. Wearing his typical jeans and t-shirt with a blue sweatshirt, the fanciest part of his attire was his blue argyle socks.

I turned to his brother. "You mentioned that you guys have to always be in a tailored suit at work. But Archie's dressed very casually right now. Your grandfather doesn't care?"

He shook his head. "Surprisingly, Grandpa doesn't care what Archie's wearing when he comes over. I think he's just happy that Archie wants to spend so much time with Aunt Dottie." He thought for a second, then theorized, "I guess at the office, it's different since he sees the four of us as representing his father."

"I can see why this was your grandmother's favorite room," my sister observed, looking around. "It's really bright and pretty in here."

"Thanks, Sarah," Neil acknowledged her with a smile.

She smiled at my boyfriend. "I'm looking forward to seeing your grandmother's decorations. I can already imagine how amazing this place is going to look when we're done." She took my hand as her focus shifted to me. "This really is a special decorating project, Abbie."

"I know, Sarah," I agreed. We both looked at Neil, and I said, "We especially want him to love how we decorate his home."

He smiled gently at us. "And he will love it. That's why he chose you."

Our attention was pulled to the parlor as we heard a feminine voice.

"How long have you three been standing there?" We looked over to see Aunt Dottie smiling at us.

"Just a few minutes," Neil answered as we walked into the room.

Archie sat up and paused the video. "Are you all done?" he asked with his typically bright smile.

"We are," my sister confirmed. "And I already have a lot of fun ideas for your room, Aunt Dottie."

"Marvelous!" she exclaimed.

"We're coming back next weekend," I said with a smile. "We'll show up bright and early and have the guys help us. We can get it all done in one day."

"Wonderful! We'll come home to a fun surprise, won't we, Lydia?"

She looked up from her book. "Yes, Dottie."

"And we can go out and have fun while these kids are working." She laughed and added, "Or at least as much fun as we can have with the old coot around!"

My sister laughed. "You're funny, Aunt Dottie." As she shared a smile with her new friend, she commented, "Right now, we're going to the carriage house to check out the Christmas decorations."

Archie's eyes lit up as he looked at his brother. "We haven't seen those in twenty years."

"I know, Arch," Neil agreed. "It'll be nice to have some holiday cheer around here again."

"Why don't you three get heading outside?" Aunt Dottie requested. "I want to have a quick word with Miss Abbie."

They gave her a hug and a kiss, then left the parlor with Lydia through the library.

She patted the couch next to her, and I sat down. She took my hand and said, "So, the old coot has you calling him Grandpa, huh?"

I couldn't help but laugh. "He told me to call him that just a few minutes after I met him."

She smiled warmly at me. "Just like Helen all those years ago." Her face softened as she looked at me. "We all see something special in you, Abbie. Especially Neil. I see the way he looks at you. His face lights right up." She squeezed my hand. "And so does yours."

"I really love him, Aunt Dottie."

"I know you do, Sugar. The two of you remind me so much of Frankie and me when we were courting all those years ago."

"I saw your wedding picture," I confessed to her. "You both looked so sweet and happy."

"And so will you and Neil," she said with a wink.

My smile brightened at hearing her words. A wave of happiness washed over me as another member of Neil's family confirmed the future I'd seen every time I looked into my boyfriend's eyes.

"Now, give me a hug and a kiss, and then you can go be with your boyfriend."

I leaned over and hugged her, delighting in her warm affection. After kissing her cheek, I went outside and found my way to the carriage house. Stepping inside, I saw Neil, Archie, and Sarah carefully sorting through decorations. I went over to join them and wrapped my arms around my boyfriend, sighing contently as I stood in his embrace.

"Did you have a nice chat with Aunt Dottie?" he asked me with an affectionate smile.

I reached up to kiss him, the emotion flowing through me. "I had an amazing chat with Aunt Dottie," I confirmed happily. "She said the best thing I've heard all day."

His smile brightened. "Good. I'm glad she made my beautiful girlfriend feel special." I was lost in my favorite brown eyes, delighting in our private moment—until my sister's voice pulled our attention to her.

"Hey, Abs, isn't this beautiful?" she asked, holding up an embroidered Christmas tree skirt.

"It is," I agreed, my smile glowing even brighter.

We continued going through the decorations, being careful with everything that means so much to Grandpa. Finding out that he wanted us to decorate his home for his wife's favorite holiday was even better than we were expecting. Hearing the way he talked about his wife made my heart so happy—the love he feels for her is so apparent.

And then hearing Aunt Dottie confirm what the daydreamer in me has been hoping for all along...I already know this is going to be the best Christmas ever.

Chapter 3

♥

"This place looks amazing, Sarah," I praised as I hugged my sister the following Saturday evening.

"I know," she agreed as she tightened her arms around me. Then she added with a whisper, "I really hope he likes it."

"He's going to love it," we heard a masculine voice whisper next to us.

Sarah and I stepped apart and looked at my boyfriend's face beaming next to us. His brother stood beside him; his face lit up with nostalgia as he looked around. Red garland decorated the railing leading upstairs, and hand-knitted stockings added Christmas cheer to both mantles. We took advantage of the guys' height, and long strands of pine boughs hung above the fireplaces and around the perimeter of the ceiling in the parlor. A large fir wreath adorned with gold balls and a red bow welcomed visitors at the front door.

My favorite part of all was decorating the two freshly cut Christmas trees. Colorful lights twinkled on the branches in the front room, placed in front of the window so passersby could enjoy the holiday cheer from outside. A gold star sat atop the tree, and gold, red, and silver ornaments shimmered against the dark-green needles. The red and white skirt embroidered with silver snowflakes at the base of the trunk was the perfect finishing touch.

And the tree in the parlor was even more majestic. Taller and fuller, streams of tinsel cascaded down the branches. All the ornaments matched in the front room, but each one in here was unique. We found a box of thirty-three different ornaments and figured they had been stored that way for a reason. So, we carefully gave each one a special place on the tree, marveling at their individual beauty. A simple red velvet skirt with white trim dressed up the base of the tree. The finishing touch was a stunning angel in a gold dress perched on top, guarding over all who entered the room.

A message beeped in on Archie's phone, and his eyes lit up as he looked at it. "They'll be here in five minutes."

We did one final sweep to make sure nothing was out of place, and we were standing at the front door as a large van pulled into the driveway. Grandpa got out of the driver's seat, and Lydia exited the passenger side. They got Aunt Dottie out with the side liftgate, and even in the darkness, I could see her face light up when she saw the house.

"Oh, Junior!" she exclaimed as he pushed her up the ramp. "Isn't it beautiful?"

"Yes, it is, Dottie," he agreed, his face also bright with wonder.

As they entered, we all gave Aunt Dottie her welcoming hugs and kisses, and Sarah and I greeted Lydia with a hug. As Grandpa hung up their coats, he gently touched the garland shimmering along the banister. His focus shifted to the wedding picture just inside the door, his eyes so full of love as he looked at his beautiful young bride.

Archie got behind Aunt Dottie's wheelchair and said, "Come on. We'll show you what Abbie and Sarah did."

We entered the front room, and Aunt Dottie gasped when she saw the stockings hanging from the mantle. Knitted in red yarn, the names *Cornelius, Laura, Dottie,* and *Frank* contrasted beautifully in white yarn.

She took her brother's hand. "Junior, look. It's Mom, Daddy, mine, and Frankie's stockings." She looked at us with tears in her eyes and asked, "Where did you find these?"

"They were in the carriage house," my sister answered with a smile. "We figured we would put them in here so they would welcome you into the house."

"It's perfect, Sweetie, thank you," she said, lifting her arm, wanting another hug from us. After we hugged her, she turned to her brother. "How did they end up in the carriage house?"

"While we were cleaning out your house when you moved in here, we noticed them in the attic," he explained. "I wasn't sure if we would ever decorate, but I knew I had to keep them. So, I tucked them into the carriage house with Eleanor's decorations."

"Thank you, Junior," she whispered, reaching up to touch his arm. He bent down to kiss her on the cheek and wiped away the tears that had escaped her eyes. Her face brightened, and her voice was full of anticipation as she said, "I'm excited to see what the girls did with the other stockings, Junior."

Sarah and I smiled at each other as she said, "Right this way."

Grandpa pushed Aunt Dottie as we led them through the library and into the parlor. The sight in here made Grandpa stop as soon as he entered the room. His gaze slowly traveled around, and I could see the memories flooding back to him. His eyes stopped as they landed on the mantle. Knitted in the same simple pattern were three stockings with the names *Junior, Eleanor,* and *Johnny.* Seeing them at the same time, Aunt Dottie reached up and lovingly squeezed her brother's hand as more tears ran down her face.

"Neil mentioned this was your wife's favorite room," my sister said quietly. "So, we decided to put these stockings in here." She added in barely a whisper, "I hope that's okay."

Grandpa finally pulled his focus from the stockings and looked at my sister. "It's perfect, Sarah. Thank you."

A look of relief came across her face as she said, "You're welcome, Mr. Rutherford." After hesitating for a second, she requested, "Can I ask you something, sir?"

He regarded her kindly as he answered, "Of course, Sarah."

"We found two boxes of ornaments in the carriage house. In one box, they all matched, and that's what we used out front. But the ones in the second box were all different. And I counted them. There were thirty-three. I'm guessing there's something special about these ornaments?"

His face brightened into a smile as he responded, "Eleanor and I picked out a different ornament for each Christmas we were married. She chose the matching decorations that first year in my apartment, and..." He stepped up to the tree and scanned it for a minute. Carefully removing an ornament, he returned to show us a ceramic cardinal and said, "This one."

"Eleanor loved cardinals," Aunt Dottie remembered fondly.

"Yes, she did," Grandpa agreed as he lovingly gazed at the vibrant bird in his hand. A moment later, he returned to the tree and delicately placed it back where he found it. Then, his focus moved to the fireplace. After admiring the stockings, silver trees, and reindeer on the mantle, he turned to us. "And thank you for putting our stockings in here." His focus switched to his grandsons as he said, "You boys might not remember, but your grandmother always hung our stockings just like this."

He returned to stand next to his sister, took her hand, and said, "Our grandmother made matching stockings for all of us, including our spouses and children. John's was the last one she made."

"That was a very special Christmas, Junior," she reminisced, smiling at her brother.

Grandpa's smile brightened as he explained, "It was our second Christmas together and the first one in our new home. Eleanor was due to have John in late November, and she wanted to decorate the house before he was born."

"So, we all pitched in and helped," Aunt Dottie said.

Grandpa's eyes were full of love as he recalled, "John was born on Thanksgiving, and when the three of us got home from the hospital, everyone was here waiting for us."

"I still remember the look on Eleanor's face as she noticed Johnny's stocking," Aunt Dottie said, her smile brightening even more. "Grammy added his name when you called with the good news, and we hung it up as a nice little surprise."

"I remember too, Dottie," Grandpa replied, smiling at his sister. "It meant the world to Eleanor and me." He looked at us and said, "Our grandmother passed that following summer, so we were grateful she got to share John's first Christmas with him." He paused for a second, remembering back, and then his facial expression changed as a realization came to him. "All the women in our family called him Johnny." He looked at his sister. "You're the only one left, Dottie, who still calls him that."

She held her brother's hand to her cheek. "I know, Junior."

Grandpa looked at his sister with the same gratitude I've seen Neil and Archie look at each other with. It made my heart so happy to see how much all the siblings in their family love each other. And it makes me even more grateful for my own sister. I reached over and squeezed her hand, and her matching smile confirmed she felt the same.

Grandpa's voice switched from nostalgic to happiness for his sister as he said, "So, would you like to see what Abbie and Sarah did in your room?"

She beamed at us with a smile full of anticipation. "Yes, we're so excited, aren't we, Lydia?"

Lydia's smile matched Aunt Dottie's as she answered, "We've been daydreaming out loud all day about what our rooms will look like."

"Let's start with yours," Aunt Dottie suggested, taking Lydia's hand.

"Okay," she agreed cheerfully.

Sarah and I led the way to a closed door, and we stopped and smiled at the eager faces. My sister pushed the door open and announced, "Ta-da!"

Grandpa pushed Aunt Dottie into the room as Lydia followed. Their eyes glowed brightly as they looked around. Turquoise sheets perfectly contrasted the orange comforter that cheered up her bed. Faux fur zebra and leopard print throw pillows were arranged throughout the room, adding some fun life to the space. A light-pink velvet chair sat next to the window, giving her a private yet comfortable place to read. Sheer turquoise curtains bordered the window, and the dreamer in me pictured them flowing happily in a warm summer breeze. We topped it all off by having the guys hang up a few pictures of vibrant flowers encased in golden frames.

"Oh, Lydia!" Aunt Dottie exclaimed. "I love it!"

"Me too," she agreed excitedly. She picked up the leopard print pillow and brought it over to Aunt Dottie. "And feel this pillow."

"Ooh," Aunt Dottie gushed as she ran her hand over the plush cover. "This might just find its way into my room."

Lydia laughed good-naturedly as she hugged her excited friend. Then she came over and hugged Sarah and me. "Thank you," she said with a grateful smile. "It's perfect."

Sarah and I beamed at each other, and then we turned to our new friend as she said, "You're welcome, Lydia. We were hoping you would like it."

"I love it," she confirmed with a bright smile. Then she looked at Grandpa and said, "Thank you, Mr. Rutherford."

"You're welcome, Lydia," he replied. His focus switched to his sister. "Are you ready to see your room?"

"Yes, Junior," she said excitedly as Lydia returned the pillow to her bed.

Sarah and I stood on either side of the adjoining door with bright smiles. This time, it was my turn to open the door for the big reveal, and I excitedly announced, "Dorothy Buchanan, come on down. You have just won yourself a new room."

She giggled as her brother pushed her into her bedroom. As soon as they entered, she reached for his hand, excited about the transformation. Floral sheets and a plush golden comforter were a beautiful complement to her yellow quilt. Several vibrant-colored throw pillows cheered up her room, making it feel more welcoming. Sheer ivory curtains embroidered with yellow flowers framed her windows, brightening the entire space. We found some snowmen and Santa Claus figurines tucked in with her Christmas decorations, so we added some holiday cheer to her room as well.

"Oh, Junior!" she exclaimed, her eyes glowing brightly as they landed on a stunning crystal vase filled with an assortment of carnations. "Look!"

"I see, Dottie," he commented, picking up the vase and bringing it over to his sister so she could smell the flowers.

She closed her eyes and peacefully inhaled the beautiful scent. When she opened her eyes, they were so full of love as she looked at her brother. "Thank you, Junior, for remembering my vase," she whispered.

"You're welcome, Dottie," he replied softly. "I saw it on your dresser as we were packing up your bedroom, and I knew you would want it." His voice turned apologetic as he continued, "I'm sorry it was in the carriage house for almost four years. I didn't go through each box once we got them here, and I forgot about the vase."

She pulled his face toward her to kiss him on the cheek. "It's okay, Junior. It's in here now."

"Neil and I recognized it immediately as we were going through boxes," Archie said to her with a gentle smile. "We picked up the carnations this morning, remembering how special they are to you and Uncle Frank."

Aunt Dottie's smile glowed brightly as she looked at her great-nephews. Then her eyes shifted to Sarah and me as she explained, "Frankie wanted to get me flowers for our first date, but he wasn't sure what kind to buy. So, his mom told him to call me and ask about my birthday. I thought it was so strange when I got a phone call, and all he said was, 'When is your birthday, Dottie?'" She paused to reminisce with a small laugh. "I told him January twenty-first, so his mom suggested a bouquet of carnations. Thirty minutes later, he showed up at the house with the prettiest assortment of colors."

"That's so sweet, Aunt Dottie," I gushed, loving her story.

"Thank you, Abbie," she replied with a smile. Her expression turned playful as she grinned at her brother. "That even won Frankie brownie points with the old coot!"

Grandpa smiled gently at her as the rest of us shared a good laugh. Aunt Dottie was quiet for a moment as she lovingly touched the petals and ran her fingers down the vase.

She looked at Sarah and me with tears in her eyes and said, "This vase was given to Frankie and me as a wedding gift. Every time he brought home carnations, we would set them in this vase on my dresser. And seeing this vase again makes me feel like my Frankie is still here with me." She closed her eyes and indulged in their beautiful scent one last time; then Grandpa returned them to her dresser.

My sister took my hand, and we smiled at each other; then we turned to her, and I said, "We're so happy to hear that, Aunt Dottie."

Sarah's gentle smile turned bright with excitement as she added, "And we have another surprise outside for you, too. Abbie noticed birds fluttering around the backyard, so we had the guys hang up some birdfeeders that we found in the carriage house. It's dark right now, but you can enjoy them in the morning."

"Come here, you two," Aunt Dottie said to her great-nephews as she raised her arm for a hug. After they hugged her, she praised them, "Thank you for helping the girls. And thank you for remembering my special vase." Then she smiled at her brother and added, "And Eleanor's birdfeeders."

Even though it was dark outside, Grandpa was looking out the window like he could see the birdfeeders. He turned to his grandsons and agreed, "Yes, thank you, boys. Your grandmother always loved feeding and watching the birds. But after she passed, I put the feeders away. So, it will be nice to see them again."

"You're welcome, Grandpa," Neil replied with a gentle smile.

Grandpa looked at Aunt Dottie and Lydia. "I'm happy the two of you love what Abbie and Sarah did with your rooms. I'm pleased with it, too." His expression softened as he turned to Sarah and me. "And I especially love seeing my wife's decorations around the house again. I agree with my sister. I can feel Eleanor around here in a way that I haven't felt in twenty years. This is the first time since she passed that it truly feels like the home we made together. So, thank you."

Sarah and I beamed at him as she replied, "You're welcome, Mr. Rutherford. We were hoping you would love everything we did."

"And I do," he confirmed with a grateful smile. He reached into his pocket and pulled out his wallet. Taking out a check, he held it out to us and said, "And that's why I want to give you this."

My sister and I glanced at each other, and then we looked back at him as she said, "We can't take that, Mr. Rutherford."

"Why not, Sarah?" he questioned her.

"Because we were decorating your home," she answered as if stating the obvious.

"But it's what you do for a living. And you were paid for decorating the resort, and I'll pay you for your time at the office as well."

"But that's different, sir," my sister continued her refusal.

"How so?" he countered.

"Because they're both businesses. And they feel like businesses. But this is your home, Mr. Rutherford. And we cannot take your money."

I was impressed with her firmness and how she maintained eye contact with him the entire time she spoke to him.

"But how will you support yourself, Sarah?" he challenged her.

A proud smile spread across her face as she answered, "You don't have to worry about that, Mr. Rutherford. Thanks to Neil here, we've already gotten three more homes to decorate in Westport."

"Thanks to me?" Neil questioned her with raised eyebrows.

"Robyn loved what Abbie and I did at her home so much that she recommended us to three of her friends,"

Sarah explained with a grateful smile. "So, thank you, Neil."

His raised eyebrows turned to a bright smile as he praised her, "That's great, Sarah. But I still don't see what that has to do with me."

"It's because you believed in me, Neil." Her focus switched to Grandpa as she continued, "Mr. Rutherford, Abbie tried to convince me for three years to look for decorating jobs in Fairfield County. But I was always too nervous that the people here wouldn't like my designs. And then Neil had Archie give my phone number to one of your employees."

Grandpa looked at Neil, and he replied, "Dan Moore in risk analysis."

"Neil has believed in Abbie and me ever since he first met my sister, and we're very grateful for every job we've gotten because of your family," my sister acknowledged thankfully.

"And decorating my home was a job, too, Sarah," Grandpa pointed out.

"This was different, sir." The firmness in my sister's voice grew stronger every time she spoke to him. "This time, it didn't feel like we were working. This time, it felt like we were decorating rooms for our sweet aunt and her friend." She smiled at Aunt Dottie and Lydia, then returned her focus to Grandpa. Her voice turned gentle as she said, "And we felt like we got to know your wife while we were putting up her Christmas decorations. Abbie and I really wish we could have met her."

"I wish that too, Sarah," he agreed with the same gentleness.

"So please don't be mad at us for not taking your money, Mr. Rutherford."

His face softened a bit as he asked her, "Why would I be mad at you, Sarah?"

"Because Neil told us that no one says no to Cornelius Rutherford. But we don't see you as Cornelius Rutherford, sir. We see you as our family."

"You do?" he asked with a hint of surprise in his voice.

I nodded in agreement as my sister answered, "Of course we do, sir. You have my sister calling you Grandpa; we're both in love with your sister, and my sister is completely in love with your grandson." She looked at my boyfriend, her face full of exasperation, and said, "Just buy her a ring already, Neil."

This got a chuckle out of everyone but Grandpa. He just looked at the two of us with a softness in his eyes. Then he focused on my sister and said, "I would still like to compensate you for your time, Sarah."

"Your family has already been more than generous, sir." My sister paused for a second, and her demeanor changed as she looked at me with a resigned sigh. "The Catholic is coming out of me, Abbie." Her focus returned to Grandpa as she said, "I have a confession to make to you, Mr. Rutherford."

His face softened further as curiosity mixed with compassion took over his features. "What's that, Sarah?"

She fidgeted with the hem on her shirt as she admitted, "When Abbie sent Neil the invoice for decorating the resort, he paid us a few days later. And he included a bonus above the amount we had charged."

His eyes softened even more at hearing her admission. And that softness was in his voice as he replied, "I know, Sarah. I wrote that check myself."

"Oh," she said quietly. "You did?"

He nodded.

She thought for a second, then said, "Can I ask you something, Mr. Rutherford?"

"Of course, Sarah."

"The amount of the bonus...it wasn't a round number. Was there a significance to that number?"

His eyes brightened as he answered, "It's the year Eleanor and I got married."

"Aww, Junior," Aunt Dottie gushed. "You old softie."

"That is really sweet, Mr. Rutherford," my sister agreed. She returned to her fidgeting as she continued, "But the part I have to confess to you, sir, is what Abbie and I did with the money."

His blue eyes had a look of admiration as he watched my sister—who managed to maintain eye contact with him this entire time.

"We didn't feel right taking the money, but we didn't want to offend anyone by giving it back. So, we donated it to your family's foundation."

Grandpa continued to look at my sister for a second; then, his expression turned more serious as he looked at Neil. "Did you know about this?"

"Yes, Grandpa," he answered. "Abbie and Sarah asked me the name of our foundation, and after I told them, I asked why the sudden interest." He smiled at me as he said proudly, "That's when they said they wanted to donate the bonus they had been given."

We looked at Grandpa to see him smiling fondly at us. "Good," he answered. "I'm glad the two of you aren't keeping secrets." Then his focus switched to my sister. "And thank you for telling me, Sarah, but I already knew you had donated the money."

Her eyes grew huge as she looked at him. "You did, sir?"

He nodded. "Every week, Helen and I sit down to discuss foundation matters, and she tells me every time an anonymous donation comes in. She mentioned that we had gotten one in a rather unusual amount, so I asked her how much it was. And I immediately recognized the number."

This got a laugh out of Neil. "I told you Grandpa has eyes and ears all over southern Connecticut. I guess that even includes my mom." Suddenly, his laughter stopped as a look of realization came over his face. He looked at Grandpa rather stunned and said, "Wait, Mom tells you every time an anonymous donation comes into the foundation?"

Grandpa's eyes had a look of pride in them as he confirmed, "Yes, Neil. She does." They continued looking at each other for a moment until my sister's voice pulled everyone's attention back to her.

"So please, Mr. Rutherford, do not be mad at us. Abbie and I honestly feel like we cannot take your money. And it's not just because you've already been more than generous to us. It's because..." She hesitated for a second, then admitted, "Mr. Rutherford, it's because even though we haven't known you all that long, you already feel like a grandfather to us."

Grandpa's facial expression barely changed as he heard my sister's words. He remained silent as he looked back and forth between the two of us.

Sarah took my hand, and her eyes were full of emotion as she looked at me. We turned back to Grandpa as she spoke for us, "Mr. Rutherford, Abbie and I said goodbye to our last grandparent a few years ago. But having you around...it's like we get to have a grandparent again. And I know you told Abbie to call you Grandpa, so it would make sense that she feels that way about you." She fidgeted with my fingers as she quietly added, "I hope it's okay that I feel the same way about you, too, sir."

Grandpa didn't say anything as his focus switched solely to my sister. His blue eyes softened ever so slightly as he looked at her, but he didn't say a word.

My sister's eyes stayed locked on his, and they silently stared at each other—until suddenly, her facial expression changed. Her eyes were full of conviction, and she let go of my hand. She squared her shoulders and stated with firm defiance, "So anyways, Mr. Rutherford, we are not taking your money, and that is that! I truly hope you are not mad at us, sir, but if you are, you will just have to deal with it. I am not backing down. And I am even willing to pay the ultimate price. I will give you my parents' phone number, and you can call my mom and tell her everything I just said to you. And I guarantee you, Mr. Rutherford, my mother will go up one side of me and down the other for disrespecting an old person."

I whipped my head to the side, glaring daggers at my sister. "Sarah Caroline!" I scolded her loudly. Reaching over, I gave her a swift whack on the backside—hard enough so she lurched forward.

Her focus switched to me, and the scornful look on my face made her fully realize what she had just said. She looked back at Grandpa and said quietly, "Or my sister could just do it now, sir."

I looked from my sister to the man standing before us, ready to offer him some sort of an apology. But as soon as my eyes landed on him, I was caught off guard by something I wasn't expecting. Instead of looking angry, his expression was one of...humor, maybe? His arms were crossed, his lips were pulled in, and he was holding his breath like he was trying to suppress what he was really feeling. Finally, losing control of his steadfast discipline, his face lit up in a smile, and he started to laugh. And the longer he laughed, the harder and more uncontrollable it became.

"Junior!" Aunt Dottie gasped, clutching her chest with her left hand. "I've already had a stroke. Are you trying to give me a heart attack, too?"

"I don't get it," my sister said, looking back and forth between the two siblings.

"Sarah," Aunt Dottie said, looking at her with huge eyes. "In my entire seventy-nine years, this is only the third time I've ever seen my brother laugh."

"It's our first time," two masculine voices said next to me.

I looked over to see Neil and Archie staring at their grandfather as if they were looking at a ghost. Both white as a sheet, they stared at their stoic disciplinarian with huge eyes, unable to recognize the man standing before them. They slowly turned and looked at my sister—their faces full of astonishment at her ability to bring out a side of their grandfather they had clearly never seen before.

Once he got his laughter under control, Grandpa looked at my sister and reassured her, "Sarah, when I do meet your parents, I promise I will have nothing but good things to say about you and your sister. Now, if you will all excuse me, I'll be in my study making an anonymous donation to the Barrington-Rutherford Foundation." He headed toward the door, and as he got there, he turned around and looked at my sister. "You are something else, young lady," he said, smiling and shaking his head. Then he disappeared into the hallway.

The six of us looked at each other wide-eyed.

"What was that?" Archie expressed everyone's shock.

"I know, Arch," Neil agreed. He looked at my sister and said, "Grandpa's right, Sarah, you are something else. You seem to have a way with Grandpa all your own."

"Thanks, Neil," she said with a smile of pride. Her focus switched to me as she gave me her '*See? Somebody appreciates me*' smirk.

My focus switched to Archie, whose blue eyes were huge as he looked at my sister. The brothers just saw an entirely different side of their grandfather all because of Sarah. The longer he looked at my sister, though, his expression went from shock to what looked like admiration. His eyes softened to a look of genuine fondness, impressed at my sister's ability to not only make his grandfather laugh but stand up to him as well. My attention was pulled to Aunt Dottie as I heard her voice.

"Lydia, honey, it's just as well we're in my room. I think I need to lay down."

"Are you okay, Aunt Dottie?" Neil asked with a concerned tone.

"Yes, Sugar," she answered with a gentle smile. Her focus switched to my sister. "This pretty girl just gave me the shock of my life, that's all."

"I've got it," Lydia said reassuringly. "Why don't you guys go?" She looked at my sister and me. "Thanks again for everything."

The four of us gave Aunt Dottie a quick hug and kiss, then we left. It was a relatively quiet ride back to Westport as the brothers were still processing what had just happened. We got changed for the gym and were back in New Canaan before we knew it. Even though it had been a long day, it was also one of the best days I'd had in a long time. It felt like we got to know Neil's grandmother through her decorations, and seeing the joy on Grandpa and Aunt Dottie's faces was priceless.

And my unfiltered sister struck again. But this time, her impulse to say whatever was on her mind brought out a completely different side to a man that I think his family enjoyed seeing. Although shocked at first, the two brothers seemed genuinely happy to see that side of their grandfather. The entire time they were in the weight room, they kept looking at each other with amazed expressions, and I knew what their conversation was about. And every time Archie glanced at my sister on the elliptical next to me, his admiration for her seemed to grow. And seeing him look at Sarah like that makes me even more grateful for the affection my sister feels for our new grandfather.

Chapter 4

♥

"I CAN'T BELIEVE IT'S Christmas Eve already," I said, leaning my head on my boyfriend's shoulder as I sat next to him on the couch.

He smiled as he gave me a kiss. "You and Sarah did an amazing job decorating. My home has never looked so festive."

We gazed across the room at the majestic Christmas tree standing tall in front of the window. Colorful lights twinkled against the branches, reflecting beautifully off the gold and red ornaments. A quilted skirt surrounded the base, and the golden star shimmering on top was the perfect finishing touch. Red and green garland sparkled around the windows, joyfully framing the winter scenery outside. Romantic flames happily danced in the fireplace; our stockings hung safely on either side.

"So, you never decorated before now?" I asked.

He shook his head. "No, we always celebrated the holidays at the country club, and then we would go to my parents' house afterward. So, there was no need to decorate here." He gazed at me fondly and said, "Besides, I was waiting for the right woman to come along and really make this place feel like home." He kissed me again. "And you definitely make my home feel extra special, Abbie."

I snuggled closer against him, feeling wonderful that his house felt like a home because of me. I grinned at him and admitted playfully, "Tomorrow will be my first time celebrating Christmas at a fancy country club."

His expression mirrored mine as he said, "Even Grandpa bites the bullet and goes to the country club willingly for Christmas brunch."

I laughed. "I can't wait to see him there, based on what you and Archie have said about his dislike of the place."

He joined in my laughter as he said, "And my dad wasn't kidding. You should see the way he handles the girls who hit on Archie." He thought for a second, then added, "The ones that approach him, that is. The girls seem to have radar for when Grandpa's around and avoid our table."

"And poor Archie won't have his new friends there since I think my parents are planning to stay home tomorrow. And Sarah will probably go up to Windsor to see them."

"It's nice that we saw them yesterday," he commented with a smile.

"Yeah, since my dad's birthday is two days before Christmas, we always make sure to celebrate it separately from the holiday. I don't think he minds too much, but we try not to make him feel cheated out of a birthday." I smiled at my sweet boyfriend. "And they understand that we're celebrating with your family tomorrow. So, you're right. It was nice to see them yesterday."

He gazed at me lovingly as he ran his fingers through my hair. "And I already know this is going to be my best Christmas, Abbie. And it's all because of you."

"I agree," I said, leaning forward to kiss him.

"And I'm looking forward to spending Christmas Eve with my beautiful girlfriend. A private celebration for just the two of us." He kissed me again and suggested, "Why don't we get dinner started?"

"Sure," I agreed as we stood up and headed for the kitchen.

"I figured we could make panko-crusted salmon for dinner tonight if that sounds good," he said as he gathered ingredients from his refrigerator and pantry.

"That sounds wonderful," I agreed happily.

Surveying his items, he lifted the lid on the Parmesan cheese and looked at me with a scrunched-up nose. "I think this cheese has gone bad. And it's the perfect addition to the panko crumbs."

"I could run out for some more," I offered. Then I added with a playful grin, "And all it'll cost you is a kiss."

"That is my favorite form of payment," he said with a gentle laugh as he wrapped his arms around me and pulled me in for a kiss. He smiled at me and acknowledged, "Thank you, Abbie, for offering to go out."

"You're welcome," I responded with a smile. Suddenly, my expression changed as something occurred to me. "Since it's Christmas Eve, do you think the stores are still open?"

"Let me check," he said, taking out his phone. After doing a quick search, he looked up with a smile. "The grocery store in the Westport Plaza is open until six, and it's five o'clock now. I'll give them a call to make sure they have the cheese in stock."

I went to get my coat, and when I returned to the kitchen, Neil smiled at me and said, "I'm on hold. A nice lady is checking for me." I put on my scarf while I waited, and a moment later, my boyfriend's face lit up. "Great, thank you, Patty. I'll send my girlfriend right down. She'll be the stunning brunette in jeans and a black wool coat. Her name is Abbie." He paused for a second to listen, then responded, "Merry Christmas to you too."

He hung up his phone and came over to help me with my coat. He brushed my hair over my shoulders and said, "I'm glad I called. They have one container of the brand I buy left in stock, and they're holding it for us. Go to the service desk and ask for a nice lady named Patty and tell her your boyfriend Neil sent you to pick up the Parmesan cheese. She'll know what you're talking about."

"Sounds good," I said, giving him a quick kiss.

I grabbed my bag, headed out the door, and pulled into the parking lot fifteen minutes later. I went up to the service desk and was greeted by two smiling faces. A blonde about my age wore a name tag that read *Stacy,* and a middle-aged brunette's name tag said *Patty.*

I approached them with a smile and said, "Hi, Patty. You're just the lady I'm looking for. My name is Abbie, and my boyfriend Neil sent me to pick up some Parmesan cheese. He said you're holding it for us."

The two of them smiled at each other and then looked at me. "It's nice to meet you, Abbie," Patty said, her smile growing. "We've been eager to meet you."

"Okay," I replied, a bit stunned. Neil just called them a few minutes ago and only sent me to pick up cheese. And they seem very excited to see me.

Patty reached under the counter, retrieved a large white rectangular box with a red bow wrapped around it, and set it on the counter. "Neil said to give this to you."

I just blinked at their smiling faces. "No," I said after a moment. "He sent me down here to pick up cheese. What's this?"

"We've been wondering the same thing," Stacy replied, her blue eyes glowing.

Patty pushed the box toward me and excitedly said, "Open it!"

Still a bit confused, I untied the bow and lifted the lid. My eyes brightened as soon as I saw what was inside. Underneath a card was a black sheath dress and a fuchsia scarf. And I immediately recognized them.

"What is it?" Stacy asked.

I set the card on the counter, picked up the dress, and said, "I was wearing this exact dress and scarf when I met my boyfriend. I ran into him carrying my coffee and made a huge mess out of his perfectly tailored gray suit."

"Aww," Patty gushed, her hazel eyes full of delight. "And he remembered."

"What does the card say?" Stacy wanted to know.

I smiled at them, their faces so eager and happy for me. I opened the envelope and read the card out loud, *"My beautiful Abbie. My life changed six months ago when you ran into me wearing this dress. Bring the dress back home and go to the space that belongs to you. There, you'll find your next clue."*

"It's a scavenger hunt!" Stacy exclaimed. "How exciting!"

"And so romantic," Patty gushed.

"Your boyfriend is amazing," Stacy raved. "When he came in here last week and asked if we would help him with a Christmas Eve surprise for his beautiful girlfriend, we jumped at the chance to be involved."

"So, he set this up a week ago?" I asked, looking at their bright faces.

"Yeah," Patty answered. "And then he showed up with this box and asked us to hold onto it. And to be very careful because there was something special inside. I even put it in my car so nothing would happen to it until we were back here at the desk." Her smile brightened even more. "And we have been on pins and needles waiting to meet you and hoping you would open it in front of us."

"So, thank you for sharing your surprise with us," Stacy said as they came out from behind the counter and hugged me.

"What do you think his next clue is?" Patty asked.

"I'm excited to see, too," I answered. "I'll have to come back in and tell you."

"Or you could just call us," Patty said with a grin as she took out her cell phone and waved it around.

My eyes got huge with realization as I watched her. "So, Neil called your phone and not the store?"

She nodded. "I gave him my number and told him to call me directly so we would know when you were coming."

"And I wasn't even on the schedule for tonight, but I had to come in and meet you," Stacy said, her eyes glowing with fondness. "The way your boyfriend talked about you..." An affectionate smile took over her face. "I just knew I had to meet this sweet girl that he is clearly in love with."

As I looked at their huge smiles, another realization occurred to me. "So, there is no Parmesan cheese?"

They both laughed. "No, that was just a way to get you to the store to see us," Patty answered with a gleam in her eyes.

"So go home and see what your next clue is!" Stacy exclaimed.

I gave each of them one last hug, then grabbed the box and headed eagerly out the door.

I OPENED THE DOOR to Neil's house to find all the lights off, the cheerful Christmas tree casting a festive glow around the living room. Two candles happily flickered on the coffee table, adding extra romance to the fire burning warmly across the room. Doing just what the clue told me, I went upstairs to the room where Sarah and I had been decorating and flipped on the light. A folded card sat on a small table next to a vase of red roses. My smile grew even more as my eyes landed on the fuchsia heels sitting next to the table, and I once again recognized them from the morning we met. My heart swelled with love at seeing just how much he remembered from that first moment. I picked up the card and read:

Welcome home, my sweet Abbie. This has always been my favorite outfit on you since meeting you was the best moment of my life. Bring everything into the bedroom next door, and there you'll find your next clue.

I excitedly gathered everything and flipped on the light in the adjacent bedroom. Red rose petals were scattered all over the white comforter, and a smaller box sat on the edge of the bed. Also wrapped in a red bow, the tag on it said, *Open me*

I lifted the lid, and a laugh escaped me as soon as I saw the contents. I reached in and picked up a hot-pink lacy bra, marveling at his craftiness. I opened the card in the box and read:

My sexy Abbie. Okay, so this was what you were wearing for my absolute favorite moment. Taking our relationship to the next level was very special for both of us, and I will never forget our first time together. Put everything on and come downstairs, and you'll find your next clue in the Christmas tree.

My heart swelled with even more love at reading this card. It meant the world to me knowing that our first time together was as special to him as it was for me. And realizing this bra made such a lasting impression on him made me feel very sexy and desired. I quickly changed my clothes and headed back downstairs.

The lights were still off; just the Christmas tree was illuminated. Right out front, tucked in one of the branches, was a simple card that read: *May I have this dance?* And that's when the music started.

I turned around to see my boyfriend standing a few feet behind me, looking so handsome in the light-gray suit he was wearing when we first met. His face glowed with happiness as he walked toward me and took me in his arms. We silently danced together for a few minutes, swaying back and forth to the rhythm of the slow jazz music.

When the song finished, he tilted my chin toward his face and lovingly gazed into my eyes. His brown eyes were so full of affection as he said, "You look so beautiful, Abbie."

"Thank you, Neil," I replied, reaching up and kissing him. A playful grin came across my face as I said, "Sorry, but I forgot the Parmesan cheese."

He laughed gently. "Thank you for offering to go to the store. I was going to ask you to go out, but you're so thoughtful that I didn't need to." He leaned down and kissed me again. "And that's just one more thing I love about you."

"Stacy and Patty are delightful," I complimented them with an affectionate smile. "They were so excited that I opened the box in front of them."

His smile matched mine as he said, "I knew they were the perfect people to help me. They're always so nice to me every time I go in there, and I knew that when the time came, I would approach them and ask for their help."

Just then, a timer went off in the kitchen.

"Do we want to have dinner?" Neil asked me.

"I would love to," I replied, taking his hand and interlacing our fingers.

We walked into the dimly lit kitchen, illuminated by two candles happily flickering on the table. Another vase of red roses sat between them, with dinner plates and crystal glasses set for a romantic dinner for two.

I looked at my sweet boyfriend to see him smiling as he watched me. “Thank you,” I said, wrapping my arms around him.

“You’re welcome, Abbie.” His expression turned to a playful grin. “And there is Parmesan cheese mixed in with the panko crumbs.”

“So, you had some here the whole time?” I asked with a laugh.

He nodded. “It was tucked in the back of the fridge.” His eyes sparkled with mischievous pride as he added, “I needed a way to have this place all to myself for a little bit.”

He led me over to the table and pulled out my chair. As I sat down, he took our plates to the counter and removed dinner from the oven. A moment later, he returned with panko-crusted salmon, potatoes, and green beans. Then he took a bottle of sparkling red grape juice out of the refrigerator and filled our glasses.

He sat down across from me with a smile and raised his glass. “To our first Christmas together.”

“To our first Christmas together,” I echoed as we clinked glasses and each took a celebratory sip.

After we finished dinner, Neil took our plates to the sink. As he opened the dishwasher, I got up to help him.

“Why don’t you let me take care of the dishes?” I offered with a smile. “Since you were so sweet to cook us dinner.”

"Thanks, Abbie," he beamed. Giving me a kiss, he said, "I love that we make such a great team. While you're doing this, I'll go check on the fire."

He left the kitchen, and as I loaded the dishwasher, I marveled at his skilled plan to get me out of the house. I honestly thought I was going out for cheese, and instead, Neil sent me on a fun scavenger hunt. I am already loving the way this Christmas is starting.

"Why don't you come with me?" a masculine voice said softly as two warm arms wrapped around my shoulders.

I turned around to see my boyfriend beaming at me. "Where else are you taking me?" I asked playfully.

"I want to dance with my beautiful girlfriend by the Christmas tree again."

He took my hand with a smile and led me back into the living room. The music was softer now, and fresh logs added to the fire made the space even more romantic and intimate. Neil pulled me in close, and I rested my head against him as I gazed lazily at the lights on our tree.

Just as I was getting lost in a romantic daydream, something new in the tree caught my eye. A petite gold ornament had been hung on a branch, and there was a small tag attached to it. I stopped dancing and looked into my handsome boyfriend's brown eyes, now sparkling with enjoyment.

"Did you see something that caught your eye?" he asked playfully.

I looked at the tree again, then back at him, my smile growing.

"Here, let's take a closer look," he suggested.

He took my hand and led me the few steps to the tree, and the instant I was close enough to read the tag, I gasped with happy surprise. In very delicate handwriting were the words: *Will You Marry Me?*

"Neil," I breathed, tears of joy coming to my eyes.

He took the ornament off the tree and opened the little gold trinket. Inside was a stunning round diamond, surrounded by several smaller diamonds set in platinum. I looked from the ring up to his eyes, sparkling as brightly as the brilliant gemstones.

He carefully hung the ornament back on its branch and turned to face me. He took my hands and smiled at me, his white teeth gleaming with happiness.

"Abbie Perkins, when I first saw you in that coffee shop wearing this dress, you took my breath away. And then, as you were frantically wiping your coffee off this suit, you amused me and impressed me all at the same time."

He stopped talking for a second as we shared a good-natured laugh. He wiped the tears of joy from my cheeks, gazing lovingly at me. Then he took my hands again and continued.

"And I instantly knew you were the woman for me. Your sweet and kind personality, along with your natural beauty, is a rare combination. You were the exact lady

I had been looking for, and I couldn't believe you were standing right in front of me."

He tilted his head to the side as he lovingly ran his fingers through my hair, gently trailing them down the entire length.

"And you made me the happiest man alive when you accepted my dinner invitation a few weeks later. And then our first kiss on the beach..." He closed his eyes and exhaled peacefully. When he opened his eyes, the love radiating from them was even stronger. "And as our relationship has continued to progress, it's just gotten better. My home now feels like our home, and I can't wait to make a life here with you."

He let go of my hands and retrieved the ornament from its branch. He smiled at me as he took the ring and got down on one knee.

"I am the happiest man alive, and it's all because of you. And there is only one thing that could make me even happier. Abbie Perkins, will you marry me?"

"Yes," I whispered as tears of joy streamed down my face.

Neil slipped the ring on my finger, then stood up and wrapped me in his arms. He held me tight against him, and I could feel the happiness radiating from him. As I stood in his warm embrace, my feelings matched his, so excited for this next step in our relationship. When he let me go, he gave me the sweetest, happiest kiss yet, and I indulged in the romance of the moment.

I opened my eyes and looked from his shining brown eyes to the ring happily sparkling on my finger. My smile grew as I watched the diamonds glistening in the lights of the Christmas tree. But as I continued to admire his beautiful gift, my smile fell a bit as a realization came to me.

Seeing my expression, Neil slid his hand under my chin and tilted my face up to meet his. There was such compassion in his features as he observed, "Abbie, your pretty smile disappeared. Why the long face?"

More tears escaped my eyes—this time from feeling guilty. He sweetly wiped them away, patiently waiting for my reply.

"It's just...," I began, then hesitated, overwhelmed with a feeling of selfishness. I looked into his kind eyes and said, "We agreed we weren't going to get each other Christmas gifts. And you sounded so convincing." My voice was barely a whisper as I admitted, "So, I didn't get you anything." My focus switched to the ring on my finger, and my smile instantly returned. "But then you gave me this gorgeous ring." I looked at his face to see his smile matching mine. "And I love it."

He took my left hand and kissed it, my ring glistening next to his shining smile. He clutched my hands to his chest, his eyes and smile softening as he looked at me. "You did give me a gift, Abbie. The best gift of my life. You said *yes* to my proposal. And that is the only gift I need."

He wrapped his arms around me and pulled me in for a long, affectionate kiss. And the way he kissed me and held me in his arms confirmed that he meant it. Asking me to marry him, and my response of *yes* was the best gift either of us could ask for.

After a moment, he pulled his face back, and I opened my eyes to see him gazing fondly at me—his eyes full of dreams for the future. As I looked at the ring on my finger again, I remembered that I did, in fact, have something else just for him.

I smiled at him playfully and teased, "And I do have another gift for you. One that *you* get to unwrap." I slid my arms over his shoulders, my smile growing. "I put on everything in the boxes of clues, just like you requested."

His eyes sparkled with desire, knowing exactly what I was talking about. "Well then," he said, picking me up in his arms. "Why don't we go to the bedroom so I can enjoy my gift."

Our smiles met for a loving kiss as my fiancé carried me down the hall. We entered the bedroom, and he set me down, my heart swelling with even more love for him as I looked around. The lights were dimmed, and several candles filled the room with an intimate glow. The same soft music was playing in here, and a vase of red roses sat on the dresser. Rose petals were scattered all over the white comforter, taking me back to a very special moment we shared.

I looked at my fiancé, his face radiant as he gazed lovingly at me. I took his hand, intertwining our fingers, and admired, "Just like our first time."

"Of course," he replied, his eyes glowing. "There's no way I could forget that night."

His smile glowed softly in the candlelight as he pulled me into his arms, and we swayed gently to the music. Leaning my head on his shoulder, I delighted in his touch as he ran his hand down my back. Tracing his fingers up my arm, he tilted my face to meet his kiss. As his kiss deepened, his fingers trailed through my hair, slowly running down the entire length. His hands gradually worked their way back up, and a swell of anticipation surged through me as he unzipped my dress, and it fell to the floor...

Chapter 5

♥

"MERRY CHRISTMAS, BEAUTIFUL," A deep voice said the following morning as strong arms held me close.

"And a Merry Christmas it is," I agreed, leaning in for a kiss.

I looked at the ring on my finger and smiled, still elated from last night. Neil pulled me closer, and we admired the sparkling diamond together.

He kissed me on the side of my head and commented, "This is the first morning I've skipped the gym in years." His smile turned mischievous as he added, "Archie told me yesterday that he wasn't expecting me last night or this morning."

"So, he knew you were going to propose last night?"

He nodded. "He's known for a long time. But nobody else in my family knows yet."

As he said that, something dawned on me. "I'm excited to tell your family during brunch this morning. And I would love to tell my parents and Sarah today as well.

But this isn't something I want to do over the phone." I rolled over and looked at him, propping myself up on my elbows. "Can we go up to Windsor today and see my family?"

He kissed me and answered with a smile, "Anything for my beautiful fiancée."

I kissed him again and sighed happily. "I love hearing you call me your fiancée." Then I checked the time. "We should probably get in the shower now and get dressed for the country club."

"That sounds good," he agreed. "I can't wait to tell everyone that you are going to be my wife."

An hour later, we were out the door. Neil looked handsome in a red sweater, gold tie, and khakis, and I felt beautiful in a dark-green sheath dress. We pulled into the parking lot of the country club and parked next to a Volvo wagon.

Neil grinned at me. "Archie's already here. And he never gets here before me." He picked up my hand and kissed it. "Can I make a request?"

"Anything for my handsome fiancé," I replied with a smile.

"Why don't you take your ring off for now, and we'll surprise everyone with a big reveal."

My eyes brightened at hearing his suggestion. "I love it!" I agreed, slipping my ring off and handing it to him. Then I looked at my empty finger, my smile falling a bit.

"Don't worry," he reassured me, kissing my hand again. "We won't wait long."

We entered the country club hand-in-hand to see Helen looking as classy as ever in a black dress and heels. John stood beside his wife in a light-blue button-down shirt, navy-blue blazer, and black pants. Wearing a dark-blue sweater over a white shirt and gold tie paired with khakis, Archie's smile was blazing as he noticed us.

"Abigail! Cornelius! Merry Christmas," Helen greeted us as she kissed us hello.

"Merry Christmas, Mom," Neil replied. He looked at his brother. "It's nice to see you here already, Arch."

"Of course," he said, kissing me on both cheeks. "I didn't want to miss anything." His smile faded a bit when he noticed the ring missing from my finger and looked at his brother. Neil discreetly patted his pocket, and Archie's eyes brightened back up.

After we handed our jackets to the coat check, the door opened, and three more people walked in. My eyes were as bright as Archie's as I saw my parents and Sarah dressed in their best Christmas attire. I looked at my fiancé, his smile glowing brightly as he watched my reaction.

"Valerie, Michael, Sarah," Helen greeted them in her typical way. "What a lovely surprise."

My dad beamed at the man standing next to me. "A couple of nights ago, Neil suggested that I bring Val and Sarah to celebrate with all of you." There was a glimmer in his eyes as his focus switched to me.

"Merry Christmas," John said as he shook my dad's hand and kissed my mom and Sarah on both cheeks. "It's wonderful to have you join us."

"Yeah," Archie chimed in, excitedly greeting my parents. "The country club is so much better with you here." His smile brightened even more as his focus switched to my sister. "Merry Christmas, Sarah."

"Merry Christmas, Archie," she replied brightly.

They stepped aside for a moment to check their coats, and as soon as my sister slipped off her thick winter coat, she transformed into a completely different woman. She had put some loose curls in her long brown hair, which she gathered over her left shoulder, and I watched as her fingers shook new life into her hairstyle. Her makeup was barely detectable, and her only accessory was a silver bracelet on her left wrist. But the real showstopper of her Christmas look was the dark-blue sheath dress perfectly hugging her feminine curves. And wow, did she look stunning! Figuring someone else noticed, I glanced over at Archie. Sure enough, his blue eyes were glued to her figure, captivated by her beauty as he slowly scanned her up and down.

He leaned over and whispered to his brother, "Wow, Neil! Look at Sarah. Just when I thought she couldn't get any prettier." After a moment, he pulled his eyes from my sister to see both of us grinning at him. His face instantly flushed with embarrassment, realizing I heard him too.

Wanting to save Archie from any further awkwardness, I quickly turned to my parents and complimented them, "The two of you look very nice."

"Thanks, Abbie," my dad said, sliding his arm around my mom's shoulders and smiling at her. "I think your mother looks quite beautiful."

I smiled at my dad's compliment of my mom, always saying she was the most attractive lady in the room. Sarah had given our mom a shimmering ivory scarf to accent her burgundy dress—my dad's favorite color on her. He looked so sharp in his funeral jacket over his button-down shirt, his dark-blue pants clean and presentable.

I smiled at my sweet fiancé. "Thank you for inviting my family."

His smile matched mine as he replied, "Of course, Abbie. You know how much family means to me. And I already consider them my family." He leaned in and whispered, "And I can't wait until they're my family officially."

I was lost in my private moment with my fiancé, tuning out the chatter around me, until I heard my sister's voice. "Helen, this place looks amazing. It's so beautiful and festive."

"Thank you, Sarah," Helen replied with an appreciative smile. "Besides handling the flower arrangements, we ladies also decorate the country club for each holiday."

Looking around, I agreed with my sister. The entryway felt so festive and welcoming, with red and green garland framing the windows. Fir wreaths decorated with silver bows, red ornaments, and pinecones cheered up the paneled walls, filling the room with a fresh, evergreen scent. A large poinsettia sat in the middle of the grand walnut table, surrounded by gifts wrapped in shimmering golden paper. Winter sunshine streamed in through the windows, brightening the foyer with holiday joy.

As I finished scanning the room, my focus landed on my sister, whose eyes were glowing with excited anticipation. She leaned in and discreetly said, "I hope I get to see my favorite new person today, Abbie."

As if on cue, the door opened, and in came three more people. My sister's eyes lit up even more as her Christmas wish came true. I did a double-take as I realized her focus was not on the lady in the wheelchair—but on the man pushing the wheelchair.

Dressed in a dark-gray suit, Grandpa helped Lydia remove Aunt Dottie's coat, and my smile instantly grew when I saw her Christmas outfit. Wearing a vibrant red dress and black boots, a festive Santa hat was the perfect finishing touch. Looking beautiful in a plum-colored dress, Lydia's brown hair was styled in a French braid, and her makeup was light and natural. As she stepped aside to check their coats, Grandpa pushed his sister closer, her smile brightening as she noticed two new friends.

Curious to see my dad's reaction to the man approaching, I glanced over at him. Just like I figured, his demeanor became serious as he scanned the family disciplinarian. Practically standing at attention, his rigid posture looked like a new recruit arriving at basic training. I giggled to myself, waiting for the salute.

Needing no introduction, Grandpa stepped from behind the wheelchair with a commanding presence. He approached my dad with his hand extended. "Cornelius Rutherford."

"It's nice to meet you, Mr. Rutherford," my dad replied, his voice full of respect. "Mike Perkins." After shaking his hand, my dad slid his arm around my mom's shoulders and introduced her, "And this is my wife, Val."

"It's a pleasure to meet you, Val," Grandpa acknowledged her kindly as he shook my mom's hand. He returned to his sister and said, "I would like the two of you to meet my sister, Mrs. Dorothy Buchanan."

My parents smiled at the lady in the Santa hat, and my mom reached out her hand. "It's lovely to meet you, Mrs. Buchanan."

Aunt Dottie's smile fell as she looked at my mom's outstretched hand. Her eyes moved to her brother as she said, "Now I know where their girls get it from, Junior." Her focus shifted back to my parents' faces, and she playfully scolded them, "And I'm going to tell the two of you what I told your daughters. Put that hand away and save that formal nonsense for the old coot!" Her bright smile returned as she said, "Both of you are to call me Aunt Dottie." She raised her left arm and welcomed them, "Now get over here and give your new auntie a hug and a kiss."

My dad chuckled as they hugged and kissed her. Standing back up, he commented to Sarah, "I like this lady already."

"I know," my sister agreed. "Isn't she great?"

"Junior, where's Lydia?" Aunt Dottie asked her brother.

"I'm right here, Dottie," Lydia answered, stepping beside her.

Aunt Dottie took her hand and smiled at my parents. "Mike, Val, I want you to meet my friend Lydia." She smiled at Lydia and said, "These are Abbie and Sarah's parents."

Lydia exchanged pleasantries with my parents, while the rest of us indulged in the affection we got from Aunt Dottie. As I watched everyone smiling and laughing with one sibling, I realized Helen was the only person talking to her brother—until I heard my sister's voice.

"Merry Christmas, Mr. Rutherford," Sarah said to him with a warm smile.

"Merry Christmas, Sarah," he replied kindly.

Out of the corner of my eye, I caught John and Helen sharing a glance—obviously surprised that someone would speak willingly to the family patriarch. Their raised eyebrows turned to warm smiles as John took his wife's hand, and they admired my sister.

After a moment, Helen's focus turned to all of us, and she suggested, "Now that everyone is here, why don't we go into the dining room?" She took my sister's arm and said, "Wait until you see the decorations in here, Sarah."

The dining room was even more stunning than the foyer. A magnificent Christmas tree towered in the middle of the room, with gold, red, and silver antique ornaments glistening in the morning sun. A dazzling gold star crowned the top of the tree, radiating happiness throughout the room. A large red and white tree skirt circled the base, with more golden-wrapped presents waiting to be opened. A warm fire blazed in the grand fireplace, just as romantic as I had imagined.

Poinsettias sat in the middle of every table, surrounded by glistening silver and gold ornaments. Full-place settings framed each plate, with a gold charger plate adding a festive layer. Alternating red and green napkins adorned with gold rings were the perfect finishing touch to the holiday tablescape.

The hostess led us to a large table close to the fireplace, and I excitedly pulled Neil to the seats in front of the romantic flames. Gloriously warm and cozy, it was the perfect atmosphere to announce our engagement. He pulled out my chair for me, and I watched as Grandpa and Lydia settled Aunt Dottie between them. My parents sat across from them, and as the seats filled up, Archie quickly took the chair next to my dad. With only three seats left, that's when I realized they were the ones on the other side of Grandpa. I figured Helen would sit next to her father-in-law—but someone else got there first.

Scampering over to the chair closest to him, Sarah pulled it out and smiled brightly at John. "I'll sit next to your dad if that's okay with you two."

He smiled at my sister and replied, "By all means, Sarah. Go ahead."

"Thanks," she said cheerfully.

Grandpa had been focused on getting Aunt Dottie comfortable and just now realized who had claimed the seat next to him. His eyes softened as he watched my sister slide her chair up to the table, and he got up to help her.

"Thanks, Mr. Rutherford," she said with a smile.

"You're welcome, Sarah," he replied kindly as he returned to his seat.

John and Helen shared a warm smile, obviously loving my sister's acknowledgment of the man that so many people avoid. Once again, somebody else had noticed this too. Archie's eyes were glued to my sister, but this time, his expression was different. Instead of admiration for her beautiful figure, his eyes were full of amazement as he watched Sarah interact so easily with his grandfather.

After the waitress took our order, I smiled excitedly at Neil, and he nodded in agreement. The two of us stood up and held hands, facing our families with bright smiles.

"Abbie and I have exciting news to share," Neil announced, making everyone's focus turn to us.

We turned to face the romantic fire, and he pulled my ring out of his pocket. He slipped it back on my finger with a kiss, and we both turned around. I excitedly thrust my hand out for everyone to see the diamond sparkling on my finger as I exclaimed, "We got engaged last night!"

A roar of cheers went around the table as everyone jumped up and came over to congratulate us. Lydia wheeled Aunt Dottie over, and everyone hugged us as the ladies gushed over my ring. I realized we were missing a person in all the commotion when a deep voice called out across the table—making all the excitement instantly quiet down.

"Neil?" Grandpa stood with a commanding presence, his features glaring with authority as he focused on his grandson. "I trust you had a conversation with Abbie's father?"

"Yes, Grandpa," he answered.

"And you looked Mr. Perkins in the eye and addressed him formally?"

"Yes, Grandpa," he repeated.

He continued to look at his grandson for another moment, his piercing blue eyes locked on Neil's calm, dark-brown eyes. Then, Grandpa's focus shifted. Just like an authoritative drill sergeant singling out a recruit, he was now looking solely at my dad. Unlike my fiancé, however, my dad didn't maintain eye contact with him for long. He glanced at my mom with an expression that clearly said, '*This guy is intense.*'

After a second, my dad's focus returned to Grandpa as he slid his arm around my mom's shoulders, a proud smile taking over his face. "Mr. Rutherford, I assure you, Neil has been nothing but polite to Val and me ever since we first met him. And when he pulled me aside a few nights ago, I did not hesitate to give him my blessing."

"So, you knew about this?" my mom asked him with an inquisitive yet slightly annoyed look.

My dad grinned at Neil. "When you told me you wanted to talk to me in my man cave, I thought you wanted to hear more of my Army stories." His expression turned serious as his focus returned to the family patriarch. "But instead, he told me how much he loves my daughter, and he wanted to ask her to marry him. And he wanted my blessing, which I instantly gave him." His focus switched to Sarah and me as he said, "Not that you girls need my permission to do anything because you don't." He looked back at Grandpa and praised, "But I appreciate Neil coming to me and showing me a level of respect I've never seen before."

Grandpa's face softened a bit as he regarded my dad. "Thank you, Mike. Nothing pleases me more than hearing people talk nicely about my boys. And I'm happy to hear that you gave Neil your blessing so quickly."

"Of course, Mr. Rutherford," my dad replied as we returned to our seats. "Val and I have been impressed with Neil since the moment we first met him."

"Thank you, Mike. Thank you, Val," Grandpa graciously acknowledged my parents. "And I have felt the same way about your girls since the moment I met them, too."

"Thank you, Mr. Rutherford," my mom expressed her happiness, putting her hand over her heart.

Grandpa's face softened as he looked at Neil and me together. "I heard so many wonderful things about Abbie, and I understood why as soon as I met her. She has a level of gratitude that I rarely see in people. I knew instantly how much she appreciates the quality of man that my grandson is. But what truly affected me was when she thanked *me* for why Neil treats her so well. Only one other young lady has ever thanked me for how well one of my boys treats her." He smiled at his daughter-in-law. "And that was Helen."

Helen reached for his hand behind my sister's chair, and I could see the love they feel for each other as they shared a smile. After a moment, their focus was pulled to my mom's voice across the table.

"What about Sarah?" she asked tentatively.

"Mom!" my sister protested, offended at my parents' lack of faith in her.

"I'm sorry, Puddin' Pie," my dad said, "but you have a tendency to speak without thinking."

"Dad!" she scolded him through clenched teeth, glaring at him across the table.

"Puddin' Pie!" Aunt Dottie repeated my dad's nickname with a laugh. "I love it, Junior!"

Grandpa smiled at his sister, then turned to my parents. "Mike, Val, I assure you both that Sarah has impressed me from the moment I first met her. I instantly noticed something in her that I see in very few people."

My parents glanced nervously at each other. "What's that, Mr. Rutherford?" my dad asked cautiously.

Grandpa looked at my sister and said, "Sarah is one of a handful of people who is able to maintain eye contact with me." His focus returned to my parents as he explained, "My father raised me always to look a man in the eye when I'm speaking to him—whether it's business or personal. And almost everyone looks away from me when they're speaking to me, including my own boys."

His focus switched to my fiancé as he continued, "Except for Neil. You have never had a problem looking me in the eye." He paused for a second, sharing a quiet moment with his grandson. Then, his focus switched to John. "But it even took my own son eighteen years to be comfortable with it. I noticed the change as you were heading off to college." He stopped speaking again as John calmly looked at him, seeming very much at peace looking his father in the eye.

"What about Archie?" my dad asked.

Grandpa's attention switched to my dad as he answered, "Archie is twenty-eight years old, and he still needs his father and brother to remind him to look me in the eye." His eyes shifted to his younger grandson, who instinctively glanced away.

"That's because you're an intimidating old coot, Junior!" Aunt Dottie accused, glaring at her brother.

Grandpa smiled at his sister, then redirected his attention to my parents. "The two of you have nothing to worry about. I find Abbie and Sarah to be incredible young ladies in their own ways."

Just then, our waitress showed up with our brunch. I smiled as I watched my dad, who knew right off which fork to start with. As everyone started enjoying their Christmas meal, my mom suddenly looked across the table with an excited smile.

"Helen, you will not believe the Christmas gift I got this morning."

"What's that, Valerie?"

"When Mike and I showed up at Sarah's apartment to pick her up, there wasn't a single dirty dish or article of clothing to be seen."

"Oh, Sarah!" Helen exclaimed, running her hand down my sister's arm. "How wonderful!"

"Thanks, Helen," she beamed at her.

"I knew you would get there. Can I ask what prompted you to clean your home?"

My sister's smile fell as she looked down, and her posture slumped. Her voice was full of reluctance as she said, "I can't believe I'm going to say this." She looked across the table and admitted with a sigh, "You were right, Mom."

—*clang!*—

My mom was so shocked at hearing my sister's admission that she dropped her fork on her plate. She stared at her wide-eyed, then looked at my dad with disbelief. Finally, she turned back to my sister and said, "Thank you, Sarah. Can I ask what exactly I was right about?"

My sister perked back up as she smiled at the man beside her. "I needed to meet Mr. Rutherford."

"Oh," Grandpa said, with the same tone of surprise as my mom. He looked at my sister and acknowledged, "I feel like you're giving me credit for something, Sarah, but I'm not sure what."

"The last time we were here, our moms were comparing notes about how messy Archie and I are," Sarah explained. "And when Neil mentioned that Archie had cleaned his apartment, my mom suggested that Helen should send you over to my place—that maybe you could light a fire under me. But Helen said you wouldn't feel like it was your place to discipline me."

Admiration took over my sister's face as she continued, "But then I met you, sir. And I instantly saw the discipline that I've heard so much about, and I found it inspiring." Her voice was quiet as she added, "And then

Abbie and I went to your home, and that's when I was truly inspired."

Grandpa's face softened as he asked, "What was it about my home, Sarah?"

"Mr. Rutherford, you trusted Abbie and me with your wife's Christmas decorations, which we knew right off meant a lot to you." She looked down at her plate and started pushing her food around with her fork. "And then I got home that night, and I walked into my messy apartment, and I felt ashamed." She looked at Grandpa. "Here you were, trusting us to take care of your home, and I wasn't even taking care of my own home. So, I decided I would clean my apartment before we returned to decorate."

Sarah looked across the table at Archie. "Does your apartment feel better now?"

"It does," he admitted with a proud smile. "It feels good to open my door and see a clean living room."

"I know. It's amazing how much better I feel going home now," she agreed with a smile that mirrored Archie's. "I'm not sure what your incentive was to clean your apartment, but I know what mine was." She smiled at Grandpa. "It's because of you and your wife, Mr. Rutherford."

"Thank you, Sarah," he replied, his voice full of genuine honor. "I'm happy that trusting you with Eleanor's decorations inspired you to clean your home."

"And she would be happy about it too, Junior," Aunt Dottie said, smiling at her brother.

"Yes, she would, Dottie," Grandpa agreed, returning his sister's smile. "Now I'm even more convinced that having Abbie and Sarah decorate was the right decision." He smiled at my sister. "I'm proud of you, Sarah."

"Thanks, Mr. Rutherford," she beamed at him.

"Your mother and I are proud of you too, Kitten Mitten," my dad praised her.

"Oh, Junior!" Aunt Dottie laughed. "These names keep getting better and better!"

My sister shook her head as she laughed good-naturedly. "I'll give you that one. And thanks." Suddenly, her expression changed, and she looked at Neil and me with huge eyes. "I am so sorry you guys. We're supposed to be celebrating your engagement today. Not me cleaning my apartment."

Neil smiled at her. "It's okay, Sarah. We can celebrate two big milestones today."

"And besides, Sarah," I jumped in. "You're going to play a big part in our wedding. I need a Maid of Honor."

Her eyes lit up at my invitation to give her such a meaningful title. "Thanks, Abbie!"

My focus switched to my fiancé, and I looked back and forth between him and Archie.

Neil grinned at his brother. "Archie and I worked this out more than twenty years ago." He looked at his parents. "Do you remember when Mr. Davenport's youngest son got married?"

Helen's eyes lit up. "I do remember. His bride was so beautiful. And, Sarah, you should have seen the way they decorated."

Archie grinned at his parents. "Do you remember his brother's Best Man speech?"

John and Grandpa exchanged a look with raised eyebrows as Helen put her face in her hands. "Now that you mention it, I do," she said, shaking her head. She looked at my parents and explained, "Our boys were so well-behaved that we could take them anywhere, and they were the only two children allowed at that wedding. Even the Flower Girl and Ring Bearer were ushered out after their part of the ceremony."

"I remember when Tim got up to make his speech," John recalled, laughing. "I think he forgot there were two children present because he told some rather inappropriate jokes for young ears."

"We had no clue what he was talking about since we were six and eight," Neil said to his dad. "While you were tucking us into my bed that night, Archie asked you who the funny guy was. You told us he was Steven's Best Man, and we asked what that meant. You said that meant he was Steven's best friend in the whole wide world."

The two brothers smiled at each other as Archie said, "So after Dad tucked us in and kissed us goodnight, he turned out the light and shut the door. That's when I said, 'When I get married, Neil, you'll be my Best Man.'"

Neil's smile grew as he looked at his brother. "And then I said, 'And you'll be mine too, Arch.' And then we fell asleep."

I kissed my sweet fiancé on the cheek. "So, the two of you have always been best friends."

"Always," he confirmed with a smile.

My attention was pulled from my favorite brown eyes when I heard a surprised voice a few feet away.

"Do my old eyes deceive me, or is Junior Rutherford out socializing?" An older gentleman dressed in a black suit walked up to Grandpa with a big smile on his face.

Grandpa stood up and greeted him with a handshake. "Mr. Weston. How nice to see you, sir." After introducing my family and me, he said, "Our families have been doing business together since my father and Mr. Davenport were in charge."

"I've known Junior here since he was about ten years old," Mr. Weston remarked, putting his hand on Grandpa's shoulder. "And he looked like a miniature business owner even back then, sitting next to his father at his desk, looking so serious in his suit." He smiled at Grandpa. "It's nice to see you celebrating the holidays, Junior."

"And our family has more than just Christmas to celebrate this year." Grandpa smiled proudly at the two of us. "Neil and Abbie got engaged last night."

"Congratulations!" Mr. Weston exclaimed, his hazel eyes glowing with happiness. He looked at the two of us together for a moment; then, his focus switched to just

Neil. He slid his arm around Grandpa's shoulders and admired, "There's nothing like a man in love, is there, Junior?"

"No, Mr. Weston, there's not," he agreed.

He smiled at Grandpa and said, "I still remember the first time I saw you with Eleanor." He looked at us and recalled, "I had known Junior for twenty years at that point, and that was the first time I ever saw him smile. I didn't even recognize him at first. I turned to my wife and said, 'Get a load of Junior. It turns out he can smile without his face breaking.'" We had a good laugh as he smiled at Grandpa. "And then we saw the prettiest little brunette on your arm. Eleanor sure was a special lady."

Grandpa's face lit up in a smile as he agreed, "Yes, she was."

Mr. Weston's expression turned to a look of sorrow as he continued, "I lost my wife back in the summer. We had just celebrated our seventieth wedding anniversary." He paused for a second as everyone gasped with amazement. "And while that might sound like a long time, I will tell you right now, seventy years wasn't nearly long enough with her."

"I know how you feel, Mr. Weston," Grandpa empathized. "I had thirty-three years with Eleanor, and it went by in the blink of an eye."

Mr. Weston smiled at Grandpa, then turned his attention to Neil and me. "May the two of you enjoy a long and happy marriage as well."

"Thank you, Mr. Weston," Neil graciously accepted his well wishes.

Then he regarded my family and kindly acknowledged, "It was nice meeting all of you."

"You as well, sir," my dad replied.

Mr. Weston's smile grew as he looked at the lady in the Santa hat. "Merry Christmas, Dottie," he said, kissing her on the cheek.

"Merry Christmas, Mr. Weston," she replied.

After he had left, I turned to Neil. "Seventy years. That's amazing."

He nodded, his smile beaming with fond memories. "His wife was such a sweet lady. And just like Grandpa, he was always smiling around her." He slid his arm around my shoulders and looked at his grandfather. "A great woman will have that effect on a man. Even the strictest disciplinarian."

I rested my head on Neil's shoulder, watching peacefully as our families continued to visit since everyone had finished eating. As a realization occurred to me, I looked at my fiancé. "We made it all the way through brunch without one girl hitting on you or Archie."

Neil grinned at me. "That's because they all sense someone's presence." He looked at his grandfather again. "People tend to stay away when Grandpa's around." Just then, something caught his attention, and his smile disappeared. "Although there are some exceptions."

I followed his line of sight and immediately recognized who was coming our way. Wearing a low-cut red dress that showed off her voluptuous curves, Arabella Shaw was making her way through the dining room—her eyes fixed on my fiancé. Her long brown hair flowed luxuriously over her shoulders, and she strutted with confidence in her six-inch stilettos. Moving like a woman who knows what she wants and how to get it, her hourglass figure exuded all the hypnotic sex appeal of Jessica Rabbit.

Neil took my hand and said, "I apologize now for whatever she's going to say."

She sauntered around the table and stopped behind us. "Hi, Neil," she said with a suggestive smile.

"Hi, Arabella," he replied politely. He smiled at me and said, "I'd like you to meet my fiancée, Abbie."

Her smile disappeared as she eyed me up and down with disgust. "Well, at least the two of you are only engaged. There's still time for Neil to come to his senses and leave you to marry someone within his social status."

"No, Arabella," Neil stated firmly, looking directly at her. "Abbie is the woman I've waited my entire life for." He smiled gently at me and said, "And I can't wait to make her my wife."

"We'll see," she said with a dismissive wave of her hand. "I'm used to getting what I want." Her focus moved a few seats over, her eyes brightening as they landed on the available brother. Archie was sitting perfectly still, hoping she wouldn't see him, but he wasn't so lucky. "And besides," she declared, her seductive smile returning, "you're not the one I really want."

Neil leaned over and whispered, "Watch this." I looked at him to see a big grin on his face. "She'll see just how much she's going to get with Cornelius Rutherford here." We looked across the table to see a stone-cold face intently glaring at the brunette bombshell, shaking her curves as she pursued the target of her desire.

She slid her hands over Archie's shoulders and leaned down so her cleavage was right next to his face. "Hi, Archie," she said seductively.

"Hey, Arabella," he replied nervously, his eyes darting around.

"You look really nice today, Archie." She tucked her face into his neck and inhaled his scent. "And you smell good too."

"Thanks," he said, his blue eyes growing huge with panic.

"What are you doing for New Year's Eve?" she asked him, sliding her left hand up to play with his hair.

"Um, probably working."

"On New Year's Eve, Archie?"

"Uh-huh," he answered quickly.

"I'm going with some friends to Times Square. You should come with me, and we can ring in the new year right."

"Um, no thanks."

"Come on, Archie," she coaxed. "I already have a room booked at the fanciest hotel in the city." Her voice lowered to just above a whisper as she said enticingly, "I promise it'll be a night you'll never forget."

Suddenly, Archie's eyes stopped darting around, and his focus locked on a very unlikely person. Blue eyes that matched his instantly read the pleading look for help, and everyone's attention was pulled to the sound of someone clearing their throat.

The tempting seductress instantly vanished as Arabella noticed the piercing blue eyes glaring at her. She stood up quickly and yanked her hand from Archie as if he were on fire.

"Mr. Rutherford."

"Miss Shaw."

"I didn't see you there, sir," she admitted, looking away from him.

"Yet here I am," he replied matter-of-factly. "How is your father?"

"He's good, sir, thank you."

Grandpa's eyes were laser-focused on her, but all she would do was occasionally glance at him.

Finally, looking clearly uncomfortable, she said, "Well, I should probably get back to my family now."

Grandpa's glare intensified as he informed her, "Let your father know he can expect a visit from me this week."

All the color drained from her face, realizing the severity of the consequences, and she responded timidly, "Yes, Mr. Rutherford." Her focus shifted, and a slight smile came to her face as she looked at the lady next to him. "Merry Christmas, Aunt Dottie."

"Merry Christmas, Sugar," she replied warmly.

After she slinked away like a dog with its tail between its legs, Archie exhaled all the tension he was holding. "Thanks, Grandpa," he said with a quick glance.

"You're welcome, Archie," he replied, his voice full of compassion.

I looked at Neil wide-eyed. "And I thought your mom was impressive. He barely said anything."

"Yeah, Grandpa has that effect on people. He can get his point across with very few words. He just silently stares someone down, and their discomfort instantly puts them back in their place. But there is one person who seems immune to his intimidation." His focus switched to my sister. "The truly impressive one is Sarah. The way your sister stood up to him about not taking his money..." He shook his head. "Archie and I still can't believe it." His focus returned to me. "And the way she made Grandpa laugh? That's really her gift. Your sister knew Grandpa for a week and a half, and she brought out a side of him that Archie and I didn't even know existed."

"So, the two of you never saw him laugh before that?"

His eyes grew huge as he shook his head. "No." His face softened as he laughed and acknowledged, "Archie says that's Sarah's superpower."

My laughter matched his as I agreed, "I know. I was getting ready to apologize for her. Again. But it turns out I had nothing to worry about. And Grandpa was so nice as he talked about us to our parents."

He laughed again. "I think your parents were worried to hear Grandpa's impression of Sarah."

"My poor sister," I sympathized, feeling a bit bad for her. "Her lack of a filter has always gotten her into so much trouble. And I know she appreciated your grandfather's kind words about her."

A warm smile spread across his handsome face. "It was nice hearing Grandpa speak so well of the two of you. He even told your sister he's proud of her, which he rarely does. And he's right. You and Sarah are incredible in your own ways. You're very different, but you're both genuinely good people."

My heart melted at hearing his compliment. "Thank you," I said with a smile that mirrored his. "And we're not the only siblings who are completely opposite. We can't get over how different Aunt Dottie is from her brother. Even the way they each handled Arabella. Aunt Dottie was so sweet to her."

His smile broadened. "Aunt Dottie loves everyone, and she's nice to everyone. But even she doesn't want to see Archie end up with a girl like that." He picked up my hands and held them to his chest. "And speaking of Arabella, I'm sorry for the way she spoke to you."

"Thank you," I said, rubbing my thumbs against his hands.

His eyes were so full of love as he looked at me like I was the most important person in the world to him. His soft smile returned as he said, "Thank you, Abbie. I feel like the luckiest man alive because I'm the one who gets to marry you." His smile turned to a playful grin as he added, "And I love that we've already started talking about wedding plans."

I leaned forward and kissed him, my grin matching his. "And I love everything my super organized fiancé has suggested so far."

We were pulled from our private moment as we heard Helen's voice across the table. "Michael, Valerie, after Christmas brunch, we always go back to our house to celebrate the rest of the day. Why don't you and Sarah join us?"

My parents' eyes lit up. "Thanks, Helen," my mom said. "That sounds wonderful."

"Actually, Helen," Grandpa interjected. "If you don't mind, I'd like to have everyone over to my home this year."

"Oh, Dad," she breathed, looking at her father-in-law with eyes full of love. "That would be lovely."

"And Mike and Val can see the beautiful job their girls did decorating my home."

"We'd like that, Mr. Rutherford," my dad agreed.

Aunt Dottie pulled her brother's face toward her to kiss him on the cheek. "Just like how we used to spend the holiday when Eleanor was with us." She smiled and gently complimented him, "I'm proud of you, Junior."

He smiled quietly at his sister as he stood up and pushed her into the foyer. The rest of us followed and retrieved our coats. As we got ready to go out into the cold, I noticed a warm smile on my sister's face. I knew decorating Grandpa's home meant a lot to her, but it was only during brunch that I realized exactly how much of an effect it had on her.

Chapter 6

"Wow, Abbie!" my dad exclaimed, looking at Grandpa's house as we got out of our cars. "This place is fancy."

"Wait until you see the inside," I replied with a grin.

"Wait until you see the picture right inside the door," my sister chimed in, sliding her elbow inside his and excitedly pulling him up the ramp.

We stepped into the entryway and handed our coats to Lydia, who took them to the closet just down the hall. My parents looked around wide-eyed, amazed as they observed his impressive home. I giggled to myself as I heard my mom whisper to my dad, "Don't touch anything."

And while my parents' eyes wandered around, my sister's focus was glued to one spot—a dreamy look in her eyes. I slid my arm around her shoulders, and she smiled at me. "That's my favorite picture of them, Abbie. They look so sweet and happy."

"I know, Sarah," I agreed.

Her expression switched to a playful grin as she looked at our parents. "Check out Mom and Dad. They look like they're in a museum."

I followed my sister's eyes over to my parents, still marveling at their new surroundings. As soon as my dad's focus landed on the wedding picture, he stopped and stared at it. After a moment, his eyes traveled to my future brother-in-law. He leaned down, and I heard him discreetly comment to my mom, "He looks just like Archie in that picture."

As my parents admired the photo in front of them, I noticed my sister looking in the opposite direction. She had a heartwarming smile on her face as she watched Grandpa trade out Aunt Dottie's boots for reindeer slippers with flashing lights on the antlers.

"Junior," Aunt Dottie smiled at her brother, "why don't we take Mike and Val on a tour?"

"That sounds wonderful, Dottie," he agreed, pushing her wheelchair into the front room.

"Oh, wow, Puddin' Pie," my dad marveled, taking my sister's hand. "You and Abbie did an amazing job in here."

"Thanks, Dad," she cheerfully accepted his compliment without protesting the name.

I smiled as my parents delighted in the holiday cheer, starting with the tree and then moving to the stockings. When my dad noticed the second wedding picture, he did a double-take, surprised by another joyful expression. Finally, he tore his eyes from the image and looked at Grandpa. “Your friend wasn’t kidding, Mr. Rutherford. You look like a completely different man when you’re with your wife.”

“My wife was quite the lady,” Grandpa responded, smiling at the picture.

“You can say that again!” Aunt Dottie agreed. “Eleanor had a magical way of turning this stubborn old coot into a nice man.”

My dad laughed at her wisecrack. “I like you, Aunt Dottie.”

She beamed at my dad. “Thanks, Mike. I think you’re cute too.”

“I can’t get over her,” my dad joked, smiling at my sister.

“I know,” Sarah agreed. “Isn’t she great?”

Grandpa pushed his sister through the library and into the parlor as he said, “And this was my wife’s favorite room.”

“I can see why,” my mom commented as she and my dad gazed around. Then she praised Sarah and me, “The two of you did a great job decorating.”

“Thanks, Mom,” Sarah replied, her smile glowing brightly.

Looking around, my dad remarked, “I can see why this place inspired you to clean your apartment, Puddin’ Pie.”

My sister smiled at the man responsible. “Thanks again for letting us decorate your home, Mr. Rutherford.”

“Thank you, Sarah,” he replied graciously.

Helen slid her arm through her father-in-law’s and smiled at him. “And Mom would love the way this place looks, too, Dad.”

“Yes, she would, Helen,” he agreed with a soft smile.

“Why don’t we all have a seat?” John suggested.

Looking around, Lydia observed, “We could use a few more chairs. I’ll bring some in from the kitchen.” She and Archie stepped through the adjoining door as everyone settled throughout the room.

Grandpa parked Aunt Dottie’s wheelchair beside the sofa and sat down as John and Helen joined him. My parents, Neil, and I took the armchairs as Archie set two kitchen chairs next to each other for him and Sarah. Never far from her friend, Lydia put her chair on the other side of Aunt Dottie.

“So Abigail,” Helen smiled at me, “how did Cornelius propose to you last night?”

I slipped my hand inside Neil’s and intertwined our fingers. “He sent me on a fun scavenger hunt.”

Everyone’s eyes lit up.

“Oh, Cornelius!” Helen smiled at her son. “How romantic.”

My sister looked at Neil as a realization came to her. “Is that why you asked me for the dress, heels, and scarf Abbie was wearing when you first met?”

He grinned at her. "I couldn't have done it without you, Sarah."

She laughed. "And lucky for me, Abbie's closet is neat and organized. It took me no time to find everything."

I looked at Neil. "When did you have Sarah get my clothes and shoes from my apartment?"

"I asked her a couple of days ago. And while we were at your parents' house for your dad's birthday, we snuck outside and moved everything from her car to mine."

A warmth spread through me at hearing how much he involved my family. "Was this before or after you talked to my dad?"

He smiled at my dad. "After, of course."

"So, when did you bring my dress and scarf to the store?" I asked, marveling at his thoughtful plan.

"Later that night," he answered with a playful grin. "You and Sarah were so engrossed in decorating the bedroom upstairs that you didn't even realize I had left. All the cards were written; I just needed to box up your dress and scarf. I had already talked with Patty and Stacy, so I ran into the store and handed them the box. Then I returned home to find you and Sarah looking at pictures of furniture on her phone."

My sister just blinked at my fiancé. "You left your house?" Her eyes traveled to me. "I didn't even know he was gone."

"That was all part of my master plan, Sarah," Neil commented, his proud smile growing. "I invited you to come to my place so you could keep Abbie occupied.

I've spent enough time around you two that I know you tune out everything when you're browsing at design ideas."

"My highly organized brother had every last detail planned out," Archie proclaimed with his blazing smile.

Helen looked between her sons. "So, Archibald knew last night?"

"Archie's known for a long time, Mom," Neil confirmed, smiling at his brother.

Helen's eyes brightened as her focus switched to my mom. "Oh, Valerie, isn't this exciting?"

"It is," my mom agreed. "I've been looking forward to helping my girls plan their weddings for years."

"And we have grandchildren to look forward to," Helen dreamed out loud, smiling at John.

A mischievous grin spread across my sister's face as she looked at my dad. "I'm looking forward to hearing about the boneheaded things Neil says on their anniversary."

"I still stand behind my statement; thank you very much," my dad said with his hands in the air.

My mom, sister, and I laughed as the Rutherfords turned to my dad with expectant looks.

My mom took his hand and explained, "On our twenty-fourth wedding anniversary, my loving husband informed me that he would rather be married than in prison."

Everyone laughed good-naturedly except Grandpa, who smiled slightly.

"Oh, Michael," Helen said as her laughter calmed. "Why on earth would you say that?"

"What my beautiful wife and daughters are failing to tell you is the story behind my comment. Val and I had been watching the news during dinner, and they did a story about a very young man who had committed a serious crime. And he was going to spend the next several decades in prison. Which also meant that he would miss out on all the fun stuff in life—getting married, having kids, stuff like that. So, I made the innocent comment that I would rather be married than in prison, and seven years later—" My dad cut himself off as he glanced at my mom and noticed her raised eyebrows. "Eight years later, these three still won't let me live it down."

"It makes sense to me," Archie agreed, smiling at my dad.

"Thanks, Archie," my dad beamed at him. He looked at my mom and said, "See? Archie gets me." Taking my mom's hand, he smiled at our new family members. "And marrying Val is still the best decision I've ever made."

"Nice save," my mom acknowledged him with a smile.

Wanting to get the attention off my poor dad, I told our families, "And Neil and I have already started talking about wedding plans."

Everyone's focus switched to us as Helen exclaimed, "Oh, Abigail, that's so exciting. What are you two thinking?"

I smiled at my sweet fiancé. "Last night, Neil showed me a picture of a cute little resort that will take care of everything for us. We can have the ceremony there as well as the reception, and anyone who wants to stay the night is more than welcome."

"So, you don't want to have your ceremony in one place and arrive at your reception in a helicopter?" Archie asked us with a grin.

My sister's eyes brightened with excitement. "That sounds so cool, Abs."

The Rutherfords, on the other hand, had a much different reaction to Archie's suggestion. John and Grandpa glanced at one another as Helen shook her head with her face in her hands. "I remember that wedding," she murmured.

"Okay, we have got to hear this story," my sister said with an amused smile.

Helen looked up, and I could tell just by the expression on her face that she felt terrible for the couple. She reached over, took John's hand, and began, "A young couple from our country club got married a few years ago, and the bride insisted on arriving at the reception in her father's helicopter."

My family and I looked at each other with raised eyebrows. Of course, it was my sister who asked, "The guy owns a helicopter?"

John grinned at my dad. "I'm sure he would love to meet you, Mike. He's always looking for a reason to take it out and have fun."

"Like a wedding?" my sister asked, grinning at Neil and me.

This got a laugh out of my fiancé. "While it sounds fun in theory, the reality wasn't so fun for the bride."

"Why? What happened?" she asked.

"Her father tried to talk her out of it," Helen explained, "but she threw an absolute fit. So, he gave in and let her have her grand entrance." She smiled at my sister. "You should have seen their decorations, Sarah—they were breathtaking. All the tables were set with the finest crystal, and there were gorgeous flowers everywhere."

"But what the bride failed to realize was what the strong blast of wind from the helicopter blades would do to those decorations," John continued the story. "Until it was too late."

My sister's eyes grew huge with understanding. "You mean?"

"Yup," Archie answered with a laugh. "Blew their entire flower display to smithereens in a matter of seconds."

My mom gasped. "That poor bride must have been devastated."

"And it only got worse from there," Helen confirmed. "She jumped out of the helicopter as soon as it was on the ground, and the still-spinning blades completely tangled her gorgeous hair—that I heard took two hours to style."

"And then she threw an even bigger fit," John chimed back in. "Especially when she noticed all the dirt that had been kicked up, completely ruining their wedding cake. No one could calm her down. Not even her new husband."

"That poor guy," Archie sympathized, glancing at his brother.

"Okay, then," my sister said, changing her original thinking. "When you put it that way, I don't think you should come in on a helicopter, Abbie."

"I agree," I said, smiling at my handsome fiancé. "Besides, Neil and I want to keep things rather simple. And having everything in one location makes it easier for us and our guests."

"And the old coot is going to help you pay for everything," Aunt Dottie announced, glaring at her brother.

Neil and I looked at each other wide-eyed, then turned our focus to the man being scrutinized by his sister. "Grandpa," Neil said, shaking his head. "You don't have to—"

"Yes, he does!" Aunt Dottie cut him off, still glaring at the man next to her. "If somebody gives me a crowbar, I will pry my brother's wallet open myself. I still have one good hand."

Grandpa smiled at his sister, then turned to address the two of us. "Neil, Abbie, I would be honored to help the two of you pay for your wedding." His focus switched to my parents as he stated, "I just don't want to step on Mike and Val's toes."

"Oh, Mr. Rutherford," my dad responded, a bit surprised. "We just don't want to..." He trailed off, looking at my mom, not sure how to finish.

"Take advantage of your generosity," my mom helped him complete their acknowledgment of the family patriarch.

"Generosity? Ha!" Aunt Dottie's scorn intensified, her eyes burning holes through her brother. "I know you make these boys negotiate their salaries every three months. You should be ashamed of yourself, Junior!"

Grandpa smiled at the lady glaring daggers at him, then turned to my parents. "Mike, Val, thank you, but you don't need to worry. We are a family, and I want to do whatever I can to make Neil and Abbie's big day as special as possible." He smiled at the two of us, then his focus switched to his sister. His smile softened as he reminded her, "Just like how I made sure you and Frank had the best wedding you could have—considering the circumstances."

"Oh, Junior," Aunt Dottie's scowl instantly vanished. "I remember." She pulled her brother's face toward her to kiss him on the cheek, then explained to my family, "Our caterer called two days before our wedding to cancel, realizing they had been double-booked for that day. Well, as soon as this one here got word, he picked up the phone, called the caterer, and lit right into her. At that point, our father had only been gone a few years, and people already knew what it now meant to get a phone call from Cornelius Rutherford."

"And the lady on the phone asked about the other couple," Grandpa expanded on the story. "And while I did not want my sister's wedding guests to go hungry, I also didn't want that for the other couple. So, I came up with a last-minute solution to please both couples."

Aunt Dottie smiled at her brother. "Junior called all his employees into an emergency meeting and explained what was happening. He offered to pay any employee double time if they would help at either wedding."

"Oh, Mr. Rutherford," my sister gushed. "That's so sweet."

"Yes, it was, Sarah," Aunt Dottie agreed with a grateful smile. "Both of us couples were so grateful to Junior and the forty employees who agreed to help. And none of them accepted his money. They were all just so happy to make our day special."

"Dad and Mr. Davenport certainly hired the best people, didn't they, Dottie?" Grandpa asked with a smile that matched his sister's.

"Yes, they did, Junior," she affirmed. Turning to my family, she said, "Frankie and I were married for almost sixty years, and every time we talked about our wedding, we always remembered how special Junior and the employees made us feel." She kissed her brother's cheek again. "And that feeling was priceless."

As my family listened to the story, they smiled as they learned of Grandpa's dedication to his sister. Suddenly, Sarah's facial expression changed like a realization was occurring to her.

She smiled brightly at Aunt Dottie and said, "And you have another special day coming up in less than a month." She looked at my parents and told them, "Aunt Dottie's going to be eighty on January twenty-first."

"Oh, Sarah, honey," Aunt Dottie breathed. "You remembered my birthday."

"Of course I remembered," she stated the obvious. "I couldn't forget my favorite new auntie's big birthday."

As John and Grandpa smiled warmly at each other, my mom asked, "So, do you have any exciting plans for your birthday?"

"Oh, yes!" she exclaimed happily. "My daughter and two of my granddaughters are taking me out for a spa day."

"Oh, wow!" my sister's enthusiasm matched Aunt Dottie's. "That sounds like so much fun."

While my family reveled in her excitement, the Rutherfords had much different facial expressions. Grandpa looked at John with eyes full of anger as Helen eyed her two sons expectantly. I instantly read her universal 'Mom Look,' which clearly said, *'Say something nice. Now!!!!!'*

Picking up on the silent communication, Neil smiled and said, "That sounds like a great time, Aunt Dottie. How sweet of them to take you out and give you the royal treatment."

"Yeah," Archie chimed in, his smile blazing. "You'll come home looking like an all-new lady. We might not even recognize you."

As Helen smiled her approval at her sons, I looked at Neil inquisitively. His smile for Aunt Dottie's benefit disappeared as he leaned in and quietly explained, "Aunt Dottie's kids are notorious for making plans with her and then bailing at the last minute. She gets her hopes up every time, and every time they call and say something came up—or worse—they forgot. And then she starts crying, and Grandpa starts yelling."

I looked at Grandpa and noticed the angry scowl. "Grandpa already looks furious," I discreetly commented.

He nodded. "I know what he's thinking. It's what we're all thinking. They're not going to show up." Neil's focus switched to Aunt Dottie's beaming face. "I really hope we're wrong this time."

Our attention was pulled to my sister as we heard her ask, "So, Mr. Rutherford, did you do anything exciting for your eightieth birthday?"

As soon as she heard the question, Helen gasped with realization. "Dad!" She turned to John with a panicked expression, then slid down the couch next to her father-in-law and took his hand. "Oh, Dad," she said, her voice full of regret. "I'm so sorry. We didn't do anything for your eightieth birthday."

His eyes were full of love as he smiled at his daughter-in-law. "Actually, Helen, you did do something for me. You gave me the best gift I had gotten in years."

Grandpa turned to us and said, "Our new family members might not be aware that my birthday is eleven days after Dottie's. And her stroke happened right in the middle."

"That's right, it did," John said, voicing his family's realization as they all looked at each other. He turned to his father and admitted shamefully, "But...I don't remember what we did for you, Dad."

Grandpa's face was soft with gratitude as he answered, "You moved my sister into my home."

"That was on your birthday?" Helen asked in a whisper.

He nodded and replied gently, "Yes, Helen." He looked at his son and grandsons and said, "And the care you boys took with your Aunt Dottie meant everything to me."

"We were more than happy to help, Dad," John commented as he slid across the couch to sit beside his wife. "But we're sorry we didn't realize it was your birthday."

"It's okay," Grandpa said. "It had been a long day for all of us. That morning, Neil and Archie finished installing the ramp as John and I went to pick up the van. And then, after Lydia agreed to move in, the four of you helped to pack her belongings as I filled out Dottie's discharge paperwork. All of you were in the driveway, waiting for us when we arrived. And you stayed to make sure that everything was set up perfectly for Dottie and Lydia."

"I remember it was late when we left here that night," Neil recalled.

"I remember when they left too, Junior," Aunt Dottie said, grinning at her brother.

Grandpa smiled at his sister. "It was just after nine o'clock. I thanked Lydia for all of her hard work and told her she could relax for the rest of the night." He paused and smiled gratefully at the lady sitting next to his sister. "I figured you would appreciate some much-needed rest. And as much as I appreciated everyone's help, I wanted some time alone with my sister."

"So, did the two of you stay up for a while after I went to bed?" Lydia asked the siblings.

Grandpa and Aunt Dottie smiled at each other, then he got up and left the parlor momentarily. When he returned, he was carrying his sister's yellow patchwork quilt.

"We cleaned out most of Dottie's possessions from her home in the spring," Grandpa explained to my family. "But I asked John and Helen to make sure that a few of her things were here when she moved in—especially this quilt."

He draped it over his spot on the couch as John and Helen moved to the other end.

"Then I took my sister out of her wheelchair..." He scooped her up and set her on the quilt.

"And then he wrapped me up like a little burrito!" Aunt Dottie joked as he folded the quilt around her.

We all laughed with Aunt Dottie except for Grandpa, who smiled as he sat next to his sister.

"Then I put in the tape of Casablanca and sat next to my sister and held her close to me." Grandpa put his arm around Aunt Dottie, and she rested her head on his shoulder.

Aunt Dottie smiled at her brother. "And that's when I said, 'Happy birthday, you old coot.'"

Everyone shared another good-natured chuckle as Grandpa smiled at his sister. "And I kissed you on the forehead and said, 'Thank you, Dottie.'" His focus switched to us as he continued, "And then I started the picture, and about fifteen minutes later, my sister drifted off. And I smiled as I listened to her peacefully snoring—"

"Junior!" Aunt Dottie cut him off, lifting her head to glare at him angrily. "You take that back! I do not snore!"

Grandpa kissed her on the cheek, then tucked her head back onto his shoulder. "Anyways, I sat here, enjoying Casablanca, knowing that all was right with the world. My sister was alive and healthy and with me where she belonged."

He was quiet for a moment, leaning his head against his sister's. He closed his eyes and sighed peacefully, then opened his eyes and looked at his family.

"That was the best birthday I'd had since Eleanor passed, and all of you helped to make it special. For me and for Dottie. So, thank you."

Everyone smiled at the two siblings as John replied, "You're welcome, Dad."

Neil's attention switched to his brother. They shared a look of regret as Archie whispered, "I can't believe we forgot Grandpa's eightieth birthday."

"I know, Arch," he agreed so quietly that only Sarah and I heard their exchange.

They looked at their grandfather with a combination of love for him mixed with remorse at having forgotten his milestone birthday. And while I could understand their sorrow over not celebrating his big day, as I looked at Grandpa, I don't think he minded. Watching him with Aunt Dottie, I got the feeling that he was sincerely happy just to have his sister with him.

We continued to celebrate for the rest of the day—our families blending so beautifully together. My parents went from looking like they were out of place in a fancy museum to seeming like they felt at home here. And I know everyone felt the warm presence of Neil's grandmother, even those of us who hadn't gotten the privilege of meeting her. Just by having her decorations around, their home felt warmer and more inviting than when Sarah and I first arrived a month ago. Grandpa's home truly felt like one more place where I knew my family and I belonged.

Chapter 7

♥

"THIS PLACE DOESN'T LOOK the same without all the Christmas decorations," I commented, standing on my tiptoes to kiss my sweet fiancé in his kitchen.

"I know," he agreed, wrapping his arms around me. "I wonder what you and Sarah have up your sleeve for decorating our home next."

I grinned at him playfully. "We've been collecting a lot of fun and romantic Valentine's Day decorations."

"Mmm," he sighed contentedly, giving me another kiss. "I can only imagine the surprise I'll come home to." There was a twinkle in his eyes as he added, "And I already have our date planned for that night."

I couldn't help the smile that took over my face. "I love having such a sweet and thoughtful fiancé." I gave him another kiss. "And organized, too. Your surprise of New York City to ring in the New Year was perfect."

"It was my pleasure," he said, his voice deep and sexy. "You were the most beautiful woman in the entire city."

"Thank you," I accepted his compliment as my smile glowed brighter. My smile turned to a mischievous grin as someone came to mind. "And I'm sure we enjoyed our New Year's Eve in the Big Apple better than Archie would have."

He laughed. "Grandpa really saved him. Besides, Archie had fun hanging out with Aunt Dottie, watching the Three Stooges like they used to when we were kids."

"So, Grandpa gave him the night off from work?" I asked, my laughter matching his.

"Amazingly, yes. But probably because Aunt Dottie yelled at him." As our laughter calmed, he tilted his head to the side and gazed lovingly at me. "That really was my favorite New Year's Eve, Abbie. I loved celebrating with my beautiful fiancée."

Neil brushed my hair over my shoulders, and just as he leaned in for a kiss, his phone rang on the counter. He glanced at it with a grin and silenced it.

"Archie must know we're talking about him. I'll call him back in a bit."

Just as Neil's soft lips made contact with mine, his phone rang again.

This time, we both looked at his phone. "It's okay if you want to answer it," I assured him, feeling a bit concerned. "It might be something important."

He answered the call and put it on speaker as a grin spread across his face. "It's only been two hours since you saw me at the gym, Arch. You miss me already?"

"Neil," Archie said, his voice full of concern. "It's Aunt Dottie."

Neil's grin instantly disappeared. "What's going on?"

"They bailed on her. Just like we knew they would."

His head slumped. "That's right—today is Aunt Dottie's birthday. How is she doing?"

"She's devastated, Neil. I came by to tell her happy birthday and to offer to drive the van for them. Just as I got here, the phone rang."

"What was their excuse this time?" Neil's tone was a mixture of curiosity and dread at hearing the answer.

"They forgot." Archie's tone was a mixture of sadness and annoyance. "They had made other plans for today and only remembered when the spa called on Thursday to confirm the appointments."

"And they waited until this morning to let her know?"

"That's what they always do," Archie said. "They call really quick and then say they have to go. When she started crying, Brittany jumped in and said, 'Don't cry, Grammy. They said they're not going to charge you.'"

Neil's eyes got huge. "I'm guessing that's when Grandpa started yelling?"

"He's furious, Neil. I had to come outside to call you because he's yelling so loud. I think he's even angrier now than when Aunt Dottie had her stroke."

His eyebrows raised with understanding. "Wow! That bad, huh?"

"Yeah, I just got off the phone with Mom and Dad. They're on their way over to try and calm him down."

My heart broke as I listened to their conversation. Aunt Dottie already means a lot to me, and I remembered how excited she was on Christmas. As an idea occurred to me, I grabbed my phone from the counter and stepped into the living room.

A few minutes later, I returned to the kitchen with a hopeful smile. "Hey, Archie?" I asked.

"Hi, Abbie."

"Where's Aunt Dottie?"

"In the parlor."

"How long until she could be ready to leave the house?" I asked, as my fiancé's eyebrows raised with curiosity.

"She's ready now," he answered, the curiosity in his tone matching the look on his brother's face. "She's in her wheelchair, and Lydia even made sure she's wearing her favorite dress."

"Perfect!" I exclaimed, my eyes glowing brightly as I looked at Neil. "I just got off the phone with the salon where Sarah and I get our hair done. They had a bunch of last-minute cancellations this morning." A grin spread across my face as I explained, "They had a wedding party to take care of, but the couple ran off and eloped yesterday. So...they have the morning free now to pamper a sweet lady on her eightieth birthday."

"Abbie!" The usual brightness returned to Archie's voicc. "That is so nice of you. She's going to be thrilled."

Neil kissed me on the cheek as an appreciative smile took over his handsome face. "Yeah, Abbie," he agreed. "Thank you so much for wanting to make Aunt Dottie's birthday special."

"Of course," I answered, a feeling of warmth spreading through me. "My family and I already love Aunt Dottie as much as you guys do."

"I'm heading back in the house now," Archie said, sounding as excited as a kid in a candy store. "I can't wait to tell her. Text me the address, and Lydia and I will get her in the van. Thanks again, Abbie. I'm so happy Neil found you."

As his brother hung up, my sweet fiancé wrapped his arms around me. "I'm so happy I found you, too," he agreed with a smile. "This is so thoughtful, Abbie. I know it's going to make her day."

My smile brightened as I said, "And this is just the first part of my plan to make her feel special." I took his hand and led him out of the kitchen, grabbing my bag on our way out the front door. "Come on. We'll call my sister from the car."

He opened my door for me with a kiss. "I am so lucky to have you." As he got in on his side, he smiled at me and requested, "At least tell me which direction I'm driving."

"Milford," I replied, taking out my phone to call my sister.

"Hey, Abs," she answered cheerfully. "What's up?"

"Today is Aunt Dottie's big birthday."

"Oh, that's right! Today is the twenty-first. Is she excited about her spa day?"

"Her kids bailed on her," I answered sadly.

She sighed. "The poor thing." Pausing momentarily, the brightness returned to her voice as she said, "Well, we'll make her big day special then."

I smiled at Neil. "I'm already working on that, Sarah. I called Heather at the salon. They had a big cancellation this morning. They were supposed to take care of a bridal party, but the couple ran off and eloped."

She laughed. "Well, Heather and the girls will definitely give her the royal treatment." She paused again, and I knew her wheels were turning. "We can stop at the bakery near The Green and pick her up a cake. And we have a bunch of decorations at the office."

"You're reading my mind, Sarah," I said, loving how great of a team we make. "Neil and I are on our way to Milford right now. We should be at your place in about half an hour."

She laughed again. "Good thing my apartment is still clean." She paused briefly, and when she spoke, her voice was full of concern. "Hey, can I talk to Neil for a second?"

"I'm right here, Sarah," he answered. "You're on speaker."

"How is your grandfather doing?"

"Angry," was his one-word answer. "Archie had to step outside to call me because he's yelling so loudly. My parents should be at his house by now, trying to calm him down."

"Do you think you could get him to leave his house?" she asked with a hopeful tone.

Neil laughed. "There was only one person who could get Grandpa to do anything, and she died twenty years ago."

"Please, Neil?" she kept trying.

He glanced at me, and I could see my curiosity mirrored in his expression. "Well...," he said, trying to come up with a solution. "I guess if anybody has a chance now, it's my mom. I'll give her a call and see what she can do."

"Thanks, Neil," she responded brightly. "I'll see you guys soon."

As Sarah hung up, Neil asked the exact question I was wondering. "What is she up to now?"

"I can only imagine!" I said with a laugh. "But knowing her, it could be anything."

After Neil called his mom, I made one more phone call of my own. And we were at Sarah's apartment before we knew it.

"OH, WOW, PUDDIN' PIE!" my dad praised, looking around wide-eyed as he stepped into the parlor through the kitchen. "This place looks amazing."

"Thanks," my sister answered brightly.

"You two really outdid yourselves," Neil complimented Sarah and me as he slid his arm around my shoulders. "It's impressive what you pulled off on such short notice."

I gave my sister a high-five. "We Perkins sisters make an amazing team." Then, looking at Neil and my parents, I added, "But Sarah and I can't take all the credit. We're making Aunt Dottie's birthday special as a family."

My mom smiled at Neil. "When is the guest of honor due home?"

He checked the time. "Any moment now," he replied eagerly.

We opened the front door a few minutes later as a large van and a Volvo SUV pulled into the driveway. We stepped onto the ramp with excited smiles as Aunt Dottie was lowered down on the liftgate. As soon as my sister saw her, she ran down the ramp, and we all followed.

"Oh, wow, Aunt Dottie!" Sarah exclaimed, giving her a hug and a kiss. "You look amazing!"

"Thank you, Honey," she replied with a glowing smile. Her focus switched to me. "And I hear you're the one responsible for my spa day." She raised her left arm for a hug. "Come here, Sugar."

"Happy birthday, Aunt Dottie," I said, relishing in the warmth of her hug despite the cold weather.

"Thank you, Abbie," she whispered, kissing me on the cheek.

Standing up, I scanned her beautiful appearance. Her face looked so fresh with the lightest amount of make-up, and her gray hair was exquisitely styled. Mostly pulled up in a loose bun, a few curls framed her glowing face. Radiant with happiness, it was hard to believe that she was beside herself with tears of sadness just a few hours ago. I stepped back so everyone could take turns hugging her, and her eyes got even brighter as her brother bent down to kiss her on the cheek. Just seeing the expressions on their faces, I knew they were both happy with how the day turned around.

Grandpa's focus switched to me, his face full of gratitude. "Yes, Abbie, thank you. My sister looks completely different now, and I don't just mean the hair and makeup. A few hours ago, she was inconsolable. But then, because of your thoughtful phone call, Dottie's birthday turned around instantly. And she is absolutely glowing."

I smiled at them. "You're welcome." My expression turned to a mischievous grin as I looked at just her. "And we have a few more surprises for you inside."

"Oh, Junior!" she exclaimed, reaching for his hand. "Can you believe there's more?"

He kissed her on the cheek again. "Do we want to go inside and see what they did for you?"

"Yes!" she replied excitedly. "You know I love a surprise!"

Sarah ran to the front door and flung it open as Grandpa pushed his sister up the ramp, and we all followed behind. As soon as we entered, Aunt Dottie started crying again. But this time, I knew they were tears of joy.

A large *Happy Birthday* banner hung above the wedding picture with gold streamers framing both sides. Silver garland wrapped around the banister sparkled happily in the mid-day sun. As Aunt Dottie was delighting in the decorations, Grandpa took off her coat, and Sarah slipped a hot-pink *Birthday Girl* sash over her green and yellow floral dress.

Aunt Dottie's eyes glowed brightly as we proceeded through the front room into the library, lifting her hand to touch the streamers hanging from the ceiling. She giggled as her brother pushed her into the parlor, tickled by the long strands of snowflake garland that hung in the doorway. More streamers dangled from the ceiling, and even Grandpa smiled as they brushed over his shoulders as he walked.

Aunt Dottie's face beamed with happiness as she looked around, and as soon as her eyes landed on the coffee table, she gasped. "Oh, Junior! Look!" Grandpa picked up the crystal vase filled with yellow carnations and brought it over to his sister. After peacefully delighting in their scent, she smiled at Neil. "You remembered."

Neil's face was soft as he said, "Uncle Frank always bought you an assortment of colors—except on your birthday. Then he would get you just yellow since it's your favorite color."

"Come here, Sugar," she said, raising her arm for a hug.

As he stood up, he looked at her with a bright smile. "And while we were decorating, Mike and Val were in the kitchen making macaroni and cheese for you."

"My favorite!" she exclaimed happily. She beamed at her brother. "Oh, Junior, aren't our new family members so sweet?"

"Yes, they are, Dottie," he agreed, returning the vase to the coffee table. As he set down the flowers, something else on the table caught his eye, and he looked at us curiously.

Sarah and I grinned at each other, then turned to Aunt Dottie with bright smiles and announced together, "But wait! There's more!" We scampered over to the table and lifted the lid to a bakery box. Inside was a cake beautifully decorated with yellow flowers and a blue border. Delicately scrolled in pink icing were the words: *Happy 80th Birthday, Dottie!*

Aunt Dottie raised her left hand to her mouth, unable to speak, overcome with emotion.

"Happy birthday, Aunt Dottie," Neil said gently.

She just nodded her appreciation, still too emotional for words. The look on her face said it all, though. We stepped forward to hug and kiss her, and I could feel the love and gratitude radiating through her.

As everyone was hugging Aunt Dottie, I watched as Archie went over to the coffee table, his smile blazing as he looked at the cake. Suddenly, his expression changed as he saw something nobody else had noticed.

"What's in the other box?" he asked, looking at Sarah, Neil, and me.

Neil grinned at his brother. "Open it, Arch."

As Archie lifted the lid, Helen gasped, covering her heart with her hands. "Oh, Dad!"

Grandpa was so focused on his sister that he didn't realize what was happening until he heard Helen's voice. Looking at her with a questioning expression, she came over to him, slid her arm through his, and gestured toward the coffee table.

"Dad, look what they did for you," Helen said, her voice full of emotion.

Grandpa looked where Helen was pointing, his face instantly softening. Inside the second bakery box was a cake decorated with an exquisite cardinal gracefully drawn with red icing. Next to the cardinal were the words: *'Happy Birthday, Junior'* carefully written in green icing. Grandpa silently admired the cake for a minute; then, his focus switched to Neil as he broke the silence in the room.

"Actually, Mom, there's only one person who can take the credit for Grandpa's cake. And it isn't me." His expression was apologetic as he looked at his grandfather. "Sorry, Grandpa."

Grandpa's blue eyes switched to me, and I shook my head. His focus moved to my sister, who was smiling brightly. "Sarah?" he asked, still processing this unexpected discovery.

"Surprise!" she exclaimed, her cheerful voice matching her facial expression. She continued smiling at Grandpa for a moment before her focus switched to Aunt Dottie. "I hope you don't mind that I got a cake for your brother, too, since it is your birthday today."

Aunt Dottie looked from the cake to my sister, her face full of emotion. "Oh, Sarah, honey. Of course I don't mind." She raised her arm for a hug. "Come here, pretty girl."

After my sister indulged in a loving hug, she stood up and smiled at Grandpa. "I was hoping the bakery would have an extra cake since I know your eightieth birthday wasn't celebrated in the typical way. When we were here on Christmas, I could tell you were okay with how you spent your birthday, but I know your family felt bad for not celebrating with you."

Helen tightened her arms around Grandpa and smiled at him. "I'm so happy Sarah did this for you, Dad."

Grandpa remained silent as he smiled at his daughter-in-law, then his focus returned to my sister as she continued, "While Neil and Abbie were getting Aunt Dottie's cake decorated, I pulled one of the girls aside and told her I needed another cake. When she asked how I wanted it decorated, I told her I wanted a cardinal because your wife loved them so much."

Grandpa remained silent, his face softening further the more my sister talked.

Sarah's smile brightened even more. "She was so sweet. She loved that I wanted something that would remind you of your wife, so she took her time and drew the cardinal really delicately."

Aunt Dottie reached up and took her brother's hand. His focus switched long enough to smile at his sister; then, his eyes returned to Sarah as she continued speaking.

"And when she asked me what she should write for a name, that's when I had to stop and think. I didn't think Mr. Rutherford would be appropriate for a birthday cake. And I know the only person who called you Cornelius was your wife. So I went with Junior, knowing that's what your sister calls you. And I figured since this could be a celebration for both of you..." She paused for a second, then said quietly, "I hope that's okay."

"It's perfect, Sarah, thank you," he replied, his eyes still focused on her. After a moment, he looked at the cake. "And thank you especially for choosing the cardinal. You're right. I love anything that reminds me of Eleanor."

"Junior, why don't we have our picture taken together?" Aunt Dottie suggested.

"I think that's a great idea," Grandpa agreed, stepping behind his sister's wheelchair.

"And we'll make sure to get both cakes in the picture, too," John commented as he and Neil rearranged the cake boxes on the coffee table.

Grandpa leaned down so his face was right next to his sister's, and he wrapped his arms around her shoulders. "Happy birthday, Dottie," he said, kissing her on the cheek.

"Happy birthday, Junior," she replied, her face glowing with happiness.

We took several pictures of them, laughing as Aunt Dottie's expression kept changing. Of course Grandpa's face barely changed; he just smiled softly the entire time. Sometimes, he was looking at us; other times, he gazed at the cake Sarah got for him. Afterward, we took turns showing them the photos, Aunt Dottie's laughter increasing with each picture.

As I watched our families gushing over Aunt Dottie, I realized we were missing a person in all the commotion. Looking around, I noticed Archie standing off to the side, looking at his grandfather's cake with a different expression. His typically blazing smile was replaced with...affection? Fondness? Amazement? Maybe all three?

I watched as his blue eyes moved from the cake to my sister. As everyone else was making a fuss over Aunt Dottie, she was showing Grandpa the pictures she took. Seeming very at ease with the family patriarch, Sarah gave him her assessment of each image. The longer Archie watched the two of them together, the more his facial expression changed. His obvious attraction to my sister seemed to be evolving into something deeper. And the longer I watched him, I came to a realization of my own, and a huge smile took over my face.

Archie must have sensed my eyes on him because suddenly, his attention switched to me. His face instantly flushed with embarrassment as he noticed my smile. He quickly glanced around, and I knew it was to make sure no one else saw him. Then, he darted over to Aunt Dottie, his blazing smile returning as he showed her the pictures he had taken.

"What's that grin for?" Neil asked me discreetly.

I looked at him and noticed the intrigued expression on his face. "Oh, just a little plan I dreamed up for our wedding," I replied nonchalantly.

"Mmm," he sighed happily, leaning in for a kiss. "A plan for our wedding. I can hardly wait to see what it is."

"Dorothy," Helen's voice pulled our attention back to our families, "you look absolutely stunning. How did you enjoy your morning at the salon?"

"Oh, Helen, it was lovely!" Aunt Dottie gushed. "Those ladies were so sweet to us, weren't they, Lydia?"

"Yes, they were," she agreed with a bright smile. "And even though it's Dottie's birthday, they insisted on making both of us feel special and pampered."

"Oh, Lydia," my sister acknowledged her. "I'm so sorry. None of us noticed." Her smile brightened as she surveyed Lydia's hair. "These highlights look amazing."

"Thanks," she accepted my sister's compliment with a smile. "And let's show everyone our nails, Dottie."

Lydia held out her hands as Aunt Dottie raised her left hand and playfully wiggled her fingers. "They gave us matching manicures!" Aunt Dottie exclaimed. "Check out these fun snowflake decals. They sparkle!"

As everyone ooh'd and aah'd over their nails, Lydia grinned at my future brother-in-law. "Even Archie got the royal treatment."

Archie's smile blazed brighter as he said, "Yeah, one of the girls felt bad for me just sitting there with a bunch of women, so she ran next door to get her dad. He showed up and said, 'Come on, kid, I have a barber shop next door. I'll give you a break from all these cackling hens.'"

Grandpa smiled affectionately as everyone laughed. Neil went over to his brother, took his jaw, and turned his face side-to-side. "Wow, Arch, that's a close shave."

"I know," he agreed with excitement in his voice. "I felt a little bad not shaving after the gym this morning, but I'm glad I didn't. And I like the way he cut my hair." He looked at Aunt Dottie and Lydia. "We should keep going back to them."

"I agree, Sugar," Aunt Dottie said with a bright smile.

"And they would not let Archie pay," Lydia chimed in. "None of them. Not even the barber."

"They all fell instantly in love with Aunt Dottie," Archie explained, smiling at her. "They were all just so grateful they could be a part of her birthday and make her feel special."

Grandpa glanced at John and Helen, then turned to Sarah and me. "Thank you, Abbie. Thank you, Sarah. The two of you really came through for my sister this morning. And then to include me in this celebration..." He smiled at his sister. "We are truly grateful. Aren't we, Dottie?"

"Oh, yes, Junior!" she agreed without hesitation. She paused briefly, then said, "And just like your eightieth birthday was your favorite one since losing Eleanor, my eightieth has been my favorite since losing Frankie."

Aunt Dottie paused again, taking her brother's hand and smiling at him gently. Her voice softened as she continued, "And I know you spent time with Eleanor this morning. I knew as soon as I saw you. It was written all over your face." She kissed her brother's hand. "John and Helen took you to the diner."

Grandpa silently nodded as John said, "It works every time, Dad."

Aunt Dottie's focus switched as she explained to my family, "Whenever Junior is sad, or angry, or just needs a pick-me-up, John and Helen take him to the diner where he met Eleanor."

Grandpa smiled at his sister. "My life changed instantly in that diner all those years ago."

"I know it did, Junior," she agreed gently. "A cute little waitress saw something in you that no one else did." Her eyes moved to her nephews. "And it's because of that cute little waitress that we have you three boys and the beautiful women that you love."

John smiled at Helen as Neil smiled at me.

"And it's because of you boys and your special ladies that my birthday was saved today. Not only did you make my birthday special, but you included my brother as well. And I am forever grateful for all of you."

"And we're grateful for you too, Aunt Dottie," my sister said. She smiled at Grandpa and added, "And your brother."

A warm smile spread across Grandpa's face as he looked at my sister. I know he appreciates everything we did today. And I know he's especially grateful that Sarah included not only him but his wife as well. And somehow, I get the feeling that he's thankful for her beyond what she did today. Between decorating his home for Christmas and being so willing to interact with him, I think he enjoys having someone around who seems genuinely comfortable with him.

As our families celebrated with macaroni and cheese and two birthday cakes, I paid close attention to how everyone interacted—especially regarding my sister. John and Helen kept looking at Sarah with a mixture of disbelief and gratitude. I don't think they're used to seeing the way she seems so comfortable around Grandpa—a man that so many people avoid.

And every time I noticed my parents looking at Sarah, they seemed genuinely proud of her. Between her thoughtfulness and her recent maturity, I know they're impressed with all the progress she's making in her life.

As everyone mingled from one conversation to another, Sarah stayed rather close to Grandpa for the rest of the evening. Every time I watched her talking to him, her face was lit up with joy. She was so excited in the bakery to show Neil and me the cake she had decorated for him. And the brightness in her eyes of surprising him stayed with her for the rest of the day.

And that same brightness was in Grandpa's eyes whenever he looked at my sister. And as I thought back, it started before today. When we were in Aunt Dottie's bedroom, and Sarah told him that she sees him as a grandfather, his expression changed ever so slightly. But there was a spark that brightened his typically sharp blue eyes. And I think that one statement has made the most significant impact on him out of anything she has said or done so far.

But the biggest difference I saw today was in Archie. Every time he looked at my sister, I knew he was being drawn in further by her. Several times, I caught him looking at her, his blue eyes mesmerized by her beauty—and not just her physical beauty, but the beauty of her kind personality. And during one of the times when he watched her talking to Grandpa, he looked like he was just dying to walk over to her and tell her something. And my heart instantly melted because I knew exactly what he was thinking. And that, dear reader, was my favorite moment of this entire day.

Chapter 8

♥

"So, ARE YOU EXCITED for today?" my handsome fiancé asked me as we sipped our morning coffee.

A huge smile spread across my face. "I am very excited." I leaned in and kissed him. "And I'm excited that we've already confirmed one big detail for our wedding. And I love that we did it together."

"Me too," he agreed, his voice deep and sexy. There was a gleam of desire in his eyes as he asked, "So my beautiful fiancée loved my Valentine's Day surprise?"

"Yes, I did," I replied, wrapping my arms around his shoulders and pulling him in for another kiss. "And as much as I love planning our wedding together, I'm looking forward to spending today with just the ladies." My smile turned playful as I added, "My super organized fiancé deserves at least one surprise at our wedding."

"Mmm," he sighed happily. "And thankfully, I have less than four months to wait." He tilted his head to the side, gazing at me with eyes full of love. "I can't wait to make you my wife, Abbie."

"And I can't wait to become your wife," I agreed, reaching up for another kiss. As I was lost in my little moment, enjoying his soft lips on mine, we heard the front door open.

"Good morning," Helen's voice called.

"Come on," Neil said, taking my hand. "Even though they're here for you, I'll say good morning too."

We walked into the living room to see my mom, Sarah, and Helen, all with bright smiles on their faces.

"There's our bride-to-be!" my sister exclaimed. "See? It says so right here!" Her smile glowed brighter as she held up a silver sash with the words: '*Bride-to-Be*' in hot-pink lettering. As she slipped it over my head, she asked excitedly, "Are you ready to go dress shopping?"

My heart swelled with love as I watched my sister's obvious excitement. Even though she's not a hopeless romantic like me, she is already the best Maid of Honor I could ask for.

"Of course, Sarah," I replied with a playful grin. "You know I've been daydreaming about my wedding dress since junior high."

She laughed as she looked at Neil. "Abbie's been planning her entire wedding since we were kids. All that was missing was you."

"Well, I'm glad she found me," he said, his eyes bright with love as he admired the sash.

After I hugged my mom and Sarah, Neil kissed them both hello. As Helen took my hands and greeted me in her typical fashion, she declared, "Abigail, you are positively glowing this morning."

"Thanks, Helen," I accepted her compliment, my smile brightening. "I'm happy you recommended that dress shop. The lady I spoke to was so sweet when I called to make the appointment."

"Of course," she replied, glancing at her son with a smile. "They are the best bridal store in all of Fairfield County."

"Hi, Mom," Neil said as he kissed her hello on both cheeks. Smiling at me, he added, "And I agree, the lady you spoke to was very kind to you. I already know you're going to have a great time there."

Checking the time, I said, "We should get going in a few minutes. I just need to grab my bag from the kitchen."

"And I wanted to take Mom upstairs really quick," my sister commented. "I want her to see everything we've done to your special room so far."

As she took my mom's hand and excitedly pulled her up the stairs, I went to the kitchen and made sure I had everything I needed. Looking at the sash, my heart flooded with love and gratitude for our families. We haven't even left the house yet, and I already feel like a million bucks.

I walked into the living room as my mom and sister got to the bottom of the stairs, and Neil and Helen were talking on the couch. Everyone's faces brightened even more when they saw me.

"Ready?" my mom asked cheerfully.

"Ready!" I confirmed.

Neil walked us to the door and gave me a kiss. "Have fun," he said, leaning in the doorway. He waved as we pulled out of the driveway in Helen's car, Sarah and I giggling in the backseat.

"So, Helen?" my mom asked. "Where is this dress shop?"

"New Canaan," she answered.

Sarah and I glanced at each other. Even though Neil and I have been together for several months, I'm still in awe every time we go somewhere in his hometown. Being with a man from the wealthiest town in our state has been something to get used to. But, while his family is quite well-to-do, they are certainly much different than the rest of the people in their social standing.

"So, Abigail?" Helen asked me, looking in her rearview mirror. "What did Cornelius do for Valentine's Day?"

I felt a bright smile taking over my face. "He brought me to the resort where we're getting married."

"Oh, Abs!" my sister exclaimed. "That's so romantic!"

"Wait until you see this place, Sarah," I daydreamed out loud, taking her hand. "The landscaping is beautiful, and their grand ballroom looks like something right out of a fairy tale."

She laughed. "That sounds perfect for you."

"So, have the two of you set an official date?" my mom asked, looking around her seat.

I nodded. "The second Saturday in June."

All three sighed happily, and then my sister's expression became more serious as she looked at me. "That's less than four months away."

"I know," I agreed with a grin. "We have a lot of planning to do."

She laughed again. "Good thing you found such an organized man."

"You can say that again!" my mom agreed, her laughter matching Sarah's.

We continued to dream about my upcoming wedding all the way to New Canaan. As Helen pulled into a parking lot, Sarah and I glanced at each other again. "Even the outside of this place is fancy, Abbie," she whispered.

"I know, Sarah," I replied quietly, taking in the grand brick building with expansive windows. Stunning white and ivory dresses were on display in every window—some with sequins, others with lace—and they all looked like they belonged on a runway. A very expensive runway.

Helen led the way and opened the door for my mom, Sarah, and me. While the three of us looked around wide-eyed, Helen seemed rather at ease in such a fancy establishment. Golden drapes framed the floor-to-ceiling windows, and the mid-morning sunshine danced on the sequins of the gowns. Several racks of dresses lined the interior walls, and cozy sofas sat throughout the room for each bridal party. A few other families were browsing at dresses, as brides stood on pedestals outside their dressing rooms while their bridal parties gushed over them. As I marveled at the grand chandeliers hanging from the ceiling, I felt like I was back at the country club. My attention was pulled to an approaching voice as a slender brunette about my age in a red dress made her way toward us.

"Mrs. Rutherford!" she greeted Helen with a bright smile.

"Hello, Jacqueline," Helen replied, kissing her on both cheeks. "How lovely to see you again."

As I listened to them, a realization occurred to me. "You must be Jackie," I said with a smile. "You were so nice to me when I spoke to you on the phone."

Her blue eyes switched to me and instantly brightened when she noticed my sash. "Oh my God!" she exclaimed, covering her heart. "You're the girl who's marrying Neil Rutherford!"

I extended my hand to her. "Abbie Perkins."

She shook her head. "Oh, no, I have to hug you," she declared with a bright smile, pulling me into a tight embrace. As she let me go, she eyed me up and down. "I can't believe I'm finally meeting you." She looked over her shoulder and called out, "Hey, Cindy, get over here."

Another brunette, wearing a dark-blue dress, looked over from where she was arranging dresses on a rack. Coming over, she immediately recognized the lady with us.

"Mrs. Rutherford!" she said, extending her hands.

"Hello, Cynthia," Helen replied, greeting her as usual.

As soon as Helen finished her greeting, Jackie grabbed her friend's elbow and excitedly pulled her to face me. "Cindy, this is Abbie Perkins. The girl who's marrying Neil Rutherford!"

Cindy's hazel eyes were huge with delight as she pulled me into her arms and hugged me tightly. Letting me go, she smiled and said, "Welcome to our store." Looking at her friend, she proclaimed, "Jackie, we have to take care of this girl ourselves."

"I agree," she said, slipping her arm into Cindy's. "The two of us have been best friends since the first grade, and we own this store together. We grew up with Neil and Archie, so we are giving you the royal treatment today!"

A wave of fondness surged through me as I looked at them. Jackie was delightful enough over the phone—but meeting her and Cindy in person? In just a few short minutes, they made me feel like the most important customer in their entire store.

"Thank you so much," I replied. Gesturing toward my family, I said, "And this is my mom, Val, and my sister and Maid of Honor, Sarah."

The two girls hugged them as well, and then Jackie turned to Helen. "So, we already heard Neil was getting married. What about Archie?" she asked with a hopeful tone.

Helen smiled gently at her. "Archibald is still single."

"Yes!" Cindy exclaimed. "There's still hope for the rest of us!"

As we shared a laugh, Jackie offered, "Feel free to look around and grab any dresses that catch your eye. While Cindy sets up a dressing room, I'll get you some water." Looking at Helen, she asked, "And how does some tea sound?"

"That sounds perfect, Jacqueline. Thank you," Helen replied kindly.

As the two of them scampered off excitedly, the four of us started browsing. My eyes glowed with happiness as I took in all the glittering sequins and delicate lace. Even though I had checked out several bridal magazines, I still wasn't sure about the exact style I wanted. As I gazed at the various silhouettes, I imagined how Neil would feel seeing me in each design. Suddenly, a beaded gown with a sweetheart neckline caught my eye, and I draped it over my arm with a smile. As I was on my way to the next rack, that's when I saw my sister.

"Sarah!" I exclaimed with a laugh. "How many dresses are you holding?"

After taking a quick count, she proudly announced, "Five." Then she counted the ones heaped on my mom and said, "And I gave Mom six to hold on to." She looked at me with a blazing smile that reminded me of someone else.

I shook my head and laughed. For someone who's not very romantic, my sister has gotten right into helping me plan my wedding.

Jackie and Cindy appeared, also laughing as they saw my poor mom buried under heaps of tulle and chiffon. "Let us help you with those," Jackie offered as they lightened my mom's load. "We have a dressing room all set up for you."

After we hung up the gowns, Helen showed up with two more. She placed them with the rest and joined my mom and sister on a luxurious white leather sofa. I giggled as I watched my sister pick up her tea and sip it with her pinky out—just like Moe Howard taught her.

"So," Jackie said with a smile, "where do we want to start?"

"How about the one with the fluffy skirt?" my sister suggested with a grin. "I picked that one, knowing how princessy you are."

As we laughed, Cindy retrieved the dress and looked at me. "And why don't we have your sister come in the dressing room with us? Since she'll be helping you on your big day."

Setting down her tea, Sarah sprang up off the sofa with a huge smile. "Let's do this!" she exclaimed, picking up the bottom of the dress and helping Cindy carry it into the dressing room.

"See? She's already helping," Jackie said humorously as we followed behind them.

Taking the dress off its hanger, Cindy asked, "So, how did you meet Neil?"

"Sarah and I own an interior decorating business, and we decorated a resort that his family's firm acquired," I answered as I stepped into the dress.

My sister crossed her arms and looked at me with raised eyebrows. "Abigail. That is not the moment you and Neil met."

"Okay," I admitted shyly. "I may have spilled my coffee all over him earlier that morning, not realizing he was the man we were making our big pitch to."

Cindy and Jackie looked at each other wide-eyed. "You did that to him?" Jackie asked as she zipped up the dress.

"Yes," my sister jumped in. "And Neil gave us the job on the spot. He even intercepted his grandfather before he left the office so we wouldn't have to make our presentation to him."

Cindy raised her eyebrows. "Wow! Sounds like he was into you right from the start."

As Jackie fluffed the ruffles on the skirt, she commented, "Well, he and Archie were raised to be polite. Extremely polite."

The four of us looked at me in the mirror and laughed. "This dress looks ridiculous on you, Abbie," my sister voiced what we were all thinking.

"I know," I agreed. "Let's show Mom and Helen and bring in a couple more."

We stepped out of the dressing room, and I climbed onto the pedestal. "What do you think?" I asked with a big grin.

My mom just shook her head as Helen said, "No, Abigail. That is not the dress for you."

"Come on," my sister teased. "Wouldn't Neil love to see her walking down the aisle looking like the giant dust bunnies that were under my couch?"

My mom shook her head again as Helen waved for us to go back into the dressing room. Sarah took my hand and helped me down as Cindy and Jackie followed us, each carrying two more dresses. Cindy was about to take one off its hanger when my sister stopped her.

"Not that one. I didn't see all these buttons down the back." She looked at me. "We need your dress to be something that Neil can help you out of. My Maid of Honor duties end when the two of you go back to your room for the night."

I had to laugh at my sister. "Good point, Sarah."

Scanning the other three dresses, Cindy and Jackie set aside two others with the same long line of buttons down the back. As they unzipped the fourth dress, Sarah helped me out of the fluffy one.

"So, what were Neil and Archie like growing up?" Sarah asked Cindy and Jackie as they helped me into an ivory gown.

They smiled at each other as Cindy praised, "Neil and Archie were the nicest guys at our school. And all of us girls would have dated either one of the Rutherfords."

"Did they date much?" Sarah asked.

Jackie thought for a second. "Not really. They both went to prom and would take girls to the movies occasionally, but they spent a lot of their time working."

"And when they did go out with a girl, they were both perfect gentlemen," Cindy added as she zipped my dress.

"And we all know why that is," Jackie said, shaking her head. "Their grandfather was intense. Whenever he came to school events, we all behaved better—just because he was there."

"Yeah, I noticed his commanding presence in family pictures," I acknowledged. "And then I instantly felt it when we met Grandpa in person."

Jackie and Cindy stopped fussing with the dress and looked at each other wide-eyed. Their eyes were still huge with amazement as they looked at me, and Jackie asked, "Did you just refer to Mr. Rutherford as 'Grandpa?'"

"He told Abbie to call him that about ten minutes after he met her," my sister said with a proud smile.

"Wow, Abbie!" Cindy exclaimed. "You really are a special girl. Not only did you land one of the Rutherfords, but you also won over the hardest man we've ever met."

A warmth spread through me at hearing her compliment. "Thanks, Cindy." I slid my arm around Sarah's shoulders and grinned at them. "And I'm not the only one who's made an impression on Neil's grandfather. My sister here is able to look him in the eye, and she'll stand up to him."

Jackie and Cindy's jaws hit the floor, their eyes growing even wider as they looked at my sister.

"What?" she said like it was no big deal. "I like Mr. Rutherford."

"Now that's something we've never heard anyone say before," Jackie said with a laugh. "You two are unbelievable."

We turned toward the mirror and surveyed this dress. An ivory gown with an empire waist, glittery beads shimmered down the entire length.

"This one isn't bad," my sister commented. "Let's show Mom and Helen."

We stepped out of the dressing room, and my mom's eyes brightened when she saw me. "That one's pretty, Abbie."

"Thanks," I replied. Looking at Helen, I asked, "What do you think?"

She shook her head. "That is not the dress for you, Abigail."

Sensing a pattern, Cindy mentioned, "Well, we still have a few more on the rack here." Checking them for complicated buttons, she set aside three and brought the rest into the dressing room.

"So, Neil and Archie really did work all the time growing up?" Sarah asked as she unzipped my dress.

"Yeah," Jackie answered, taking a lacy dress off its hanger. "Their grandfather kept them quite busy." Thinking for a second, she continued, "But I think they both liked working for the family business. And Archie's so good at math, I think he preferred doing financial analysis over anything else after school."

"Neil said Archie was a total nerd in school," I commented, stepping into the dress.

"That's an understatement!" Cindy said with a laugh. "He took our school's math league all the way to nationals and won."

Sarah and I looked at each other wide-eyed. "They didn't mention that part," I remarked.

Jackie grinned at us. "A Rutherford does not brag."

"And they said they didn't play any sports," Sarah commented as she zipped the dress.

Cindy laughed. "You're lucky, Abbie, that Neil started working out in college. They were both skinny in high school."

"Really?" my sister asked.

Jackie nodded. "They looked nothing like they do now."

Sarah eyed me up and down. "This isn't the dress for you, Abbie."

I turned and surveyed myself in the mirror. Delicate white lace in a floral pattern adorned the entire length of a spaghetti strap gown. "I agree, Sarah." Turning to

Cindy and Jackie, I gave my assessment, "Too much lace. And it's a bit scratchy."

"Well, we don't want that," Cindy commented as she unzipped me. Setting aside two more lacy dresses, Jackie took a chiffon dress off its hanger.

"And the guys mentioned they had to work for everything," my sister said, pulling up the chiffon dress so Cindy could zip it.

"There's another understatement!" Jackie laughed, shaking her head. "Nothing was handed to them. As all the kids we went to school with were given cars on their birthdays or going on fancy vacations for Christmas, Neil and Archie..." She looked at Cindy. "What did they do?"

She shook her head. "I don't know. Probably worked." She looked at me with a curious expression. "Does Mr. Rutherford still make them negotiate their salaries on a regular basis?"

"Yeah, Neil got called into his office a couple of weeks ago for his quarterly negotiation."

"And?" Sarah, of course, asked as all three of them looked at me.

"And we've already put the money to good use," I answered with a smile.

My sister batted me playfully on the arm and teased, "Is Neil buying you a car? That way, the two of you can have matching Volvos?"

"That's right, his family has always owned Volvos," Jackie commented. She laughed as she added, "I remember that station wagon Archie bought when we were in high school."

"He still has it," Sarah told her with the same amused tone.

The four of us looked at this dress in the mirror. A strapless gown with an A-line silhouette flowed effortlessly to the floor. "I'm not sure about this one, Abs," my sister commented. "Let's see what Mom and Helen think."

We stepped out of the dressing room to see Helen walking toward us with a few more dresses. As she approached, she eyed me up and down. Shaking her head, she said, "That is not the dress for you, Abigail." She handed Cindy the dresses she was carrying and offered, "I found a few more that you ladies might like to try."

"Sure, Mrs. Rutherford," she replied politely. As an employee showed up with fresh mugs of tea, she asked, "Are you ladies enjoying your tea while you wait for us?"

"Yes, Cynthia," Helen answered kindly. "Your staff has been more than hospitable to Valerie and me. And I appreciate you remembering that I prefer tea."

"Of course, Mrs. Rutherford," Cindy acknowledged her with a smile.

As Helen sat down on the sofa, my mom commented, "I agree with Helen, Abbie. That's not the right dress."

"Well, thankfully, we have a few more to try on," my sister commented cheerfully. "And Helen does have the best fashion sense out of all of us." Smiling at my future mother-in-law, she took the dresses from Cindy and led us back into the dressing room.

As Jackie unzipped a satin gown, she quietly told us, "Normally, we offer mimosas to our brides and their families. But we know what Mrs. Rutherford went through losing her father and brother."

"It brought tears to my eyes when Neil told me the story," I said, stepping into another dress. "He seemed relieved when I told him I'm not a drinker."

"That would be a deal-breaker for both Neil and Archie," Cindy confirmed. "They've always felt that way about alcohol. When we were growing up, they didn't even come to parties." As she zipped the dress, she added, "Well, except for at the end of the night when we all needed a ride home. Even if there were sober guys at the party, we still called them."

Sarah and I looked at each other. "What do you mean?" she asked.

"We knew Neil and Archie were the safest guys to call," Jackie explained. "We knew there was never any risk of them taking advantage of us. Every one of us girls trusted them completely."

"Wow!" my sister said, her face glowing with admiration. "So even in high school, they were responsible?"

"Responsible doesn't even begin to describe those two," Jackie praised them. "They have always been so kind and thoughtful to everyone. Even the guys who teased them."

"Why would the guys pick on them?" I asked, my voice full of concern.

"As the other guys would be bragging about how many girls they had scored with, Neil and Archie had nothing to contribute to the conversation, so the guys would tease them," Cindy explained with a tone of disgust.

"That's horrible," my sister replied, her voice full of compassion.

"Tell me about it," Jackie agreed. "But I think what bothered them more than being teased was listening to how the other guys talked about the girls." As she adjusted the straps on the dress, she thought for a second. "I think the real reason the guys were so mean to Neil and Archie was because they were jealous of them. All of us girls wanted to date a Rutherford, and they knew they couldn't compare."

As we turned to look in the mirror, a smile of admiration spread across Cindy's face. "And as a further testament of his character, even though all the guys picked on Archie, he still helped every one of them with their homework."

"Neil is a great guy, Abbie, and we're so happy for you," Jackie beamed, smoothing down the dress. "But I think the truly lucky girl will be the one who lands Archie. I can't believe how sweet he is."

As Cindy and Jackie made adjustments to the dress, my focus was on my sister's reflection. My heart melted as I noticed her expression—an expression I instantly recognized. It was the same look Archie had on his face at Aunt Dottie's birthday party as he watched Sarah and Grandpa so easily interacting and enjoying each other's company. At this moment, I realized the exact same thing was happening to my sister. As I stood there and watched her, I was flooded with happiness. Trying on wedding dresses might be fun and exciting, but it doesn't compare to seeing my sister like this. Now I'm even more eager for my wedding, and not just because I'm marrying the man of my dreams. I cannot wait to put my master plan into action.

"I don't know about this one," Jackie's voice broke me from my trance. "What do you think, Abbie?"

My focus switched from my sister's reflection to mine. Surveying the white satin gown, I sighed. "I don't think this one is for me. It's too plain. What do you think, Sarah?"

"Huh?" she asked, still mesmerized by her daydream.

"What do you think of Abbie's dress?" Cindy asked.

She eyed me up and down. "Not my favorite." Seeming to be back in the present, she laughed and suggested, "Let's see what Helen thinks of one of her latest finds."

We stepped out of the dressing room, and Helen immediately shook her head. "Oh, Abigail, get that dress off now."

This got a laugh from all of us. "Well, at least there was a little variety to her response this time," my sister joked as the four of us turned around.

As Cindy and Jackie helped me out of the gown, Sarah surveyed the other dresses Helen had recommended. Suddenly, she spun around, her eyes bright with excitement. "Hey, Abs, check out this dress. It's super pretty."

She carefully removed a strapless dress from its hanger, and she, Cindy, and Jackie all helped me into it. And the moment I saw myself in the mirror, I instantly knew it was the dress for me. A beautiful white gown flowed effortlessly to the floor, hugging my feminine figure in all the right places. With a straight neckline and just a touch of sparkly beading at the bodice, it was the perfect combination of elegance and simplicity.

"Oh, wow, Abbie," my sister breathed. "Wait until Neil sees you in this dress."

"It really is stunning on you, Abbie," Jackie agreed. "It looks like it was made for you. The only tailoring it will need is a slight hemming."

"And it has a zipper," Cindy pointed out as she grinned at my sister. "So, you're off the hook for helping her out of it."

"See, Abs, it's perfect," Sarah agreed, as we all shared a good laugh. "Let's show Mom and Helen."

We stepped out of the dressing room, and my mom's eyes lit up when she saw me. "Abbie," she exhaled, standing up to hug me. "You look incredible."

"Thanks, Mom," I beamed at her. My focus switched to Helen. Still sitting on the sofa, her hands covered her mouth as her eyes welled with tears. "Oh, Helen," I said, reaching out my hands to her. "Come here."

She took my hands and kissed me on both cheeks, then pulled me in for a long, tight hug. She stepped back and scanned my gorgeous dress up close, a few tears spilling down her cheeks. "*This* is the dress for you, Abigail."

"Thank you, Helen," I whispered. "I love it too."

As Sarah, Helen, and my mom gushed over my dress, Cindy and Jackie disappeared momentarily. They returned with big smiles and a small, handheld bell.

Holding up the bell, Jackie explained, "Every time a bride finds the dress of her dreams, we give her this bell to ring and tell her to make a wish." Her smile brightened even more as she handed the bell to me. "So go ahead, Abbie. Wish for anything you want."

"What a sweet tradition," my sister gushed, looking at me with bright eyes. "So, what's your wish, Abbie?"

I had to stop and think. While I agree with my sister that it's a delightful tradition, I wasn't sure what to say at first. "Well," I began, still thinking. "I don't really have anything to wish for. All my dreams came true when I met Neil, and I don't need anything else."

Cindy slid her arm through Jackie's, and they both smiled at me. "She is totally the girl for Neil," Cindy commented fondly, leaning her head on Jackie's shoulder.

Jackie nodded in agreement. "You are the most unselfish bride we've ever had in our store. Typically, the brides wish for something outlandish, but you..." She smiled at me affectionately. "You're just happy to have a great man."

"You should at least wish for something, Abbie," my sister encouraged me. "What's the one thing you especially want for your wedding day?" Then she added quickly, "Besides Neil, of course."

I thought for another moment. "Well...I noticed a bouquet of the most amazing flowers in one of the bridal magazines. It was a simple assortment of zinnias, roses, and irises. And the rest of the floral display was peonies and lilies, and it all looked so magical. So...I guess my wish is pretty flowers."

"Then pretty flowers you shall have!" my sister exclaimed. "Now ring that bell!"

I raised the bell above my head and gave it a good shake, filling the store with the joyful announcement of finding my fairytale dress. The place erupted into cheers, and two salesladies came over to congratulate me on my beautiful choice. The enthusiasm was short-lived, though, as something caught my sister's eye as she scrutinized my dress more closely.

"Oh my God, Abbie," she whispered, looking at me with huge eyes. She angled the price tag so I could see it, and my eyes almost fell out of my head.

Panic flooded me as I looked at my mom. "This dress costs seven thousand dollars!" I barely managed to squeak out.

While we Perkins ladies were picking our jaws up off the floor, Helen looked at me very calmly. "Is there a problem, Abigail?"

I looked pleadingly at my mom. Reading my expression, she took my future mother-in-law's hand and tactfully informed her, "Helen, Mike and I didn't spend seven thousand dollars on our entire wedding."

Helen smiled gently at my mom, and then her focus switched to me. Turning me to face the mirror, my smile instantly returned as soon as I caught my reflection. *Ooh, this woman is good,* I thought.

"Abigail, you are positively glowing when you see yourself in this dress. And I know Cornelius will absolutely adore it the moment he sees you."

Hearing her mention his name made my heart leap into my throat, as I just now remembered something. "Neil was supposed to give me his credit card this morning. But once you three got to the house, I forgot with all the excitement."

Helen ran her hands down my arms reassuringly. "It's okay, Abigail," she replied with a calm smile. "We agreed to pay for the wedding as a family."

She stepped aside briefly and retrieved a credit card from her handbag on the sofa. Returning to us, she handed the card to Cindy. As Jackie removed the price tag from the dress, Cindy casually looked at the card in her hand. Suddenly, her facial expression changed, and she looked at Helen.

"Mrs. Rutherford, your husband is Cornelius the third, right?" she asked, clearly stunned by something.

"That's right," Helen confirmed.

"Because this card says Cornelius Rutherford, Junior." Cindy turned the card around to show her.

Helen smiled at her. "Thank you, Cynthia, for double-checking. But my father-in-law will be paying for the dress."

Now, my heart almost jumped out of my chest. "I can't let Grandpa pay for the dress," I squeaked, my voice full of panic.

Helen's focus switched to me. "Why not, Abigail?"

"Because..." My voice trailed off, as once again, I wasn't sure what to say. Shaking my head, I blinked several times, trying to come up with an answer. Suddenly, my mind flashed to an angry lady glaring at her brother, and I knew I had my answer. "Because I don't want him paying for it just because Aunt Dottie yelled at him."

Thinking for a second, Helen remembered that moment on Christmas. "Oh, Abigail," she said with a laugh. "That's just the way Dorothy talks to her brother."

This got a laugh out of Cindy and Jackie as well. "I bet Aunt Dottie called him a cheapskate," Jackie said through her laughter.

"My favorite line of hers is, 'You should be ashamed of yourself, Junior!'" Cindy imitated Aunt Dottie's angry voice.

"That's exactly what she said to him!" my sister chimed in, her laughter matching theirs.

I gave my sister a dirty look. "I'm glad you find this amusing."

Sarah stopped laughing and took my hands. "I'm sorry, Abbie. But you heard Mr. Rutherford. He really did say that he wanted to help pay for the wedding. He just didn't want to step on Mom and Dad's toes, that's all."

"Oh, that's right," I admitted quietly. I turned to Helen. "So, Grandpa really is okay paying for the dress?"

"Yes, Abigail," she answered gently. "When I saw him yesterday to discuss foundation matters, I told him we were coming dress shopping today. That's when he handed me his credit card and told me to make sure you find a dress that makes you feel special. Those were his exact words."

"Aww," my mom, Sarah, Cindy, and Jackie all gushed at the same time.

As we laughed, my sister acknowledged, "That really is sweet of him, Abbie."

Cindy and Jackie looked at each other and shook their heads with disbelief. Then, Cindy looked at Helen and held up the price tag and credit card. "So, I'll take these to the register?"

"Please, Cynthia," Helen requested kindly.

"And Sarah and I will help you out of your dress," Jackie said as we returned to the dressing room. Closing the door behind us, she reassured me, "Honestly, Abbie, don't worry about him paying for the dress. Cornelius Rutherford doesn't just hand out money freely. For a man who makes his boys earn everything, he sees something exceptional in you." She paused for a second, looking at me with an admiring smile. "You and Neil aren't even married yet, and he already considers you a Rutherford."

I hugged her as a rush of gratitude flooded me. "Thanks, Jackie," I said, loving that she recognizes how much I mean to Neil's entire family.

We stepped out of the dressing room as Cindy was giving Helen the credit card and receipt. After they hugged me one more time, Jackie took my dress and said, "I'll take this out back and put your name on it. Call us next week to set up an appointment for alterations. And congratulations again, Abbie."

"Thank you," I acknowledged them with a warm smile. As they left with my dress, my smile became brighter as I daydreamed about walking down the aisle in it.

"Why don't we go out for lunch?" Helen's voice pulled me back to reality.

"That sounds lovely, Helen," my mom replied. Then she paused, scanning our outfits. "Although you're the only one dressed nicely enough for the country club."

She smiled gently at my mom. "We're going somewhere else today, Valerie. Somewhere you ladies need to see."

Sarah grinned at me. "Once again, I am intrigued."

We shared a laugh as she slipped her arm in mine, and we followed Helen out to her car. As the two moms chatted in the front seat, Sarah and I whispered in the back seat. Our conversation flowed from giggling about Cindy's imitation of Aunt Dottie to our amazement about Archie winning the national math league competition. And we gushed over the way Jackie and Cindy talked about growing up with Neil and Archie.

But the part we especially couldn't stop talking about was Grandpa's generosity. And that unbelievably sweet comment about making sure I find a dress that makes me feel special. Jackie's right. Grandpa already sees me as a Rutherford—and I already feel like one. The level of acceptance I feel from Neil and his entire family makes me feel genuinely special—even more special than I felt in my stunning dress. And that, dear reader, is priceless.

Chapter 9

♥

HELEN PULLED INTO A parking space as Sarah and I once again looked at each other wide-eyed. I knew exactly what she was thinking because I had the same thought: *What are we doing here?*

We got out of the car and turned to face a long, light-green diner with faded gray shutters surrounding the rusted metal windows. A red neon sign flickered above the front door that read: *Betty's Diner* with a banner below it proudly stating: *The Best Food and Service in All of Fairfield County*

"This is the diner where John's parents met almost fifty-four years ago," Helen explained with a loving smile.

My mom covered her heart as Sarah and I sighed happily. "Oh, Helen," I said, taking her hand. "Thank you so much for bringing us here."

"Of course, Abigail," she replied. "I figured you ladies would love to see where everything started for our family."

We entered the diner, and it was just like stepping back in time. A long counter covered with light-green Formica spanned two-thirds of the restaurant, with the kitchen visible a few feet behind. Stools upholstered with red vinyl lined the counter, all full of casually dressed patrons enjoying their lunch. Several matching tables sat throughout the room, with benches attached on either side. Windows with faded red valances lined the front and sides of the diner, drenching the entire room in late-winter sunshine. Looking around, I guessed the place hadn't been renovated in decades. This simple, outdated diner was a far cry from the fancy country club where the Rutherfords have typically brought us.

A woman in her sixties with long gray hair was filling coffee cups at a nearby table. Wearing a red apron that said '*Betty's Diner*' over a blue sweater, her hazel eyes immediately brightened when she noticed us. Setting down the coffee pot, she approached us with her hands extended. "Helen!" she exclaimed, taking her hands.

"Hello, Nancy," Helen greeted her with a kiss on each cheek.

"And who do we have here?" Nancy asked, looking at us.

"This is Valerie and Sarah," Helen answered, gesturing to my mom and sister. Then, taking my hand, she said, "And this is Abigail. She's marrying my son Cornelius."

Nancy's eyes brightened even more. "It's wonderful to meet the three of you," she said, giving each of us a hug.

"Wow, Abs," my sister whispered. "They really are friendly here."

"Welcome to our family diner," Nancy continued. "My mother started this place seventy years ago, and my sisters and I run it in her memory." Turning to Helen, she asked, "Would you like your usual table?"

"Please," Helen answered kindly.

Nancy grabbed four menus and led us to a booth overlooking the parking lot. Helen and my mom slid in on one side of the red vinyl seat as Sarah and I took the other side. I had to stifle a giggle when I noticed the long piece of red duct tape covering an obvious rip in the upholstery. The faded green tabletop was rimmed with chrome, and a warm smile spread across my face when I noticed initials with a heart around them drawn discreetly in the corner.

Nancy returned a minute later with our water and grinned at Sarah. "You're sitting in Junior's spot."

We looked at Helen as she explained, "That's the exact spot, Sarah, where Dad was sitting when he noticed Mom all those years ago."

My sister beamed at hearing her words. "Oh, wow!" she breathed as she ran her hands over the vinyl surrounding her. "I feel so special to have this seat."

"You should," Nancy confirmed. "I still remember that day like it was yesterday." She paused for a second, looking off into the distance. "I grew up working here, and I remember when they came in. They were the nicest dressed patrons to ever walk through our door. Junior was wearing a light-gray suit, and he looked so serious. He was with his mom, sister, brother-in-law, and three little kids." She shook her head and laughed. "You should have seen him holding that baby."

My mom, Sarah, and I looked at each other with raised eyebrows. "What do you mean?" my sister asked.

"When they first got here, the baby was a little fussy, but the moment Junior took him, he instantly quieted down," Nancy said with a smile.

Now, the three of us looked at Helen with questioning expressions. "Oh, Dad loves babies," she gushed, covering her heart. "You should have seen him with our boys."

The three of us just blinked at her.

A warm smile spread across Helen's face. "Dad may be a strict disciplinarian, but even he can't resist an innocent baby."

We turned back to Nancy as she continued, "And Eleanor noticed, too. She was the sweetest waitress we've ever had here."

"Did she wait on them?" my sister asked.

Nancy shook her head. "They just watched each other from afar. They didn't even speak that day. But every time they would look at each other, their faces were so bright and happy. But, of course, that's how Eleanor always looked. But Junior?" She shook her head. "He walked in here with a stone-cold face that only softened when he looked at the baby, his mom, and his sister. But the moment he saw Eleanor, he looked like a completely different man. Those sharp blue eyes of his instantly softened, and happiness radiated from him."

"Like in the pictures of them together," I said dreamily, a feeling of love flooding me as I remembered their wedding photos.

"Exactly," Nancy confirmed. "I tried to convince Eleanor to go talk to him, but she was raised in a more conservative family and didn't think it would be appropriate." She sighed. "For three months, Eleanor pined for him, hoping every time the door opened, he would walk through it. And then, finally, on a bright summer day, he did. I ran into the kitchen, grabbed her arm, and said, 'Come on, he's here!' And as soon as they saw each other..." She paused and closed her eyes, sighing peacefully this time.

Opening her eyes, she continued, "My mom told Eleanor to take the rest of the day off, but she said he went back to work, but they had made plans for dinner. And he wanted to meet her father first anyways."

"That sounds familiar!" my sister said humorously.

"Junior is uncompromising when it comes to showing a girl's father the utmost respect," Nancy praised him. "And five months later, they were married. Eleanor stopped working after they got married, but they still came by all the time and sat right here."

"What a sweet story," my sister gushed.

"They were the sweetest couple," Nancy admired, her eyes full of love. "Every time I saw them together, they were always holding hands."

Sarah and I raised our eyebrows at each other and then turned to Helen. "Dad was very affectionate with Mom," she said lovingly.

"And he's still lost without her." Nancy's voice had a sad tone to it now. "He came by here all the time when Eleanor first passed. He would sit by himself, quietly drinking his tea. It broke our hearts watching him." She paused for a second as she brushed away the tears forming in her eyes. "We know he still feels her presence here. Every time he walks through the door, his face instantly brightens." She looked at Helen. "It seems as though whatever is burdening him vanishes as soon as he steps inside."

Helen smiled. "It works every time. That's why John and I bring him here so often. We know how much this place means to Dad."

Nancy looked at us Perkins ladies and smiled. "You ladies are very special. The Rutherfords have never brought anyone here before. So, for Helen to be sharing this place with you..." Her voice trailed off, but we knew exactly what she was saying.

We looked from Nancy to Helen, and I was the one who said what all three of us were thinking. "Thank you, Helen, for sharing this special place with us."

"Of course, Abigail," she replied with a benevolent tone. "You're part of our family."

"Now, what can I bring you for lunch?" Nancy asked with a cordial smile. "We do have the best food and service in Fairfield County, after all." After taking our orders, she turned and headed toward the kitchen.

"Wow!" my sister gushed, running her hands along her seat again. "What an incredible story."

"Yes, Mom and Dad's love story is one I could listen to over and over again," Helen agreed.

"So, how did your parents meet?" Sarah asked her quietly. "If you don't mind telling us?"

Helen smiled gently at her. "My parents met in college. Like how all the Rutherfords went to Yale, my family all went to Princeton."

My mom reached over and squeezed her hand. "We were so sorry to hear about your family, Helen. I was in my forties when I lost my parents, and that was hard enough. I can't imagine losing them as a teenager and then just after college."

"Thank you, Valerie," Helen said softly. "I was very close to my mother growing up, and when she got sick with cancer, we made sure to make every moment count. It brought us even closer as a family." She paused for a moment, clearly getting emotional. "And while we were prepared for my mother's passing, losing my father and brother was a complete shock."

"Neil said you were supposed to be in the car with them," I said quietly.

"Yes," she confirmed. "But then a friend of mine wanted to give me a ride in the new car her family bought for her as a graduation gift. I wasn't sure at first about going with her since I wanted to spend as much time with my father and brother as possible. But then my father said, 'It's okay, Helen. You have fun with your friend, and we'll see you at your apartment.' Then he and my brother hugged and kissed me and said they loved me and were proud of me, and then they got into his car. As they pulled out of their parking spot, they had to wait a moment for the other cars to move. So, my brother jumped out and came over to give me one more hug and kiss, and he smiled at me and said, 'And Mom's proud of you too, Helen.' Then he got back in the car, and they left."

She paused again, brushing the tears from her cheeks. "I am so grateful to have that as my final memory of them." Rubbing her arms with her hands, she said, "I can still feel my brother's arms around mine, and I remember that smile." She brushed away more tears as she whispered, "That smile is what got me through the next six months."

My mom took her hand, the four of us now crying, as Helen continued, "I was completely lost for the next six months. I graduated college, buried my father and brother, and started a new job all within two weeks. I went back to Darien, wishing to reconnect with friends, but a lot had changed in just four short years. Many of my friends had started families, and while I was happy for them, it also made me a bit sad. As my friends would talk about having their mothers in the delivery room, coaching them and supporting them, I wondered who would be there for me when I had children."

She paused again, and when she spoke, there was a renewed hope in her voice. "And then, one day, I suddenly got my answer. I was at a charity event with a friend, and she noticed someone looking at me. She said, 'Helen, look over there. That cute guy keeps checking you out.'" She paused as we all shared a much-needed laugh. "So, I looked across the room, and that's when I saw John. He was also with a friend who was trying to nudge him in my direction."

"He told us about that," my sister remembered with a fond smile.

"The two of us kept smiling at each other across the room, but I was raised that a lady lets the man pursue her. So, I waited. And waited." We laughed again. "And finally, he came walking toward me with a smile that attempted to mask his nerves, and he told me that I had the most beautiful smile he had ever seen."

My sister grabbed my hand, and we gushed together, "Aww! That's so sweet."

"And that's when the entire room disappeared," Helen breathed, a loving smile taking over her face. "All I could see was him, and we spent the rest of the evening talking. And when the event ended, he held my hand as we slowly strolled through the parking lot. Right before we got to my friend's car, he stopped and looked at me in the moonlight. His face was glowing as he looked at me, and it made me feel like the prettiest girl alive. He asked if he could take me out to dinner, so we agreed to meet the next night. Then he gave me a hug, and as soon as I felt his arms around me, I felt like I was home." She paused to reminisce, her face full of love. "Then I got into my friend's car, and she smiled at me and said, 'Make sure to send me an invitation to your wedding.'"

Our eyes brightened at hearing her story. "Oh, wow," my sister breathed. "So, your friend knew?"

"Yes, and so did I," Helen confirmed, her face glowing. "And after our second date, John asked me how I felt about meeting his parents."

My heart surged with love, remembering a very special conversation last summer. "Neil asked me the same thing."

Helen smiled at me. "And he said he wanted to meet my family as well. At that point, I had one grandfather still alive. So, after I brought John to meet him, he took me home to meet his parents." She paused and closed her eyes, covering her heart with her hands. When she opened her eyes, they were so full of love as she said, "And they were the warmest, most loving couple I had ever met."

"And John said that Grandpa told you to call him Dad," I commented, remembering my first encounter with the family patriarch.

She smiled at me again. "Yes, Abigail, he did. And it even surprised John. He was not expecting that." She paused momentarily, her smile growing even warmer as she looked at me. "And then Dad surprised me about six months ago. And it had to do with you."

"What do you mean?" I asked, my smile matching hers.

"As you know, Dad and I get together every week to discuss foundation matters. And every time an anonymous donation comes in, I tell him about it. Most are round, even numbers, but last summer, we got an anonymous donation in a very unusual amount."

I felt my sister's hand slide discreetly inside mine. We gently squeezed each other's hands, remembering the special significance of that number.

"So, I told Dad about it," Helen continued, "and he asked what the exact number was. And when I told him, the most unusual thing happened. He actually smiled. Which, as you ladies know, doesn't happen very often. And it wasn't just a little smile either. His entire face lit up."

"That does sound like quite the surprise," my mom agreed, knowing nothing of our donation.

"And that was just the start of it," Helen went on, her face full of astonishment. "After discussing foundation matters in his study, Dad and I always go to the kitchen to visit over a cup of tea. And that was right after Cornelius brought you home to meet John and me. So, Dad asked me what I thought of you. And I said, 'Oh, Dad, she is lovely. She's warm and kind and so polite. Wait until you meet her.'"

"Oh, Helen," I breathed, reaching across the table and taking her hands. "That's so sweet of you to say."

"It's all true, Abigail," she praised, giving my hands a loving squeeze. "And that's when Dad really surprised me. He said, 'I can't wait to meet her, Helen. And I already know I'm going to have her call me Grandpa.'"

A wave of love surged through me as my eyes brightened. I looked between my mom and Sarah, loving that their expressions matched mine.

Our attention returned to Helen as she continued, "And then, back in November, I was sitting at my desk, working on foundation matters, when my phone rang. It was John and Dad, and as soon as I heard Dad's voice, I sensed a brightness. He said, 'I just met her, Helen, and I will agree with you. Abbie is the loveliest girl, and I can see that she and Neil are perfect for each other.' And then he stopped speaking for a moment, and when he spoke again, there was an emotion in his voice that I rarely hear. He said, 'And she even thanked me for how polite Neil is and told me she's very grateful for me.'" She squeezed my hands tighter. "You don't know how much it meant to Dad to hear you say that, Abigail."

A few tears escaped my eyes. "Thank you, Helen," I whispered.

"So, wait," my sister said suddenly. I looked at her to see a big smile on her face. "Abbie, the day we met Mr. Rutherford, at the end of our conversation, he told Neil and Archie that he expected them in the conference room by the time he and John got there. He said they needed to go to his office first to make an important phone call." She looked at Helen. "So that phone call was to you?"

"Yes, Sarah, it was," she confirmed with a soft smile.

My sister grabbed my hands. "Oh, Abbie! I figured that phone call had something to do with their business. But it was about you. It's so sweet that he needed to call Helen right away and sing your praises to her."

Hearing my sister say this made my heart swell with even more love for Neil's family. I smiled at Helen and agreed, "That really was sweet of Grandpa. And from the way he and John were talking, it sounds like it was just as instant for you, too."

"Oh, yes, Abigail," she exclaimed, her eyes brightening with fondness. "John's parents made me feel loved and accepted the moment I met them. They even renamed their family's foundation to include my name. They said they wanted my family to be represented as well."

I thought for a second. "So is Barrington your maiden name?"

"Yes, it is," she confirmed with a smile.

My sister's eyes brightened with a realization. "So that explains Archie's first middle name. Where did Hartsell come from?"

I looked at Sarah with furrowed eyebrows. "Archie has two middle names?"

"Yeah, I saw his degree hanging in his office. It said, Archibald Barrington Hartsell Rutherford. Just like Neil's said, Cornelius Johnson Rutherford with a Roman numeral four after it. Didn't you notice, Abbie?"

I shook my head as my mom and I raised our eyebrows at each other.

"So where did Hartsell come from?" Sarah asked Helen again.

"Archibald Barrington is my father's name, and Hartsell is my brother's name," Helen answered with a kind smile.

"I love it," my sister gushed, covering her heart.

"Thank you, Sarah," Helen acknowledged her lovingly. "It was John's idea. Just like it was my suggestion to carry on the family tradition of naming the firstborn son Cornelius."

"Neil said he and Archie were inseparable growing up," I recalled. "He told me they loved sharing their room." My heart surged with love as I pictured the two beds in their room, draped with those beautiful quilts.

Helen's face beamed with motherly pride as she said, "Cornelius was so excited when we told him he was going to be a big brother, and it was love at first sight for him. He was so attached to his baby brother that he caused me almost to have a heart attack the first night Archibald was home."

"Oh, Helen," my mom said sympathetically. "What happened?"

"We put Archibald in his crib, and then we tucked Cornelius into his bed just down the hall. An hour later, I went to check on Cornelius, and I found his bed empty."

My mom gasped and covered her heart. "I can only imagine how you felt."

"I instantly panicked, Valerie. I was on my way to the living room to get John when I noticed Archibald's door was open slightly. I walked in and found Cornelius sound asleep in his brother's crib, cuddled up next to his baby brother."

"Oh, that is so sweet," my sister breathed.

"Yes, it was," Helen agreed. "Once I realized Cornelius was safe. And then I took him back to his own room. But when Archibald woke up a few hours later, I found his brother in his crib again. This went on for a few nights, and then John asked Cornelius if he wanted his brother in his room with him. And you should have seen the way his face lit up. So, we moved Archibald down the hall, and everything was going well. Until eighteen months later, when I panicked again."

"What happened that time?" my sister asked.

"It was Archibald's first night in an actual bed. As Cornelius was brushing his teeth, I went in to check on his brother, and once again, I found an empty bed.

At least this time, my panic only lasted for a moment because I looked across the room and noticed a lump under the covers. Archibald had crawled into his brother's bed and was waiting for him."

"This keeps getting sweeter," Sarah gushed.

Helen smiled at my sister, then continued, "So then we started putting the boys to bed at the same time, and for the next seven years, Archibald's bed remained practically unused."

My sister and I looked at each other with admiration for the brothers. "Oh my God, Abbie," she whispered. "I love it."

"Me too, Sarah," I agreed.

"And while my boys have always gotten along very well, there is another pair of siblings in the family who get along equally as well. Although they do interact a bit differently."

We looked at Helen inquisitively.

"I'm talking about Dad and Dorothy." Her focus switched to just me. "You were worried earlier about Dad wanting to pay for your dress because Dorothy yelled at him. But that is just the way Dorothy speaks to her brother. And that's how we knew she was okay after her stroke."

"What do you mean?" I asked her.

"The five of us were in New York City when Archibald's phone rang. A nurse named Lydia was calling to let us know that Dorothy had a stroke. And the color instantly drained from Dad's face. We hadn't seen him that worried since he found out Mom was dying."

My mom took her hand again as Helen continued, "Dad was rather quiet on the way back to New Canaan, but that silence ended as soon as we got to the hospital. He walked in there, barking orders at nurses and demanding answers from doctors. And then we heard an angry voice yell, 'Junior, get in here!' The five of us stepped into Dorothy's room, and she glared at her brother and demanded, 'You be nice to these people right now, or I will call security myself and have them throw you out of here!'"

We looked at Helen wide-eyed. "She said that to her brother?" Sarah asked.

"Yes, she did," Helen confirmed with an amused tone. "And you should have seen Dad's face. The worry instantly vanished, and he looked so relieved. But even that only lasted for a minute. As soon as he found out her kids' plan to move her into a nursing home..." She shook her head.

"Archie told us he started yelling," Sarah said quietly.

"John and I got him out of the hospital before security really did throw him out," Helen recalled. "He yelled the entire time we were in the car, and then as soon as John turned off the engine, the yelling instantly stopped."

A smile spread across my sister's face. "You brought him here, didn't you?"

Helen's expression matched my sister's as she remembered, "As soon as he walked through the door, his entire demeanor changed. Dad cannot be angry in here. So, we ordered him some tea, and while he drank it quietly, we knew he was working on a plan. After finishing his tea, he sat back and calmly stated, 'She's moving in with me. And I'm going to hire a nurse to be her live-in caregiver. I'm already leaning toward Lydia. She was very pleasant over the phone, and she's the only one who didn't scramble when I walked in.'" Helen grinned at us. "Dad is a very self-aware man, and he knew that whoever was going to take care of Dorothy would also have to be able to live with him."

"So, he decided on Lydia that quickly?" my sister asked.

"Dad is an excellent judge of character. And the more time he spent at the hospital, the more he saw how much Lydia cared about Dorothy. And she seemed rather comfortable with him, so as Dorothy was getting discharged, he told Lydia she was coming with them."

"She told us," I said, thinking back to her recounted story. "She said she just stared at him at first, not sure what to do."

"Dad has that effect on people," Helen agreed. "But she learned rather quickly that while Cornelius Rutherford can be quite abrasive, he is also a very loving brother."

"Lydia said she noticed that in the hospital," my sister commented.

"Dad is extremely dedicated to his family, and he was going to make sure that his sister received the best of care. And Dorothy is very grateful for her brother's dedication." Helen reached across the table and took my hands reassuringly. "I promise you, Abigail, that yelling at her brother is just what Dorothy does. And the day she stops yelling at him is the day we know there is something wrong with her."

"See, Abbie?" my sister said. "You have nothing to worry about. Mr. Rutherford already loves you."

"Yes, he does, Abigail," Helen confirmed with a warm smile.

Just then, Nancy arrived at our table to gather our empty plates. "The sandwiches were delicious, Nancy," my mom praised her.

"Thank you, Val," she accepted my mom's compliment with a smile. Looking at the three of us, she continued, "It was such a pleasure meeting you ladies today. And please, come back anytime. I told my sisters who you are, and you will never pay a dime here."

We looked at each other with astonishment and then smiled at her. "Thank you, Nancy," all three of us said at the same time.

After we shared a laugh, she acknowledged, "You're welcome. The three of you are now part of a family that is very special to us here at Betty's Diner. And my mother insisted almost fifty-four years ago that we are *never* to charge a Rutherford. And we still follow that rule to this day."

As we got up to leave, we hugged Nancy goodbye, and Helen promised to tell John and Grandpa hello from her. Taking one final look around, this place is not at all what I expected when Helen told us she wanted to take us out for lunch. But I can see why their family loves this place so much. It's warm and welcoming, and Nancy's customer service was the best we've ever received.

As my focus switched to Helen, I reflected upon everything she shared about the family. The way she talked about meeting John and the instant love she felt from her in-laws made my heart so happy. And while I knew about her family's tragic losses, it moved me deeply as she shared with us her final moments with her father and brother. And I know Sarah loved it just as much as I did to hear her recall Neil and Archie's closeness right from the start.

But my favorite part of all was listening to the way Helen and Nancy talked about a sweet couple with an instant connection. And sitting in the exact spot where it all started for Neil's grandparents made me truly feel like a member of the family.

I couldn't help but wonder, though, how a family as wealthy as the Rutherfords ended up here of all places...

Chapter 10

♥

"So, has Sarah told you where she's taking you today?" Neil asked me over our morning coffee.

I shook my head. "No, I've asked her a few times, but all she would tell me is to wear something nice."

As if on cue, the doorbell rang.

Neil took my hand with a smile. "Come on." As we got to the door, he opened it and said, "You know you don't have to ring the doorbell, right, Sarah? You can just let yourself in."

"Yeah, right!" she scoffed with a horrified look on her face. "I don't want to catch you two...doing anything."

He laughed as he leaned down to kiss her on both cheeks. "Your answers still entertain me, Sarah."

"And they always will," she promised, her laughter matching his. She turned to me and scanned my indigo sheath dress and black heels. "You look nice, Abs."

"Thanks," I replied cheerfully. "I was just following your orders." My eyes ran down her navy-blue dress and nude heels. Her hair was pulled up in a ponytail, and light-pink lip gloss was her only makeup today. "You look pretty, too."

"Thanks. Are you ready to go?"

"Sure," was the only answer I could come up with, still confused about where we were going and why we were dressed so nicely.

"Have fun," my sweet fiancé said as he gave me a kiss.

I smiled at him as I stepped out the door and walked with Sarah to her car. As we got in, she asked, "So, what is Neil up to today?"

"He mentioned that he and Archie are going to do something."

She laughed. "They'll probably go to the gym for a third time today."

"Probably," I agreed with the same humorous tone.

As she drove, she chatted about the interior decorating plan that she came up with for a new client. I listened with interest, but I knew she was just making small talk until we arrived at our destination. Which, as it turned out, happened to be a fancy country club in New Canaan.

"What are we doing here?" I asked her as she turned off the engine.

She grinned at me. "You'll see."

We stepped inside the door and looked around wide-eyed. Every time Sarah and I come here, we are mesmerized by our grand surroundings. Mid-morning sun streamed in through the large windows, drenching the entryway with springtime cheer. A stunning arrangement of tulips, irises, hyacinths, and lilies decorated the large walnut table in the foyer.

I batted my sister playfully on the arm and pointed to the flowers. “Look, Sarah, your favorite. Wild hyacinths.”

Her eyes brightened as she looked at the vase. “I wonder if Archie’s seen them.”

Taking my hand, she led me in the opposite direction of the dining room. We walked into a large room with leather armchairs and bookshelves lining the walls, reminding me of Grandpa’s library. Slate flooring and antique brass wall sconces gave the room a masculine touch. While the showpiece of the dining room was its fireplace, the focal point of this room was the curved staircase leading to the second floor. Grand and majestic, the wide-plank walnut steps followed the contour of the striking walnut banister.

“Come on,” my sister said with a grin. “Let’s check out what’s upstairs.”

As we ascended the staircase, I marveled at the mahogany paneling on the walls, thinking about how much Grandpa would enjoy this room. As we reached the landing, we were welcomed by the most stunning chandelier. Sparkling crystals shimmered like prisms, filling the vaulted ceiling with colorful happiness. Leading me to a set of French doors, Sarah flung them open with all the flamboyance of Liberace. She pulled me into a grand ballroom, and I was greeted with the most beautiful sight.

"Surprise!"

My mom, Helen, Aunt Dottie, Lydia, Grace, Madison, and several friends were all beaming at me. My eyes grew even larger as I took in the magnificent ballroom. Several large white pillars towered throughout the room, and lavish gold drapes framed the windows. Round tables dressed with crisp white tablecloths and black napkins added a classy touch to the space. Fresh, vibrant flowers decorated a long rectangular table in the center of the room, with several gift bags piled nearby. Another large table sat along the wall, with a beautiful assortment of fresh fruit, finger sandwiches, and various treats for dessert. A *Congratulations* banner hung on the wall above it, and large bunches of gold and silver balloons floated happily on either side.

My sister had a massive grin on her face as she once again slipped my *'Bride-to-Be'* sash over my head. Looking at it, I asked, "Where did you get this?"

"Neil gave it to me," she declared proudly.

She pulled me further into the room as everyone came over to hug me. After indulging in their love, I went over to the lady seated at the table in the middle of the room. Hugging her a little longer, I said, "Hi, Aunt Dottie."

"Hi, Sugar," she replied with a warm smile.

As I stood up, I realized something was missing. "Where's your wheelchair?"

"The elevator is broken, so Archie carried me up the stairs. He was here to drive the van anyways, so he took my chair with him."

I thought for a second. "I didn't see the van outside."

She grinned at me. "It's hard to miss, so we told Archie to take it back to Junior's. This way, it wouldn't tip you off."

Taking my hand, Sarah led me to the head of the table and pulled out the chair. "You get the best seat in the house," she announced as I sat down.

As everyone else took a seat around the table, I gazed around with fondness. It filled my heart with happiness to see so many of my friends and family members here, full of excitement for my wedding.

"So, we know you and Neil told everyone not to get you any wedding gifts, but he didn't want you to miss out on having a bridal shower," my sister explained. "And he wanted us to have the party before you move in with him next weekend. So, he helped us come up with a list of things, just for you, to finish decorating your room for when his home officially becomes your home."

I gasped with delight at hearing her sweet words. "Really? He did that?"

"Yes, Abigail, he did," Helen confirmed. "Cornelius is the one who arranged this whole party."

I covered my heart with my hands. "Now I love him even more." Then I quickly added, "And it's not so much for the gifts. But for this sweet party. And to see all of you." I looked around again, my love for all these wonderful ladies growing even stronger.

"Why don't the two of you want any wedding gifts?" one of my friends from college asked me.

My smile fell a bit. "Because we feel guilty having people spend their money on us," I answered quietly.

Aunt Dottie smiled as she looked across the table. "She's not even married yet, Helen, and she already has a touch of the affluenza."

"Afflu-what?" my sister asked with a confused look.

Helen smiled gently at her. "Affluenza. It's the guilt that wealthy people feel about having a substantial amount of money."

"Well, some wealthy people feel it, but not all of them," Aunt Dottie clarified. "That's why Junior hates this place so much. All those gold diggers who try to sink their claws into poor Archie don't feel an ounce of guilt. All they feel is entitled." She smiled at me. "It's one more reason why we love you, Abbie, and we know you're perfect for Neil."

"Thanks, Aunt Dottie," I acknowledged her modestly.

"And you still deserve a fun party," my sister proclaimed, jumping out of her chair and grabbing a gift bag. "You are the bride, after all."

She excitedly handed the bag to me, and as I was about to peek inside, I stopped. Looking over at the glorious spread, I suggested, "Why don't we get some food first? And then I'm excited to see your thoughtful gifts."

We continued to mingle and chat as we filled our plates, and my heart swelled with even more love as I noticed the balloons up close. Customized with our names and wedding date, I gazed at them dreamily, hoping a few had been set aside for the wedding itself.

Returning to our seats, I removed the tissue paper from the gift bag sitting next to me. As soon as I saw the contents, I gasped with delight and immediately knew who it was from. I pulled a large, fluffy orange pillow out of the bag and looked at Madison. "This is just like the pillow you gushed over when Sarah and I first started decorating the resort."

Her smile was beaming as she looked at me. "As soon as I noticed it in the store, I thought of you." She looked at the other ladies and raved, "Grace and I were there to witness the spark between our happy couple on the morning they met. And we noticed it instantly."

"Well, after your initial look of panic went away," Grace added with a smile. "I know you were terrified at first, but Madison and I were so relieved when we saw Neil walk through that door."

"Abbie's own Prince Charming came to her rescue when she needed him the most," my sister joked.

Hugging the pillow to my chest, I remembered that moment. And while I certainly was terrified, Neil instantly calmed me with his smile that I love so much. "Thanks, Madison," I acknowledged her graciously. "Every time I see this pillow, I'll think of you and that first day." Then I added with a laugh, "It was a day full of so many varying emotions."

As I proceeded to open my gifts, my heart flooded with even more love for everyone's thoughtfulness. I marveled at the beautiful, golden-framed picture of an autumn landscape that Lydia gave me, knowing it would coordinate perfectly with the art already in the room. Grace's ivory, faux fur area rug made me swoon dreamily as I imagined walking on it barefoot. And I already had the best spot picked out for the stunning crystal jar with fairy lights that the girls from college so generously pitched in for.

Handing me another bag, my sister commented, "This is the last gift that's here. There's one more waiting for you; it was just too big to bring with us." Grinning at two other ladies, she said, "Mom, Helen, and I got you the chair-and-a-half that you've had your eyes on for months."

"Oh, thank you!" I breathed, knowing precisely what she was talking about. Upholstered in soft ivory fabric with golden flecks, it's the perfect size for the cozy room.

Sarah's grin increased as she looked at me. "Neil and Archie are picking it up in the van and carrying it up the stairs to your room right now."

My eyes brightened with a mixture of happiness and surprise. "So that's what the guys are doing right now?" Thinking for a second, I playfully teased, "And you knew and just made up the story about them going to the gym again?"

Her smile became even brighter, reminding me of someone else. "I needed a believable story to throw you off the trail."

I shook my head and laughed.

"Go ahead and open your last gift," my sister commented as she sat back down.

Reaching into the bag, I pulled out a stunning ivory nightgown made of delicate lace and chiffon. I held it up, and as soon as everyone saw it, they started whistling and cheering.

"Who got me this?"

"That would be me," Aunt Dottie proudly declared. "Neil told us to get you gifts for your room at his house, but I figured the two of you deserved something special for your wedding night."

"Thank you, Aunt Dottie," I acknowledged her with a grateful smile. "I love it." As I marveled at the sexy yet tasteful lingerie, I dreamed, "And I know Neil will love it too. He prefers me in something beautiful and classy."

"See, Dottie?" Lydia teased her with a grin. "Aren't you glad you listened to Archie?"

All of us looked at each other wide-eyed, then we turned to Lydia. "What does Archie have to do with this?" I asked.

"He was with us when we were shopping for your gifts. As we passed a lingerie store, Dottie said she wanted to go inside. Archie refused to go in, so I brought Dottie inside." She laughed as she recalled, "Dottie was picking up sheer nighties and lace teddies, and every time, she would turn toward the door and hold them up and ask Archie what he thought."

The room filled with laughter.

"So, what did he think?" my sister asked with a curious grin.

"He would barely glance our way, and his face kept turning a brighter shade of red with each item she held up," Lydia answered, still laughing. "I felt kind of bad for him, but he really was adorable. So finally, when Dottie held up a black lace teddy that left nothing to the imagination, that's when he came into the store. He tossed the lingerie aside and pushed her wheelchair through the maze of tables."

"And I continued picking up bras and undies along the way, and Archie kept getting more and more embarrassed," Aunt Dottie laughed. "He is so shy about that sort of stuff."

"So, when he got to the more tasteful part of the store, he told me to have Dottie pick something from that section, and then he ran out of that store like a bear was chasing him," Lydia said, her laughter increasing.

"We found him thirty minutes later hiding in the corner of a bookstore, and he was still blushing," Aunt Dottie giggled.

"And don't worry, Abbie," Lydia reassured me. "He didn't see what Dottie picked out for you."

As the laughter in the room died down, I acknowledged, "Well, even though you embarrassed him, I'm glad Archie pointed you in the right direction." I held the nightgown up again, daydreaming about our wedding night. "Neil is going to love this."

I carefully put the nightie back in its bag and set it aside, and we got up to fill our plates with some yummy desserts. As we returned to our seats, Helen asked me, "So, Abigail, what did you and Cornelius do for his birthday last week?"

I felt a bright smile taking over my face. "We spent the night at the resort where we're getting married. And this time, we stayed in their room with a king-size sleigh bed, a claw-foot bathtub, and a fireplace. We even booked it as our room for the wedding."

"How romantic," one of my college friends gushed.

"It was," I agreed. "And we nailed down a few more details for our wedding. The resort is going to take care of the food, and one of their employees enjoys photography, so he'll do our pictures."

"Oh, how wonderful," Helen beamed.

My smile got even brighter. "And the best part is the pergola in their large backyard. We already know that's where we'll exchange our vows, and then we'll have the reception in their ballroom." I looked at my beautiful surroundings and added, "We thought about having the reception outside, but their ballroom is just as stunning as this one here."

"Abbie, we're so happy for you," my mom joyfully raved.

After indulging in cupcakes, lemon tarts, and chocolate-covered strawberries, my friends from college decided to get going. As they hugged and congratulated me, I thanked them again for the crystal jar and fairy lights. As I returned to my seat, a pleasant waitress showed up with tea for us.

"This has been such a lovely party," Grace commented as she sipped her tea. "Thank you again, Sarah, for inviting us."

"Of course," my sister replied. "It wouldn't be the same without you."

"I am confused about one thing, though," Madison said, looking at Helen. "You keep talking about someone named Cornelius. Who is that?"

"That's Neil's real name," I explained. "He's Cornelius the fourth."

Grace and Madison looked at each other with their eyebrows furrowed in confusion. They looked back at us, and Grace wondered out loud, "So, John...?"

"Their middle name is Johnson," Aunt Dottie cleared up their confusion. "It was my grandmother's maiden name."

As the two of them looked at Aunt Dottie, their eyes got huge with realization. "So, this man that you keep referring to as 'Junior' is Mr. Rutherford?" Madison asked with astonishment.

"That's correct," she said with a smile.

"And you're his...sister?" Madison drew out that last word with a tone of disbelief.

"You seem surprised, Sugar."

"Well, it just..." She looked for the right words. "You're so sweet and funny, and he's—"

"Our boss," Grace quickly cut her off with a glare.

"Oh, right," she said quietly. "Sorry, Aunt Dottie."

"That's quite all right, Sugar," Aunt Dottie replied with an understanding smile. "I am well aware of my brother's personality."

"So, what was his wife like?" Madison asked, looking relieved.

"Oh, Eleanor was an absolute doll!" Aunt Dottie gushed. "I will never forget the look on Junior's face the first time he saw her."

"Helen took us to the diner," my sister said with a loving smile. "Nancy even told me I was sitting in his spot."

"Oh, yes, that is still Junior's favorite place all these years later," Aunt Dottie confirmed with bright eyes.

"The food was amazing, and the people were lovely," I praised. "But...how did your family end up there?"

Aunt Dottie laughed gently. "It was Daddy's birthday, which fell on Easter that year. We had plans to come here since our parents were members, just like John and Helen. But when we got here, the hostess informed us that our reservation had fallen through the cracks. Even though we had been coming here every week for Sunday brunch for years." She laughed again. "I swear those were the only two hours out of each week that Junior wasn't working."

"So, what did you do?" Sarah asked.

"Well, Junior barked at the hostess to speak to the manager, but Mom told him it was okay. She didn't want him making a scene, and we would go somewhere else. So, we all piled back into Junior's car, but being Easter, every restaurant in the area was packed. My kids were getting impatient, so when Frankie noticed an empty parking space outside of a diner, Junior pulled in." She laughed again. "The way those people looked at us when we walked in, you would have thought we had just landed here from Mars. Even though it was Easter, we were the only ones who were dressed up, and we clearly looked out of place. But Betty welcomed us with a smile that made us feel like we belonged there."

"That's the way her daughter Nancy made us feel," my mom said with a smile.

Aunt Dottie's smile matched my mom's. "Nancy's the one who waited on us that day. She was a sweet teenager who gushed over my children and even gave my two oldest kids crayons and coloring books to keep them occupied while we waited for our food." She looked at Helen. "That's something a young family would never get here. And my kids loved it. And we loved that they were quiet." After pausing for a second, she added, "Even Matthew was quiet, thanks to Junior."

"Is he the fussy baby Nancy told us about?" Sarah asked.

"Yes. He was three months old and had been crying all morning. We got some dirty looks while we were downstairs here, but not in the diner. I carried him to the table, and everybody we walked by commented how adorable he was. As Mom and Frankie got in on either side of the booth with Robert and Kelly, who were four and three, Junior smiled at me and held out his arms." A smile spread across her face. "As soon as he took little Matthew, that baby instantly quieted down. And I plopped down next to Robert as Junior slid in next to Kelly." She shook her head. "If you want to see a miracle worker, you should have seen Junior with her."

"What do you mean?" my sister asked in a loving tone.

"She cried the entire first year of her life. But we noticed right off that as soon as Junior took her, she would immediately settle down. One night, when she was three weeks old, Mom was at the house trying to help Frankie and me calm her. It was ten-thirty, and she was keeping Robert up, so finally, Frankie said, 'Take her to Junior's apartment. Your mom and I will stay here with Robert.' So, I put her in the car and drove by Junior's apartment, but no one was home. And there was only one other place he could be. Sure enough, I drove by the office, and the only light on in the entire building was the one in Daddy's office. By the time I stepped out of the elevator, Kelly was screaming at the top of her little lungs. And Junior came out of Daddy's office looking like a shrieking baby was the sweetest sound he had ever heard. He rushed over to me, took that baby, and held her close to him, burying his face in her blanket. Within thirty seconds, that shrieking baby was so quiet you could have heard a pin drop on the carpet. And Junior stood there in the hallway for a long time, cuddling her and talking so gently to her. It was the sweetest thing I had ever seen." She lifted her left hand and wiped away the tears streaming down her cheeks.

"Wow, Aunt Dottie," my sister breathed as we all brushed away our tears. "That is really sweet."

"Yes, Sarah, it was," she agreed with a kind smile. "I brought Kelly to Junior at least three or four nights a week that first year. And he was never at home, always at the office. I got so I wouldn't even try his apartment. Daddy had a long sofa in his office, and it's still there to this day. As Junior would sit at Daddy's desk and rock Kelly and read to her, I would get some much-needed sleep. And then, as she got a bit older, she wasn't as fussy, so I didn't go by Daddy's office much anymore." A warm smile spread across her face. "Even though that first year was tough with her, it was still one of my favorites. And I knew, just by watching my brother, that he would make a great father someday. We just had to wait a few more years."

She paused for a second, then laughed. "But they felt like rather long years to Mom and me. I would tell Frankie that all Junior did was work, and that would never get him a wife. And he would tell me to be patient. He reminded me that only a truly special girl would be able to love Junior's personality."

"And he found her in a diner," my sister said dreamily.

"And did I get the shock of my life that day!" Aunt Dottie exclaimed. "Little Robert had just shown me the picture he colored and had moved on to the next one when I looked up and saw something I had never seen before. Junior had the goofiest look on his face."

We all laughed as she continued, "I looked around the table, and Mom was busy with Kelly as Frankie was watching Robert." She laughed again. "It's a good thing he wasn't paying attention because he would have asked what was wrong with Uncle Joonie's face."

As we all laughed again, my sister said, "I am loving this story, Aunt Dottie."

"And my brother was so absorbed in what he was looking at that he didn't even notice me turn around. And that's when I saw her. The cutest little waitress was standing across the room in her red apron with a pink dress underneath it. Her hair was pulled up in a ponytail, and her brown eyes were glowing as she looked at my brother."

"Nancy told us that she tried to get Eleanor to go talk to him, but she didn't think it would be appropriate," Sarah commented.

"I tried too," Aunt Dottie said with a grin. "I went to the ladies' room, and on my way back, I saw Eleanor looking at Junior, who was busy with Matthew. So, I said, 'He's handsome, isn't he?' And she blushed the cutest shade of pink."

She stopped talking momentarily as we all shared a good-natured laugh. "And then I said, 'His name is Cornelius, he's single, and he's thirty years old. He is my brother, and that baby he's holding is mine.' And with every detail I gave her, her face lit up even more. So, I asked her a little about herself, and then I told her she should go over and talk to him. But she said that she was raised by conservative parents, and she didn't think it would be appropriate. And I could respect that. So, I returned to the table as Junior was trying to pay the bill, to find that Betty wouldn't take his money."

"Nancy told us that your family doesn't pay when you go to the diner," I said.

"Starting from that very first day," Aunt Dottie confirmed. "She told Junior at the time that Easter lunch was on the house for everyone. But she admitted to him later that she knew he and Eleanor would get married someday, and she was just so happy they met in her diner."

"Aww," we all gushed at the same time.

"So, as Mom and Frankie were wrangling the kids toward the door, I caught Junior stealing one last glance at the pretty waitress. So, I said, 'Her name is Eleanor,' and his goofy smile instantly vanished, knowing he had been caught. He asked me how I knew that, and I said it was because I had talked to her. I told him, 'She's twenty years old, she's single, and she knows you're single too.' Then I gave him a nudge and told him to go talk to her. And that's when his face fell, and he said, 'I can't, Dottie, she's too good for me.' And I said, 'That's nonsense, Junior!' And I reminded him what Daddy would always tell him: 'Your mother and I made you a good man, Junior. The right woman will make you a great man.'"

"So then, what did he do?" my sister quietly asked.

"He walked by me and went out the door to the car," Aunt Dottie answered sadly. "Several times over the next three months, I wanted to bring it up but never did." Her voice cheered up as she continued, "But then, on a sunny afternoon in July, he stopped by my house. And I knew, just from his beaming smile, that he had gone back to the diner. He told me he was taking her out for dinner after her father got home from work because he wanted to meet him first. And that was music to my ears!"

"How long until they were married?" Madison asked.

"Five months. I was one of Eleanor's bridesmaids, and as we were helping her get ready that morning, she still didn't have a plan for how to style her hair. So, I suggested she tie it up in a ponytail, just like it looked when Junior first saw her. And when it was time for all of us to walk down the aisle, I saw my brother standing at the front of the church, looking as stoic as ever. So, I took my place opposite Junior, and as everyone watched the back of the church waiting for Eleanor, I was watching my brother. And as soon as his pretty bride appeared at the entrance to the aisle, his face just melted." She paused and put her hand over her heart. "Eleanor had a way with Junior that was so special. She brought out a side of him that only she had access to."

"Oh my God, Aunt Dottie," my sister sighed happily as she brushed away a few more tears. "That is the sweetest story ever."

"Thank you, Sugar," she said with a warm smile. "And the person he was for Eleanor is the version of my brother that I love the most."

"We've already seen the way he acts differently with you, Helen, and Abbie," my sister pointed out. "The guys told us he's strict with them, and we've seen that first-hand, too."

"I get after Junior all the time for being too strict with his boys," Aunt Dottie said with an annoyed tone. "Especially Archie."

As if knowing his name was just mentioned, the French doors opened, and in walked Archie. His smile was blazing as he walked toward us and stopped behind Aunt Dottie. Leaning down to rest his chin on her shoulder, his smile shined even brighter as he looked at me.

"Did you have fun, Abbie?"

"I did," I replied with a smile. "This was such a sweet surprise."

"And this is a surprise for us, too," Madison commented, looking at Archie. "I don't know how many times I talked to you on the phone while Neil was working at the resort. It's nice to put a face with the voice finally." Then she added quickly, "I'm Madison, by the way. And this is Grace."

He looked at them with his brilliant smile. “Yeah, I’ve only been to the resort once. Grandpa doesn’t let me out of my office too much.” He laughed. “I keep waiting for the day when he locks me in and throws away the key.” He thought for a second, then added, “Although he does send me out sometimes to get coffee for the four of us.”

Helen’s eyebrows furrowed in confusion. “But your grandfather doesn’t like coffee.”

“I know,” Archie agreed. “Weird, huh?”

Madison grinned at him. “And we heard you went shopping at a certain store in the mall.”

His face instantly flushed with embarrassment as his blue eyes filled with panic. “Aunt Dottie,” he whispered loudly. “You told them I went with you?”

“Of course, Sugar,” she replied, patting his flaming cheek with her hand. As she turned to look at him, she observed, “Archie, your face is so red. Just like that lacy bra and panties set.”

“Aunt Dottie,” he whispered again, barely glancing at my sister.

I knew having this brought up in front of Sarah was making it worse for him, so I decided to help the poor guy out. “Lydia said you pointed Aunt Dottie in the right direction in the store, Archie. So, thank you. Neil is going to love what she picked out.”

“I swear I didn’t see it,” he confessed quickly, his face flushing again.

“It’s okay, Archie,” I reassured him. “Lydia told me.”

"I always feel so creepy going into stores like that, even when I have a girlfriend," he explained. "But I knew"—he glanced at Aunt Dottie—"that as soon as this one here said she wanted to get you something, I needed to guide her to the more appropriate section. Neil and I might be completely opposite, but we both have the same preference when it comes to...you know."

We shared a good-natured laugh as Aunt Dottie kissed his cheek and said, "Your shyness is so adorable, Sugar."

"Well, Neil deserves to have you looking like his bride on your wedding night, Abbie," he said to me. "And everything Aunt Dottie was holding up is not what Neil would like."

"You mean that black lace teddy?" Aunt Dottie asked him, clearly having fun embarrassing him.

"Aunt Dottie," he whispered through clenched teeth, his face turning beet-red again.

"You and you brother have always been perfect gentlemen, Archibald," Helen complimented him, which seemed to ease his humiliation. "Your father and I are very proud of you two."

"Thanks, Mom," he said, relaxing a bit. "But you really have Grandpa to thank for that."

"You mean his little chat in his office?" my sister asked with a grin.

Aunt Dottie's face was suddenly overcome with panic. "What is she talking about, Honey? What chat in Junior's office?"

"When Neil and I were teenagers, Grandpa took us to his office and set us straight about how he expected us to treat women." His eyes were huge as he shook his head. "We slept with the lights on for a week after that."

"Archie, honey." Aunt Dottie's voice was full of concern. "Did Junior threaten you?"

"Oh, no," he said, trying to downplay it, sensing her horror. "More like...making sure we were the best men we could be."

Helen thought for a moment. "You know, I remember that day. Your grandfather showed up at the house, and I figured we were all going somewhere. But then your father said, 'No, Helen, this is the day the boys become men.' And he reminded me of the conversation we had with my grandfather."

Aunt Dottie's panic was redirected across the table. "What conversation?"

"When John and I were first dating, he knew that my father and brother were deceased, so he asked me if there was a man in my family he could speak to. I told him that my dad's father was my only living grandparent, so we went to see him. And John was so polite, so respectful, and also his typical level of calmness."

She shook her head, her eyes glazed over as she remembered back. "And then, suddenly, he sat up straight, looked my grandfather in the eye and said, 'Mr. Barrington, sir.' And my grandfather and I were so stunned we just looked at each other. John then went on to tell him how his father brought him into his office when he was a teenager and told him exactly how he was to treat a lady. And he also told him what the exact consequences would be if he ever mistreated a lady."

"That sounds about right," Archie agreed. When he noticed Aunt Dottie's pale face next to him, he quickly added, "But it's okay. That conversation made Dad, Neil, and me the men we are today. And we're all grateful for it. Grandpa told us that if we are exceptional men, then we would attract exceptional women." He looked between Helen and me, his blazing smile back on his face. "And it's worked for Dad and Neil."

"And it will happen for you too, Archibald," Helen promised him with a loving smile.

Lydia reached over and took Aunt Dottie's hand. "Are you okay, Dottie?"

A bit startled, she looked at Lydia. "Oh, yes, Sugar. I think I'm past due for my afternoon nap, that's all."

Scooping her up in his arms, Archie grinned at Aunt Dottie and said, "Your chariot awaits in the parking lot."

All the ladies helped me with my bags, and after we got them into Sarah's car, Grace and Madison hugged us goodbye and left.

"Sarah," Helen said, "why don't you follow us to Dad's house? The guys had talked about having a barbecue for dinner, and we can all visit in the meantime."

"Thanks, Helen," she agreed brightly. "That sounds great."

We pulled into Grandpa's driveway a few minutes later, and I scampered up the ramp as I saw my sweet fiancé standing in the doorway.

"Thank you so much," I said, giving him a hug and a kiss. "That party was so much fun."

"You're welcome, Abbie," he replied, gazing at me with a fond smile. "I'm happy you had a good time." He glanced at Sarah. "And I'm guessing you told her about the gift already waiting for her at home?"

"Yes, I did," she confirmed with a satisfied grin. "I told her that your big plan with Archie was probably to go to the gym again, and she bought it."

"Good thinking," he laughed as our moms came up the ramp. Watching the van pull into the driveway, he suggested, "Why don't we go inside? Archie, Lydia, and Aunt Dottie will be right behind us."

We walked into the parlor to be greeted by my dad, John, and Grandpa. We were giving them exciting details about the party when the mood in the room suddenly changed.

"Cornelius Johnson Rutherford!" We heard an angry voice behind us.

Three faces turned, and as soon as we noticed John and Neil's stunned expressions, the rest of us turned around as well. Sitting in her wheelchair, a furious lady was glaring daggers at one man.

"Neil, Johnny, I don't mean you two. Everybody—out! I need to have a word with my brother."

Her eyes stayed fixed on her brother—who nodded at everyone to leave.

Stepping outside, we all looked at each other wide-eyed. "I have never heard Aunt Dottie call Grandpa by his full name," Archie voiced what we were all thinking.

"I know," Lydia agreed. "And I live with them." Glancing toward the door, she commented timidly, "And I don't want to go back in there right now."

"So come with us," Neil offered. "We'll just move the party to my place." He smiled at me. "This way, Abbie can show us all of her fun gifts."

"And if my father needs you, he'll call," John reassured her. "We can have you back here within twenty minutes."

She breathed a sigh of relief. "Thank you."

"I wonder what made her so mad?" Neil asked, shaking his head. "She's always yelling at him, but she seems genuinely angry right now."

Lydia let out a much-needed laugh. "Dottie starts her day yelling at your grandfather. And it's always the same thing: 'You be nice to Daddy's employees, Junior!'"

As we all shared a tension-relieving laugh, I could see John thinking. "There's only one employee still with the company that my grandfather or Mr. Davenport would have hired." He looked at his sons. "Ed Thompson in accounting. He started fresh out of high school, and he's been with the company for sixty-three years. And he's the only employee who calls my father 'Junior.' But

I think Dad enjoys having someone at the office who still calls him that."

"And I think I know why Aunt Dottie is so mad," Archie admitted quietly. He looked between his dad and brother. "The subject of our little chat in Grandpa's office as teenagers came up."

The three men seemed to be sharing a silent communication that only they understood. After a moment, John said casually, "Well, you know Aunt Dottie thinks your grandfather is too hard on us." He waved his hand. "And while she is angry, Dad will be fine. We all know that *nobody* intimidates Cornelius Rutherford."

We all piled into the various cars sitting in Grandpa's driveway. Archie and Sarah rode with Neil and me, and all along the way, as Sarah and I talked excitedly about my gifts, I noticed Neil glancing at his brother in his rearview mirror. As the party continued well into the evening, as the rest of us gushed over my thoughtful gifts, the three Rutherford men kept exchanging glances that I knew held significant meaning.

And based on Aunt Dottie's reaction, I'm guessing she had no clue about her brother bringing the guys into his office. But it seemed like maybe she knew something the rest of us didn't.

And I couldn't help but wonder what that something was...

Chapter 11

♥

NEIL OPENED HIS FRONT door, and he, Sarah, and I stepped inside. We walked into the living room to see Archie sitting on the couch with a troubled look on his face.

"Hey, Arch," Neil said, setting down the box he was holding. "What's going on?"

Noticing the box on the floor, Archie's eyes widened with realization. "I'm sorry I wasn't there to help you start packing Abbie's things."

"Don't worry about it, Archie," Neil reassured him. "I know something's wrong. What is it?"

Archie pointed to some paperwork on the coffee table. "I was watching Casablanca with Aunt Dottie when Grandpa came home. I immediately noticed the mistake, so I grabbed the paperwork and came here. I wanted some privacy while I traced the error." He was quiet for a second, then said, "It was Bill Anderson in accounting."

Neil picked up the paperwork and flipped through the pages. As he got to a line circled in red ink, he looked at his brother. "This is a fifty-thousand-dollar mistake, Archie."

"I know," he replied. "And Bill is my best employee." He paused again, then predicted in a worried voice, "Grandpa's probably going to fire him."

"What makes you say that?" Neil asked him.

Archie looked at his brother with raised eyebrows. "He fired Jim in accounting for his mistake last year. And that was only ten thousand dollars."

Neil smiled at his brother. "Grandpa didn't fire Jim because of that mistake, Archie."

"He didn't?"

"No, Arch. Grandpa had been looking for a reason to get rid of Jim for months. He was always late, he was rude to coworkers, and what especially bothered Grandpa was how he treated you."

Archie's eyebrows furrowed with confusion. "What do you mean?"

"He was taking advantage of your kindness, Archie." Neil looked at Sarah and me. "Jim knew that Archie couldn't say anything bad about him to Grandpa. You even saw it when he was working on his review. And Grandpa hates it when people take advantage of others—especially his family." He looked back at his brother. "Grandpa knew Jim was using your kindness as a buffer to keep him out of trouble. So, when that mistake got traced back to him, Grandpa saw it as the reason he had been looking for to fire him."

Archie was quiet for a second. "Oh, I didn't know that."

"That's because you look for the good in everyone, Archie." Neil looked at Sarah and me again. "Archie has never once stood up for himself to Grandpa. But his employees? You should see the way Archie defends them, even the ones who don't deserve it."

"That's why I started my list," Archie commented. "I already have twenty-five reasons why Grandpa shouldn't fire Bill."

Neil grabbed a pad of paper from the coffee table. He smiled as he skimmed through it, then stopped and looked at his brother with raised eyebrows. "His wife's cat died, Archie?"

"What?" he asked defensively. "She's been crying for a week, Neil. If he comes home and tells her that Grandpa fired him, then she'll really be upset."

"Grandpa is not going to fire him, Archie," Neil stated with firm conviction.

"How do you know that, Neil?" Archie asked, his voice full of doubt.

"Because you will fight for him, Archie. You, me, and Dad will go into Grandpa's office first thing tomorrow morning, and you are going to look Grandpa in the eye and tell him every one of these reasons." Neil held up the paper. "I promise you, Archie, Grandpa will not fire him."

"So, what will he do then?" Archie asked cautiously.

"He'll probably yell at him," Neil answered matter-of-factly.

Archie's eyes got huge with panic. Suddenly, his expression changed, a realization coming to him. "Wait. Why don't I ever hear Grandpa yelling at the employees? My office is right next to his."

Neil didn't say anything, his eyes shifting across the room.

Archie stood up and came over to his brother. "Neil, tell me." His voice was full of desperation.

Neil looked at the panicked blue eyes in front of him. "Because you're out getting coffee, Archie."

"Yeah, what is up with that, Neil?" Archie asked in an exasperated tone. "Grandpa sends me out to get four coffees, but we all know he hates coffee."

"And that's why he gives his to Dad or me," Neil answered simply.

"So why does he send me out then?"

"Because he knows how much you hate it when the employees get in trouble. So, I watch the parking lot from my office window, and as soon as you leave, Dad or I go and get the employee."

"And then what?" Archie's voice became more emotional with every question.

"Then Grandpa yells at them," Neil said matter-of-factly.

Archie's face drained of all color. "He does?" he asked quietly.

Neil nodded. "And this is exactly why Grandpa has you leave the building, Archie. You run three departments. He knows sending you out for coffee is a complete waste of your time. But he also knows how much it would hurt you to hear him yelling at an employee. That's why he tells you to go to the coffee shop twenty minutes away. He wants enough time."

"How long does he yell at the person for?"

Neil shrugged. "It depends. But Dad or I—and sometimes both of us—are always there to act as a buffer."

"So, you think he's going to yell at Bill?" Archie asked quietly, his voice full of emotion.

"Yes, Archie," Neil answered gently. "Grandpa is going to yell at Bill."

Panic suddenly took over his brother's face. "But what if he quits? He's my best employee, Neil."

Neil put his hands on Archie's shoulders reassuringly. "Then I will make sure Dad and I are both in Grandpa's office with him. And as Dad goes to get Bill, I will tell Grandpa how much he means to you, and I will ask him to please take it easy on him." He pulled his brother in and gave him a hug. "It'll be okay, Archie," he whispered in a calm voice.

Archie tightened his arms around his brother. "Do you promise?" he asked quietly.

"Yes, Archie, I promise," Neil reassured him. As the two brothers shared a quiet moment, an alarm went off. Neil pulled back and looked at his brother. "Is that the washing machine?"

Archie looked away as he admitted, "I borrowed some of your workout clothes. As soon as I realized who made the mistake, I needed to go for a run."

Looking at his defeated expression, I got the sense that poor Archie could use some good news. I went up to Neil and ran my hand down his back. "Do you want to show Archie what you picked up from your parents' house?"

Neil's eyes sparkled as he looked at me. "Thanks for reminding me, Abbie." He went over to the box he had carried in and pulled out something very special.

The brightness returned to Archie's eyes as soon as he saw what his brother was holding. "Great Grammy Laura's quilt," he breathed, looking fondly at the red patchwork quilt. His focus moved to his brother and me. "I'm so happy for the two of you."

"Thanks, Arch," Neil replied with a smile. "I knew you would love seeing this here."

Archie's attention moved to just his brother, and once again, the two of them appeared to be sharing a silent moment that only they understood. But unlike a week ago, this time, their communication seemed to have a positive significance to it.

Finally breaking the silence, Neil looked at me and suggested, "Why don't we go and put the quilt on our bed?" Looking at our siblings, he invited them, "Why don't you two come with us?"

Neil took my hand, and we walked down the hall to the bedroom. Handing one end of the quilt to me, the two of us very lovingly folded it and draped it across the foot of our bed. He slid his arm around my shoulders, and we admired how the red starburst pattern added a vibrant pop of color to the white comforter. Holding his hand out to his brother, Archie and Sarah stepped closer, and the four of us stood in silence for a few minutes.

"I really am happy for you, Neil," Archie whispered to his brother.

"Thanks, Arch," Neil whispered back. "I'm happy, too."

A minute later, we made our way out to Neil's car to bring in more boxes. After making another trip to Milford, the guys decided to fire up the grill as Sarah and I unpacked a few boxes in the bedroom and my room upstairs.

"We got quite the workout today," my sister commented after the dinner plates had been cleared from the deck. "Abbie and I brought our workout clothes with us..." She looked at the two brothers. "Do you guys even want to go to the gym tonight?"

"Yes," Archie answered, standing up from his chair.

"But you went for that run earlier, Archie," Neil remarked as his brother walked toward the French doors.

"And I need another run tonight, too," he said, closing the bedroom doors behind him.

"You two can change upstairs," Neil said to Sarah and me. "I'll change when Archie's done."

Ten minutes later, we were out the door. Archie was quiet the entire ride to the gym as Neil, Sarah, and I chatted about how wonderful it felt moving my things in. When we entered the gym, Archie hung up his bag on a hook, put in his earbuds, and headed toward the treadmills. Neil went into the weight room as Sarah and I jumped onto our usual elliptical machines. I noticed my sister watching Archie as she typically did, but this time, her expression was different. Usually, her eyes were full of wonder and amazement as she checked him out, but this time, they were full of concern.

After we finished on the ellipticals, Sarah and I waited for the guys on a bench. Neil showed up fifteen minutes later and sat with us as we all glanced at Archie, still running on the treadmill. Finally, the belt slowed to a stop, and a man drenched in sweat stepped off. When he turned around and faced us, we immediately noticed the change in him.

Archie had walked in here a troubled man—it was written all over his face. But now, he walked toward us with an ease in his stride, like all of his problems had vanished on that treadmill. He calmly retrieved his bag and came to sit next to his brother. Taking a moment to wipe his face with a towel, he then flipped the towel over his neck, leaned back, and looked at his brother.

"Everything is going to be okay tomorrow, Archie," Neil reassured him again.

A smile spread across Archie's face, still red from all the exertion. This time, though, it wasn't his typically blazing bright smile. His expression was calm, like a man free from his burdens. And that calmness was in his voice as he said, "I know it will be, Neil. I promise."

Chapter 12

♥

"Now my home officially feels like our home." Neil smiled at me as he pulled me in for a hug. "And I wouldn't have it any other way."

"Me neither," I agreed, reaching up to kiss him.

We turned and admired the golden-framed autumn landscape Lydia had given me as a bridal shower gift.

"That was the last thing to be hung up," my sister confirmed. Looking around, she observed, "This room looks amazing, Abbie. And it's totally you."

Neil kissed me again. "Good. That's exactly what I wanted." He stepped back and rubbed my arms. "And all your clothes have been hung up in my closet." He leaned in so his lips were right next to my ear. "So now my bedroom feels like *our bedroom*."

My sister looked at Archie. "At first, these two kind of annoyed me. But now I think they're cute."

Archie's smile was blazing as he looked at us. "I've always loved seeing them together."

We collected the tools and wrappers and headed downstairs. Once everything was in its proper place, the four of us sat down in the living room.

"So, how are your wedding plans coming along?" my sister asked. "The big day is in just under a month."

Neil and I smiled at each other. "Everything is done except for cake tasting, which we're doing today," I said, leaning in for another kiss.

Noticing the blazing smile across the room, Neil grinned at his brother. "Why don't you come with us, Arch?" Then, looking at my sister, he added, "You too, Sarah."

Springing up out of his chair, Archie bolted out the front door. The three of us laughed as he flung open the back door of his brother's car and dove inside. In his excitement, he knocked his brother's spare suit off the hanger, crushing it on the seat beneath him. Picking up the pants and jacket, he tossed them into the third row. Then he sat down with a huge smile, like an excited dog, ready to go for a ride.

"I'll bring the suit in later and give it a good steam," Neil commented through his laughter.

"Of course you will," Sarah teased my organized fiancé as we walked to the car.

"So, which bakery are we going to?" Archie asked as Neil pulled out of the driveway.

He grinned at his brother in his rearview mirror. "You'll see."

Twenty minutes later, Neil parked in front of a white brick building with a sign above the door that read: *Emma's Bakery*

"This is my favorite place!" Archie exclaimed, jumping out of the car.

"That's the main reason I chose it," Neil said, grinning at me. "If the cake expert approves, then you know it's the place to come for our wedding cake."

Archie pulled the door open, and the sound of jingling bells happily greeted us. Stepping inside was like being welcomed into a calming oasis. Light-green walls led to the front of the bakery, where cheerful white shiplap paneling decorated the space behind the counter. Several square tables were arranged throughout the room, all dressed with ivory tablecloths and gold napkins. Sunshine streamed in through the large open windows as sheer golden curtains fluttered delightfully in the springtime breeze.

A woman in her mid-fifties wearing a light-green apron over her blue t-shirt stood behind the counter. Her brown hair was pulled up in a bun, and her hazel eyes lit up the instant she noticed a certain patron. "Archie!" she exclaimed, coming out from behind the counter.

"Hey, Emma," he greeted her with a kiss on both cheeks.

"And who do you have with you?" she asked, her bright eyes switching to us.

"This is my brother, Neil, his fiancée, Abbie, and her sister, Sarah," Archie introduced us. "Neil and Abbie are here to pick out their wedding cake."

"Welcome!" she said, hugging Sarah and me as Neil greeted her in the same fashion as his brother. "So, when is your big day?"

"The second Saturday of June," I answered, taking Neil's hand.

"Well, have a seat, and I'll bring some samples over in a minute," Emma said, directing us to a table.

Looking around, I could see why Archie loves this place so much. Emma is delightful and welcoming, and the atmosphere is calm and cozy. And I can only imagine how amazing the cake will taste.

"How often do you come here, Archie?" my sister asked him.

He shrugged. "A couple times a month."

Neil laughed. "I can always tell when he's been here. His smile is even brighter, and he works extra hard at the gym on those nights."

Archie's smile was blazing. "It's worth it. Emma's carrot cake is the best I've ever had."

Arriving a minute later, Emma carried a tray of five small plates with slices of cake and four glasses of water. Setting down the plates, she described each flavor. "We have chocolate cake with peanut butter frosting, white cake with buttercream frosting, red velvet cake with marshmallow frosting, lemon cake with vanilla frosting, and…" She grinned at Archie. "Carrot cake with cream cheese frosting."

"Thanks, Emma," Archie replied with a bright smile. Looking at us, he admired, "It even looks amazing, doesn't it?"

"Thanks, Archie," she said with a laugh as she placed several forks around each plate. "Let me know what you think." She laughed again as she added, "And I was talking to them. I already know what you think." She gave Archie's shoulder a good-natured squeeze, then left us to our cake-tasting.

I grabbed a fork and took a piece of the chocolate cake with peanut butter frosting. My eyes drifted shut as I dreamily savored the perfect pairing. I opened my eyes a moment later and realized everyone was grinning at me.

"You love it, don't you?" Archie beamed at me.

"Thank you for raving about this place, Archie." I smiled at Neil. "And thank you for bringing me here. Emma is definitely making our cake for us."

"I agree," he said with a smile that mirrored mine. "So far, the lemon is my favorite."

"So, how many layers are you thinking about for your cake?" Sarah asked.

"Five!" Neil and I answered simultaneously.

As we laughed, my sister encouraged, "You should do that. And whichever flavor you like the best, make sure that's your top layer. That way, the two of you can enjoy your favorite cake on your first anniversary."

"Good thinking, Sarah," I praised her. Looking at Neil, I commended, "She has been the best Maid of Honor I could have asked for."

"Thanks, Abbie," she replied with a huge smile.

After we had tried all the flavors and had a little time to make our assessments, Archie asked, "So, which one do you think will be your top layer?"

I smiled at my fiancé. "I think it should be the lemon."

"Are you sure?" he asked me. "Isn't your favorite the red velvet with marshmallow frosting?"

"It is," I confirmed with a smile. "But the lemon is your favorite. And I want to make sure you get at least one favorite thing at our wedding."

"Aww," my sister gushed.

"I agree with you, Sarah," Neil said with a smile. Picking up my hand, he kissed it and acknowledged, "Abbie Perkins, I am the luckiest man alive. And while the lemon is my favorite cake, you are my favorite person. And *you* are all I need on our wedding day."

"You guys are too much," my sister teased playfully.

I looked across the table at my sister. "I have to tell them about Cindy and Jackie's tradition, Sarah."

"You were so adorable, Abbie," she admired with a smile. "Mom and I still talk about that."

"So, Jackie and Cindy—who raved about you two, by the way—have a cute tradition in their store. Whenever a bride finds the dress of her dreams, they hand her a bell and tell her to make a wish."

"Wait until you hear Abbie's reply," my sister cut in cheerfully.

Neil picked up my hand and kissed it again. "I hope you wished for something as amazing as you."

"Better!" my sister chimed in again. Then, calming her excitement a bit, she said, "Sorry, Abbie, go on."

"When they handed me the bell and told me to make a wish, I didn't know what to say at first. So, I thought about it and realized I didn't need to wish for anything." My smile brightened even more as I intertwined our fingers. "I told Cindy and Jackie that all my dreams came true when I met you, and I didn't need anything else."

Neil's bright smile turned to a look of honor at hearing my response. His focus switched to his brother. "Am I a lucky man, or what, Arch?"

"The luckiest," Archie agreed with a blazing smile.

"So, then I told Abbie that she deserves something special—in addition to you—on her wedding day," Sarah said to Neil. "So, I asked her what the one thing is that she especially wants for your wedding."

"And what was your answer?" Neil inquired with a warm smile.

"Well, I saw these really pretty bouquets and flower arrangements in a bridal magazine." I stared off dreamily. "Peonies, lilies, irises, roses, and zinnias. They were rather simple arrangements, but that's what made them so beautiful. There was a simple elegance to them, and

I know that's what we want for our wedding." I looked back at Neil to see him smiling softly at me.

"That sounds beautiful, Abbie. Thank you for sharing that with me."

I leaned over and kissed him. "Our wedding day is going to be perfect. And not because of cake or flowers, but because we love each other, and we're making that the focus of our wedding."

His smile glowed brighter as he clutched my hands to his chest. "Abbie Perkins, you are the best bride a man could ask for. And I can't wait to make you my wife."

We spent the rest of the afternoon at Emma's bakery. She wrote down the flavors of cake and frosting for each layer, assuring us that lemon cake with vanilla frosting would be the top layer—special just for us. When I told her about the flowers I had planned for the wedding, she offered to arrange a cheerful, blooming cascade flowing down the side of our cake. As she hugged us goodbye, she promised to deliver our cake to the resort the day before our wedding.

As we drove back to Westport, I dreamed out loud about our big day. I fantasized about flowers, cake, food, and decorating the resort. Neil would glance over at me as he drove, gently smiling as he listened to me. The only details I didn't share with him were about my stunning wedding dress. After all, I want him to have one surprise on our big day. Well, two surprises. There's also that special surprise for our wedding night...

Chapter 13

"I CAN'T BELIEVE TOMORROW is your big day," my sister said, looking at me from her ladder.

"I know, Sarah," I agreed.

Looking around, I marveled at our progress in decorating the resort. Gold and silver tulle shimmered happily against the large white pillars throughout the room. Red and pink heart-shaped confetti added a cheerful contrast to the white tablecloths, set with navy-blue napkins encircled with golden rings.

I was elated when I realized the ladies had saved several gold and silver balloons from my bridal shower, customized with our names and date. I smiled as I watched them swaying happily in the early-summer breeze, the morning air adding a fresh romance to the ballroom. The pergola outside had been wrapped in gold and silver tulle, and the only thing missing was the flowers.

As my gaze traveled around the room, my smile brightened even more when my eyes landed on the man of my dreams. Helping Archie set up a picture of us for our guests to sign, Neil looked exceptionally handsome today. In just over twenty-four hours, I will officially become Abigail Jane Rutherford. And I couldn't wait. Sensing my eyes on him, he looked up and smiled, making the butterflies in my stomach come to life—just like on the morning we met. But this time, instead of nervous butterflies, the fluttering in my stomach was excited anticipation for the happiest day of my life.

His smile grew brighter as he walked toward me. Wrapping me in his strong arms, he sighed happily. "You and Sarah are doing a beautiful job, as always," he complimented.

"Thanks," I replied with a kiss. "You and Archie have been very helpful, too."

Just then, my parents arrived. They looked around with eyes full of wonder, and Sarah got down off her ladder as she saw them come in.

"Oh, wow, Puddin' Pie," my dad marveled. "Look at this place."

Giving them each a hug, she said, "Thanks, Dad." Turning to my mom, she commented, "It's a good thing you two are here early. We're still waiting on the flowers, and Abbie and I are heading out soon to get our nails done." Looking between the guys, she added, "It'll be good to have at least one woman here to help arrange all the flowers."

We laughed in agreement as Neil assured us, "And once my mom and Grandpa are done with foundation matters, my parents will be here too."

My mom breathed a sigh of relief. "Good. Your mom is the one with an eye for fancy. She'll make sure every flower is in the exact place it should be."

My dad slid his arm around my mom's shoulders. "And I'm here to help, too. Give this Army man direction, and I'll do whatever anybody needs."

As we shared a laugh, my phone rang. I grabbed it off the table and stepped outside the ballroom to answer it. I returned a few minutes later, brushing tears from my cheeks. As soon as my fiancé noticed me, he walked toward me with his arms out.

"Abbie," he said comfortingly. "What's wrong?"

"That was the florist," I replied through my sobs. "She said the peonies didn't come in, and the only color of lilies she got was yellow, and I asked for pink." I buried my face in Neil's chest as he stroked my hair soothingly.

"Oh, Abbie," my mom sympathized, rubbing my back. "I'm so sorry."

After crying on my sweet fiancé for a few minutes, I pulled back and looked up at him. As he gently brushed away my tears, my vision cleared, and everything came into focus. Seeing the soft smile on his face made all my sadness instantly vanish. And I remembered what tomorrow is really about.

"But it's okay," I reminded everyone, my smile returning. "I have you. And like I said in the dress shop, you're all I need."

"But Abbie," my sister advocated, turning me around and wrapping me in her arms. "You said those flowers were the one thing you especially wanted."

As she let me go, I noticed the tears forming in her pretty brown eyes. "It's okay, Sarah. Honestly." I turned back to Neil. "You really are all I need."

Just then, an alarm went off on my sister's phone. Looking at the time, she commented, "It's time to get our nails done."

My sweet fiancé smiled at me. "Before you leave to get even more beautiful, give me the florist's phone number." After adding it to his phone, he looked at my sister and smiled. "She's all yours now, Sarah."

"Actually, Neil, I think I'll stay here and help," she offered. Turning to my mom, she suggested, "Why don't you go with Abbie?"

My mom's eyebrows raised with pleasant surprise. "Are you sure?"

"Yeah, I'll just slap some polish on my nails and call it good enough." As everyone laughed, she corrected herself, "Or better yet, I'll have Lydia do it. Aunt Dottie's nails always look amazing."

Neil took out his wallet and handed me his credit card. "And why don't you see if they have any available massage appointments." He smiled at my mom and me. "You two deserve it."

"Thank you," I accepted his offer with a smile and a kiss. "You may be the luckiest man alive, but I'm even more lucky because I get to marry you."

Sarah slid her arm through my dad's. "These two are so sweet, aren't they?"

"Yes, they are, Puddin' Pie," he agreed. Then he gave my mom a kiss and said, "Have fun with Abbie."

My mom hooked her elbow in mine and led me out of the resort. She smiled at me as we got into her car. "I'm really proud of you, Abbie, for how you handled that."

"Thanks, Mom," I said, leaning over the console and hugging her.

And we were off to Milford to enjoy a few hours of pampering. I felt like an absolute princess as I got my nails polished and my shoulders and back massaged. And I couldn't help but wonder what my handsome Prince Charming was doing back in New Canaan...

LATER THAT AFTERNOON, MY mom and I returned to the resort. Stepping into the ballroom, we were greeted with the most beautiful surprise.

"Oh, Abbie," my mom breathed. "Look at this place."

"I know," I agreed, unable to say anything else as tears of joy filled my eyes.

She took my hand, and we stood there for a moment, delighting in the transformation that had taken place. Crystal vases beautifully arranged with peonies and pink lilies joyfully decorated every table. The gold and silver tulle that cheered up all the pillars now sparkled with fairy lights, and roses, irises, and zinnias were tucked happily inside. As my focus landed on the rectangular table at the front of the room, the tears in my eyes escaped as I admired the sweetest sight of all. A glass vase with a picture of Neil and me on the beach lovingly displayed two gorgeous bouquets. A stunning assortment of irises, roses, and zinnias with navy-blue ribbon wrapped around the stems perfectly complemented the mixture of peonies, pink lilies, and roses exquisitely held together with sparkling silver tulle.

As I brushed away the tears, my attention drifted to a table along the wall, with balloons happily floating on either side. "Oh, Mom! Look!" I exclaimed, pointing to the five-tier wedding cake. A silhouette of a couple dancing adorned the top layer as a waterfall of peonies, irises, roses, zinnias, and pink lilies spiraled down the simple white fondant.

My mom kissed me on the cheek. "I'm so happy you got your flowers, Abbie," she whispered lovingly.

"Thanks, Mom," I whispered as she brushed away the last few tears.

Gazing around the room, that's when I saw them. Gathered along the wall opposite the cake were Neil, Archie, Helen, John, Grandpa, Aunt Dottie, Lydia, my dad, Sarah, and Emma. Gentle smiles lit up their faces, silently enjoying our reaction to the sweet surprise. Neil was the first to walk toward us, and everyone followed, with Grandpa pushing Aunt Dottie's wheelchair.

Wrapping me in his arms, my incredible fiancé gave me a kiss and smiled at me. "And there's more flowers outside, too," he said as he ran his fingers through my hair. "We had to make sure the pergola would be as beautiful as you for our ceremony tomorrow."

Tears filled my eyes again. "How...?" was all I could manage to ask.

"Cornelius Rutherford made a phone call," my sister answered with a tone that conveyed her fascination.

My hands flew to cover my heart. "Grandpa," I breathed, looking at him. "Thank you."

A proud smile spread across his face as he looked at Neil and me together. He shook his head and stated, "It wasn't me."

My eyebrows sprang up in surprise at hearing his response. Then, my focus switched to another man. "John?" I asked, my voice full of astonishment.

He smiled and shook his head.

My eyes were huge as they moved to the only other man who shares the name. "Neil?"

A gentle smile spread across his face as he looked at me. "I couldn't have you miss out on your flowers, Abbie."

I just blinked at him, still overcome with disbelief. "But you never use your real name."

"Correction, Abs," my sister jumped in. "John told Neil to use his real name, 'When it truly matters.'"

Neil took my hands and clutched them to his chest. "And nothing matters more to me than you, Abbie."

"I know just how you feel," John agreed, sliding his arm around Helen's shoulders. "Except for that clueless moment as a teenager, I have only used my real name three times." He smiled lovingly at his wife. "And all three of those times were to make something special happen for you."

Sarah put her hands on Neil's shoulders and grinned at me around him. "You should have seen your fiancé, Abbie. It was unbelievable how one phone call from Cornelius Rutherford made all these flowers appear out of thin air."

Neil looked at his dad with his eyebrows raised. "That phone call was tough." His focus returned to me, and a loving smile took over his handsome features. "But seeing your face made it all worth it."

"You should have heard that florist, Abbie," my sister marveled. "She sounded so confident answering her phone, but the moment she realized who she was talking to, her voice instantly switched to panic."

"And you handled yourself perfectly," Grandpa complimented his grandson proudly. "I could see how difficult it was for you, but you never let up on her, knowing it was to make everything perfect for the woman you love." Grandpa's face softened as he looked at us together.

Neil grinned at his grandfather. "And you handled yourself perfectly as well. I knew you wanted to jump in when she offered me that discount."

Archie laughed. "Even though she knows the name, apparently nobody informed her *never* to offer Cornelius Rutherford a discount."

"Yeah, I was wondering about that," my sister commented, looking at Neil. "Why did you refuse her offer for a discount?"

"Because Cornelius Rutherford pays his own way in life," four deep voices answered at the same time.

As the rest of us had a good laugh, Grandpa looked at Aunt Dottie with a warm smile. "There's only one place that I've ever accepted the offer of something free."

Aunt Dottie took his hand. "I know, Junior. And it surprised me that Easter Sunday to return to the table and see you so calmly and graciously accept Betty's offer." She held her brother's hand to her cheek. "But Betty knew. Just like I knew that a pretty little waitress would become your wife."

Grandpa smiled at his sister quietly for a moment. When his attention turned to Neil and me, that gentle smile remained on his face as he said, "And I hope the two of you find a place that's as special to you as that diner is to your grandmother and me."

Neil and I looked at each other, bright smiles taking over our faces as we read each other's minds. Turning back to the family patriarch, Neil replied, "That's how Abbie and I feel about this place here."

I rested my head on his arm as I dreamily shared, "It was so romantic coming here for Valentine's Day that we came back for Neil's birthday." I looked at my handsome fiancé. "And I want to keep coming back here as often as possible."

"Me too," he agreed.

I gazed around the ballroom again, absorbing the magic of my surroundings, when my focus landed on the cake. Searching for the lady responsible for such a stunning masterpiece, my eyes brightened even more as I found Emma standing next to Archie—blazing smiles illuminating their faces.

"Thank you, Emma," I said, going over to hug her. "The cake is even more beautiful than I had imagined."

She slid her arm around Archie's waist. "As soon as I got a phone call from this one here, I rushed right over."

I looked between the two of them. "What do you mean?"

"I remembered Emma's offer to decorate your cake when you told her about the flowers you had planned for the wedding," Archie explained. "So, when Neil got off the phone with the florist, I called Emma to see if she had any flowers left over."

"And when I realized that my favorite customer needed help, I jumped into action," Emma said with a laugh. "I put your cake in my van, grabbed my leftover flowers, and called my supplier on my way over. She met us here with even more flowers as your florist arrived." She laughed again. "I couldn't understand why that lady was so flustered when she got here, but then Archie explained the significance of Neil's phone call."

I looked around again. "So, some of these flowers are because of you?" I asked her, covering my heart as love surged through me.

Emma smiled gently at me. "You and Neil are the most precious couple that has ever come into my bakery. And I knew you wanted these flowers before you even told me about them. I overheard you telling Neil about your wish and how, at first, you didn't even know what to wish for. When I heard you tell him that he is all you need and all your dreams came true when you met him, my heart just melted with affection for you. So, when Archie called me and told me that you weren't going to get your simple wish, I knew I had to help."

I hugged her again. "Thank you, Emma." And then I hugged my almost brother-in-law. "You too, Archie. Thank you."

"Of course, Abbie," he replied. Smiling at his brother, he said, "All she asked for was flowers, Neil." His smile softened as his focus returned to me. "And when you realized you weren't going to get the exact flowers you wanted, you handled yourself with such poise, Abbie. You deserve all the flowers in the world."

I hugged them again as Neil came over to us. He wrapped his arms around his brother and said, "Thanks, Arch. That means a lot to hear you say that." Then he kissed Emma on both cheeks. "And you too, Emma. I'm so happy my beautiful fiancée made such a wonderful impression on you." Then he invited her with a smile, "Why don't you stay for dinner?"

"Thanks, Neil," she replied. Suddenly, her eyes brightened as a realization occurred to her. "So, does this mean I get to watch your rehearsal?"

"Since our wedding party consists of just Archie and Sarah, we decided we didn't need a rehearsal. But we still wanted everyone to get together for dinner tonight anyway," Neil explained. Taking my hand, he smiled at me, and once again, we read each other's minds. Looking at Emma, he said, "Why don't you come to the wedding tomorrow? We would love to have you as our guest."

She threw her arms up with excitement and hugged both of us together. "Thank you. I would be honored to attend your beautiful wedding."

"Oh, Abbie," my sister said suddenly. "We haven't asked the bride-to-be...how was your visit to the salon?"

My mom and I smiled at each other. "It was amazing," I raved. Holding out our hands, we showed off our French manicures. I smiled at my fiancé. "And the massages were just what we needed. Thank you for suggesting them."

"Of course," he replied. "I'm happy the two of you had such a great time."

"And check us out," my sister rejoiced, scampering over to another smiling face. Carefully placing her hands on Aunt Dottie's lap, they showed off their manicures. Polished with meticulous precision, Sarah's soft-pink nails looked delightful next to Aunt Dottie's cheerful, hot-pink fingernails. "Lydia did an amazing job, didn't she?"

"Yes, she did," I confirmed, smiling at Lydia.

Our families enjoyed good food and great conversation for the rest of the afternoon and into the evening. As the sun made its way toward the horizon, Neil brought me outside to show me the stunning flowers carefully tucked into the tulle that dressed up the pergola. I relaxed in his embrace and dreamed of tomorrow, the perfect setting for the happiest day of our lives.

We returned to the ballroom hand-in-hand, delighting in the dimly lit chandeliers and fairy lights—the romantic in me giddy with excitement for tomorrow. I was lost in my favorite brown eyes, gently swaying to the soft music in the background, when I felt someone tap me on the shoulder.

I turned around to see my sister grinning at me. "Come on, Abs. It's time to go."

"Already?" I asked, a playful pout taking over my face.

Hooking her elbow in mine, she smiled at my fiancé. "The next time you see my sister, she'll be walking down the aisle to you."

Neil sighed happily as he leaned in for a kiss. "And I can only imagine how stunning you'll be."

Pulling me out of the ballroom, Sarah and I giggled all the way to our room. It's the same room where Neil and I will celebrate our wedding night, but tonight, my sister gets me all to herself. Changing into our pajamas, we stayed up for the next several hours, giggling and fantasizing about tomorrow.

Finally, we settled under the covers and switched off the lights. My heart surged with love as I thought about everyone who jumped in to help today—from Archie calling Emma, who showed up with more flowers, to Lydia doing a fantastic job with the Maid of Honor's nails.

But the most remarkable person of all was my soon-to-be husband. I know how much it troubled him to hear that sweet lady's panicked voice on the phone all those years ago. So, to use his real name to make my ultimate wedding dream come true...that, dear reader, makes me feel truly loved.

Chapter 14

♥

"Rise and shine!" a cheerful voice exclaimed as sunlight streamed in through the windows.

I opened my eyes to see Sarah diving onto the bed, practically landing on me in her excitement. Her smile was even brighter than the early morning sunshine, her eyes glowing with happiness.

"What time is it?" I asked.

"Six!"

I laughed. "We only fell asleep four hours ago, Sarah."

"I know," she agreed. "It was so hard to fall asleep with all of our excitement. It reminded me of Christmas Eve when we were kids."

Warmth spread through my heart as I remembered her sleeping in my bed on Christmas Eve every year, even when I came home from college. We would always giggle and dream out loud about opening our presents, staying awake for more hours than we slept.

"So, do you think the guys are up yet?" she asked, pulling the covers off me. Suddenly, she stopped, realizing what she had said. "Of course they're up. They probably went for a run or something." She giggled as she flopped down next to me. "Neil gets to carry you over the threshold tonight, Abbie."

"I know, Sarah," I said, a big smile taking over my face. "I can't believe our big day is here."

She sprang up next to me. "Well then, why are you still lying in bed? We need to get you ready!"

I laughed as I got out of bed. "We still have eight more hours until the wedding starts, Sarah."

Just then, there was a knock on the door. My sister opened it, and a smiling face greeted us. A young woman with brown hair and eyes, dressed in a white chef's jacket, stood next to a cart with two covered trays, two glasses of water, and two cups of coffee.

"Congratulations on your wedding today, Abbie," she said, her eyes glowing as she looked at me.

"Thank you," I replied with a bright smile.

Sarah and I stepped aside, and the woman pushed the cart into the room. Handing me a note, she offered, "Let us know if there's anything else you need."

After she shut the door behind her, Sarah and I smiled at each other. "Open the note!" she exclaimed.

"My beautiful Abbie," I read out loud. *"I hope you had a good night with Sarah. Although I missed you, I know seeing you in your dress will be worth the wait. Enjoy*

breakfast and have fun getting ready today. I'm counting the minutes until I see your beautiful face. Love, Neil."

"Oh, Abbie," my sister gushed, wrapping her arms around me. "I'm so happy you found Neil."

"Not as happy as I am, Sarah," I beamed, love surging through me as I hugged her.

"Let's see what he ordered us for breakfast," my sister said with a big grin as she let me go.

Lifting the silver lids, we found Belgian waffles topped with strawberries, blueberries, raspberries, and fresh whipped cream, dusted with powdered sugar. A small stainless-steel pitcher of maple syrup sat on the side of each plate, garnished with chocolate-covered strawberries.

"Oh, wow, Abbie," my sister breathed. "This was so thoughtful of Neil."

"I know, Sarah," I agreed as we took everything to the table next to the window. "What a great way to start my wedding day."

Sarah and I continued daydreaming about today as we enjoyed our delicious breakfast. After we finished, she pushed the cart into the hall, and we cycled through the shower. As we each stepped out of the bathroom, we gushed over our monogrammed robes—mine embroidered with *Bride* on the back and hers with *Maid of Honor.* She was almost finished with my makeup when there was another knock on the door.

"Mom!" Sarah exclaimed, hugging our mom and pulling her into the room. Helen followed behind them and greeted my sister in her typical fashion.

Already dressed for the big event, the two of them looked exquisite. My mom's gorgeous light-blue dress with delicate floral lace looked beautiful on her. A silver barrette decorated her hair, the ideal accessory to coordinate with her silver sandals. Helen looked stunning in a floor-length navy-blue gown, which contrasted elegantly with her pearls. Her freshly straightened hair flowed effortlessly over her shoulders, and her silver handbag perfectly complemented her matching heels.

"Abbie!" my mom gushed, her eyes glowing as she looked at me. "You already look beautiful, and you're not even in your dress yet."

"Thanks, Mom," I welcomed her with a hug.

"Yes, Abigail," Helen agreed, taking my hands and kissing me on both cheeks. "You look positively radiant."

"Thanks, Helen," I accepted her compliment with a smile. "And Neil has already been so sweet to us this morning. He sent up breakfast for Sarah and me."

"Oh, Abigail," she breathed, covering her heart as tears filled her eyes. "I'm so pleased that Cornelius is taking such great care of you. Wait until I tell John and Dad."

My mom looked at her with a grateful smile and admired, "You raised a good man, Helen."

"Thank you, Valerie," she whispered, retrieving a tissue from her bag. After dabbing her eyes, she said, "I know this is the first time of many that I'm going to need these today."

"I think we all will," my sister commented good-naturedly. "And that's why I haven't put Abbie's mascara on yet. We'll do that right before we leave the room."

"Good thinking, Sarah," my mom agreed.

As my sister got to work on my hair, Helen asked, "So Abigail, do you know what you're going to do for your *'Something old, something new, something borrowed, something blue?'*"

"No," I answered in a stunned tone, realizing I hadn't even thought about those details. I turned around and looked at my sister.

"Keep your head still, Abs," she playfully scolded me. Turning my head back around, she remarked, "There's got to be things around here we could use."

My eyes traveled around the room, brightening as soon as they landed on a sleeveless midnight-blue gown with a side slit and cascading ruffle. "Sarah, your dress could be my *'something blue,'*" I suggested with a big smile.

"Abbie," she said behind me. Even though I couldn't see her face, I could hear the protest in her voice. "This day is about you, not me."

"It's okay, Sarah," I reassured her, reaching up to tap her hand. "You're my best friend and Maid of Honor. It's okay if you're part of this."

She pinned the French twist she expertly fashioned my hair into and leaned down to wrap her arms around me. "Thanks, Abbie," she beamed, kissing me on the cheek.

"Of course, Sarah," I replied, smiling at her.

As my sister stood up and moved, my mom sighed lovingly. "Oh, Sarah. You did such a beautiful job with Abbie's hair."

"Thanks, Mom," she accepted her compliment with a laugh. "Abbie told me she wanted a French twist for her wedding, so I've been practicing every day for the past month."

I looked in the mirror, and a warm smile spread across my face. "It's perfect, Sarah. Thank you."

"You're welcome, Abs," she said, smiling as she watched me gently touch my hair as I turned my head from side-to-side. Suddenly, her eyes lit up. "Your *'something new'* could be your engagement ring. That way, Neil is a part of this tradition, too."

I turned around and looked at my sister with a huge smile. "Thanks, Sarah," I loved her suggestion, my smile brightening as I looked at the diamond shimmering on my finger. "I love it!"

"And if you ladies are okay with it," Helen chimed in, "I have a *'something old'* and *'something borrowed'* for you."

My eyes lit up as I looked at my soon-to-be mother-in-law. "Of course, Helen. I would love to include you in this as well."

She reached into her bag and pulled out a dainty gold bracelet designed with open hearts alternating with diamonds. Holding it out to me, she explained, "This bracelet was given to Laura, Cornelius Senior's wife on their wedding day. And then, on the day Mom and Dad got married, Laura gave the bracelet to Mom as a gift. And then I wore it when I married John. All of us ladies who have married a Cornelius Rutherford have worn this bracelet, Abigail. If you would like to carry on the family tradition, you are more than welcome to wear it as your *'something old.'*"

"Oh, Helen," I breathed, tears coming to my eyes. "I would love to." I held out my left arm, and she attached the clasp around my wrist.

She lovingly touched the bracelet as more tears formed in her eyes. "Mom wore this bracelet every day for thirty-three years. And then, three days before she passed, she took it off her wrist and put it on mine. She held my hands and said, 'You looked so beautiful when you married Johnny. And when Neil gets married, tell his pretty bride that I love her.'" She paused momentarily, brushing away the tears that escaped her eyes. "For the past twenty years, whenever I'm especially missing Mom, I take this bracelet out of my jewelry box, and I instantly feel closer to her. This bracelet is very special to our family, Abigail, and someday, it will be yours."

"Oh, Helen," I whispered, wrapping my arms around her as tears streamed down my cheeks. "This means so much to me."

She smiled at me as she tenderly dried my eyes. "Thank you, Abigail. I knew you would appreciate the significance of our precious family heirloom."

"I do," I whispered, love flooding my heart as I gently touched the bracelet.

"That really is beautiful, Abbie," my sister said quietly, wrapping her arms around my shoulders. "It's so special that Helen shared this with you. And told you that Neil's grandmother loves you."

I just nodded and smiled lovingly at Helen, at a loss for anything else to say.

Helen smiled silently at me for a few moments, and as more tears ran down her cheeks, I knew she had more to say. She took my hands and held them tightly, trying to stop the tears from flowing. Sensing she was having difficulty, my mom and Sarah wrapped their arms around her, comforting her emotions.

"Thank you, Valerie. Thank you, Sarah," she eventually managed to whisper. Drying her eyes again, she continued, "And while this bracelet means a lot to the Rutherford side of the family, the Barrington side of the family has something equally as special."

She paused again as she reached up and lovingly caressed the strand of pearls decorating her neckline. Sliding her hands under her hair, she unhooked the clasp and held the necklace in front of her as more tears came to her eyes.

"These pearls belonged to my mother," she began. "They were given to her as a gift the day she graduated from Princeton. Her plan was to give them to me when I graduated from college, but..." Her voice trailed off.

My mom and sister affectionately slid their arms around her again as tears streamed down our faces.

"I remember one day, my sophomore year of high school," Helen continued, "my mother came to pick me up from school. She took me to the park where she used to bring me as a child. She told me that she had been to the doctor's office that day and she didn't have much longer to live. And that's when the two of us began to cry. So then..." She paused again, overcome with emotion.

Sarah and my mom tightened their arms around her supportively as she continued, "So then, she took off her pearls, slid them around my neck, and attached the clasp. She told me that she wanted me to have them while she was still alive so she could enjoy seeing me wear them. And every day, for the next two months, she would smile whenever she looked at her necklace on me."

She paused again, gazing at the iridescent beads through her tears. "And the morning my mother passed, she smiled at me and said, 'My pearls look beautiful on you, Helen. Promise me you'll wear them on your wedding day.' And I promised her I would. And then she said, 'And when you have a beautiful daughter of your own, please have her wear them on her wedding day too.'" She held up the gorgeous white strand and said, "You are my beautiful daughter, Abigail, and I would be honored if my mother's pearls would be your *'something borrowed.'"*

"Thank you, Helen," I whispered, overcome with emotion. "*I* am the one who is honored."

She held the beautiful necklace to my heart and attached the clasp around my neck. She ran her fingers over each pearl as more tears streamed down our faces. "Thank you, Abigail. They look beautiful on you." Then she pulled me into a tight hug, and my mom and sister wrapped their arms around us.

After a long, emotional embrace, the four of us parted slightly. Looking at the necklace and bracelet, my mom said, "Thank you, Helen, for sharing your special family heirlooms and the stories that go with them. And I agree with you. Abbie looks beautiful."

"Thanks, Mom," I whispered, brushing away my last few tears.

Sliding her arm around my shoulders, Sarah commented, "*This* is why I waited to put on Abbie's mascara."

As we all shared a much-needed laugh, my mom looked at my sister. "So, what are you going to do with your hair, Sarah?"

"Oh," she said, a bit stunned. She looked at me with her eyebrows raised. "We haven't talked about that, Abs. What do you think?"

Looking at my sister's pretty brown hair, I thought for a moment. Suddenly, a pair of blue eyes popped into my head, and that's when inspiration hit me. "Why don't you put a few loose curls in your hair, Sarah, and then gather it over one shoulder? That would look really pretty."

Her brown eyes lit up. "Thanks for the suggestion, Abbie."

Just then, there was another knock on the door. My mom went over to answer it, and our friend in the chef's jacket had returned. Pushing her cart into the room, a tiered serving tray of fruit, cheese, and scones was a welcome sight, along with a silver teapot and four porcelain teacups. But my favorite part of our latest special delivery was the vase with our photo. Front and center, it held two stunning bouquets—ready for Sarah and me to make our big entrance.

Handing me another note, the cheerful employee smiled at me. "That's quite the man you're marrying," she complimented him with an admiring tone.

After she had left, I smiled at Helen and my mom. Setting down her curling iron, Sarah came to join us. Opening the note, I read aloud, *"My beautiful Abbie. We have two hours left until you become my wife. And while I wait patiently to see you, enjoy these treats as you get ready for your big entrance. I'm looking forward to seeing you with your beautiful flowers. All my love, Neil."*

"Oh, Abigail," Helen gushed. "Just when I thought I couldn't be any prouder of my son."

"He really is amazing, Helen," my mom agreed with a grateful smile.

The four of us relaxed and enjoyed our tea and light lunch, courtesy of my thoughtful fiancé. Every time I looked at my gorgeous bouquet, my heart swelled with love for the extraordinary man who fulfilled my wedding day wish. Once we finished eating, my mom pushed the cart into the hallway.

After Sarah put the final touches on her hair and makeup, she looked at me with a bright smile. "Are you ready to get dressed, Abbie?"

"Why don't you go first, Sarah?" I encouraged her.

Taking her dress off the hanger, I unzipped it as she took off her robe. Stepping into the dress and slipping her arms through the openings, I pulled the zipper up for her. Then I turned her toward the mirror and gathered her hair over her left shoulder, carefully arranging her pretty curls.

"Oh, Sarah," my mom whispered. "You look so beautiful."

"Thanks, Mom," she said with a smile. Her eyes brightened as she surveyed herself in the mirror. "Thanks for letting me pick this dress, Abbie. I loved it as soon as I saw it. And thanks for the suggestion for my hair."

My heart filled with love as I admired my sister. The dark shade of blue looked perfect against her light complexion, and the cascading ruffle added a playful touch. The knee-length side slit showed just enough skin to be tasteful—and it's guaranteed to catch the attention of a certain pair of blue eyes.

"You're welcome, Sarah," I replied, wrapping my arms around her shoulders. "Mom's right. You look amazing."

She turned around and looked at me, her eyes glowing even brighter. "Now it's your turn."

She carefully removed my dress from its hanger and unzipped it as I slipped off my robe. I stepped into the dress, and my mom and Helen helped her position the straight neckline in just the right place. Zipping the dress, the four of us looked at my reflection in the mirror. And I instantly felt like a princess. The stunning white gown hugged my slender figure; the gently structured bodice fit perfectly through my hips. Flowing gracefully to the floor, the hem barely grazed my open-toed silver heels. As my gaze traveled back up, my heart flooded with love as I saw Helen's pearls resting just above the straight neckline. Glistening in the sunshine, the iridescent beads beautifully complemented the simple embellishments on my dress. Then my focus switched to my left wrist, the delicate family heirloom pulling my entire look together.

"Wow, Abbie!" my sister breathed. "Wait until Neil sees you."

I looked at Helen's reflection and smiled gently. "And this dress looks even more perfect with your mother's pearls and the bracelet that started with Laura. So, thank you."

"You're welcome, Abigail," she replied gently. "Thank you for carrying on the traditions that mean so much to my two families."

We all gazed into the mirror for a long, silent moment, loving the beautiful symbolism of the gifts Helen shared with me. A grin spread across my sister's face as she asked, "Do you think the tears have stopped, Abbie? I'll give you a little mascara, and then you're ready."

I smiled at her and nodded. She applied a light layer to my lashes, and then she went over to the vase on the table. Taking our bouquets, she came back over and handed mine to me. My smile got brighter as I indulged in their delightful scent—made even sweeter because of the man who made them happen for me.

For the fourth time today, there was a knock at the door. My mom opened it, and my dad walked in dressed in black pants and a light-blue button-down shirt. Over his shirt sat a new, dark-blue jacket, which we lovingly named his *'wedding jacket.'*

"Oh, wow, Abbie!" he exclaimed when he saw me. Coming over and hugging me, he said, "You look beautiful."

"Thanks, Dad," I replied.

He looked at my sister and complimented her, "You too, Puddin' Pie."

"Thanks, Dad," Sarah said with a bright smile.

Then, he slid his arm around my mom's shoulders and looked between Sarah and me and then at my mom. "Our girls are just as beautiful as you, Val."

My mom just smiled at him and gave him a teary-eyed kiss.

"Oh, Michael," Helen said, kissing him on both cheeks. "You are so delightful." Then, checking the time, she turned to me and offered, "I'll take the vase with the picture of you and Cornelius and put it on your table in the ballroom so it's ready for your bouquets."

"Thanks, Helen," I replied with a grateful smile. "And thank you again for the pearls and the bracelet."

She stroked my cheek as she smiled at me affectionately. She touched the necklace and bracelet one last time and silently kissed me on both cheeks. Then she picked up her bag and the vase and gently shut the door behind her.

"I should get downstairs, too," my mom said. "Archie told me he'll escort me to my seat in the front row." She kissed my dad. "That's where you'll find me." Then, giving me one final hug, she said, "I'm so happy for you, Abbie." And just like Helen, she quickly exited the room and shut the door behind her.

"They're doing a good job holding it together," Sarah praised them with a smile.

"We should get heading downstairs, too," I commented, smiling at my dad and sister.

My dad slid his arm inside my right elbow as Sarah did the same on my left side. The three of us walked through the ballroom toward the French doors leading to the backyard. My eyes glowed happily as I made my way through tables decorated with stunning floral arrangements—still in awe of everyone who helped us yesterday. As I walked past the rectangular table just inside the French doors, my smile brightened even more. The vase with our picture was front and center, awaiting our return as husband and wife.

Two staff members stood on either side of the French doors, and as we approached, they opened them with bright smiles. Nodding to another co-worker outside, he started the music.

My sister turned to me and smiled. "Congratulations, Abbie. Neil is the best guy ever, and I'm so happy you two found each other."

"Thanks, Sarah," I said, pulling her in for a hug. "I love you."

"I love you too, Abs," she whispered in my ear. Then, with one last smile, she headed out the door. Walking down the steps of the deck, she stopped as she turned to face the aisle. Blowing me a kiss, she waved as she held up her bouquet with her brightest smile yet. I blew her a kiss in return, and then she disappeared from my sight.

I rested my head on my dad's shoulder as we waited for our cue. Once my sister was in position, another employee gave us the thumbs-up. My dad and I smiled at each other and silently made our way down the deck's stairs. The glorious afternoon sunshine was warm on my face as we walked through the grass, the bottom of my dress happily grazing my toes. As we approached the end of the aisle, the music changed, and everyone stood to face us.

Turning, my dad and I stopped momentarily, and that's when I saw my handsome groom. Standing at the front of the aisle, dressed in a black suit, white shirt, and light-blue tie, his silver cufflinks sparkled in the sunshine. Clean-shaven with his hair neatly combed, his brown eyes lit up as soon as he saw me. This was the most handsome he had ever looked, and I wanted to run down the aisle to him. But I remembered his sweet words that everything—and everyone—worth having is worth waiting for, and my dad and I processed at a slow, steady pace. I could hear our guests raving about my beautiful dress as I walked past them, but my eyes stayed focused on the stunning sight in front of me.

Next to the man of my dreams stood his Best Man. Dressed in a navy-blue suit, light-blue shirt, and gold tie, Archie's smile was blazing as I walked toward his brother. On the other side of Neil stood our Justice of the Peace, a tall man with gray hair dressed in black. The beautifully decorated pergola towered above them—the colorful flowers and shimmering tulle adding to the romance. When my dad and I reached the front of the aisle, he kissed me on the cheek and took his seat next to my mom. I handed my flowers to my glowing Maid of Honor, standing under the opposite side of the large pergola.

Turning to face my radiant groom, I took his outstretched hands in mine. Admiring me up close, he caught his breath as our brown eyes met. "Abbie!" he beamed. "You are even more breathtaking than I imagined."

"Thanks, Neil," I whispered with a smile. "You look incredible, too."

Turning to our Justice of the Peace, he looked at us and smiled. Then, addressing our guests, he began, "Dearly beloved, we are gathered here to unite Abigail Jane Perkins and Cornelius Johnson Rutherford, the fourth in the sacred bond of marriage..."

Chapter 15

♥

"So, HOW DOES IT feel to be husband and wife officially?" my sister asked with a big smile.

I reached up and kissed my new husband. "It feels amazing," I breathed, my ever-present smile increasing.

"Yes, it does," Neil agreed, sliding his hands around my waist. Stepping back, his eyes lovingly scanned the length of my dress, then returned to my face. "You really do look stunning, Abbie."

"Thank you, Neil," I replied happily, leaning against him and gazing into the ballroom. Our guests were seated at the tables arranged throughout the room, awaiting our big entrance. Our DJ had set up his equipment this morning and was playing music to keep everyone entertained in the meantime. Looking around the room, my heart surged with love as my eyes passed over everyone important to Neil and me. In addition to our close friends and family members, Madison, Grace, Emma, Nancy, Cindy, Jackie, Stacy, and Patty have all become our cherished friends, accompanying us on our journey to this day. Every one of these ladies played a vital role over this past year, and I was so grateful to have them here to celebrate with us. I was lost in my daydream until Archie's voice pulled me back to reality.

"I think he's ready for us." I looked at my brother-in-law, his smile blazing from ear-to-ear as he waved at the DJ. Turning to us, he asked, "Are you two ready to make your big entrance?"

Neil and I smiled at each other. "I am more than ready to show off my beautiful wife to all of our family and friends," he said, his eyes glowing as he looked at me.

"And I can't wait to hear him announce us," I added, my smile brightening even more.

Archie turned back toward the DJ and gave him a thumbs-up, and we heard him announce, "Ladies and gentlemen, please put your hands together for our wedding party." While our guests applauded, he continued, "First up is the groom's brother and Best Man, Archie Rutherford!"

Archie ran into the room, his smile even more prominent as he gave high-fives to every guest he passed. Reaching the table in front of the French doors, he stood on the right side and turned around to face us. His smile lit up the entire room as he looked at Neil and me.

"And next up," continued our DJ, the sequins on his jacket shimmering under the flashing lights of his display, "we have the bride's sister and Maid of Honor, Sarah Perkins!"

Sarah's face was glowing as she danced her way through the room, waving her bouquet over her head. Stopping briefly to kiss Aunt Dottie, she arrived at the table up front and stood opposite Archie.

"And ladies and gentlemen, please stand for our newlyweds!" our DJ exclaimed happily. Grandpa turned Aunt Dottie's wheelchair around as our guests all stood to face the entrance of the ballroom. "Please join me in welcoming our newly married couple, Neil and Abbie Rutherford!"

The room erupted into applause as Neil and I entered hand-in-hand. Making our way through the tables, we hugged the smiling guests congratulating us, love surging through me for these fantastic people. Reaching the table at the front of the room, Sarah took my bouquet and placed hers with mine in our special vase. Stepping behind the table, Neil pulled out my chair for me, and Archie pulled out the seat next to me for Sarah. After pushing our chairs in for us, Neil sat beside me, and Archie took the chair next to his brother. Our guests sat back down, still smiling as they looked at the four of us basking in the late-afternoon sunshine.

I leaned my head on my husband's shoulder. Gazing at the happy faces, I praised, "We have some amazing people in our lives, don't we?"

"The best," he agreed, giving me a kiss.

As our guests chatted amongst themselves, I looked around the room, my eyes eventually landing on the smiling face next to me. "You look so beautiful, Abbie," my sister complimented me. "Your face is glowing. And you and Neil looked so perfect together while you posed for the family photos."

I reached over and hugged her. "Thanks, Sarah." I pulled back and smiled at her, running my fingers through her loose curls. "And you look gorgeous today, too."

Her brown eyes glowed as she looked at me. "Thanks." She leaned in and whispered, "I feel really pretty."

My smile grew even brighter the longer I looked at my sister. I'm so happy she chose that dress and took my suggestion for her hair. And somebody else approves of her wedding day look, too. Several times today, I've caught a pair of bright blue eyes discreetly checking her out when he thought no one was looking. Turning in the opposite direction, I smiled as I watched my handsome groom laughing with his best friend. Scanning Archie's freshly shaven face, I thought, *I cannot wait to put my plan into action.*

After we had enjoyed the chicken and beef, the resort's excellent staff cleared the plates, ensuring everyone was all set with their water. Then we heard the DJ's voice again.

"Ladies and gentlemen," he announced. "I think it's time our happy couple cuts their cake. What do you think?"

The applause taking over the room was the only answer we needed. Neil and I went over to our gorgeous wedding cake as Archie stood up and acknowledged the lady who made it for us. Our guests chuckled as Neil and I smiled at Emma, now blushing with embarrassment.

Neil picked up the knife next to our culinary masterpiece, and I smiled at him as I wrapped my hand around his. Sliding the blade through the bottom layer, my smile brightened as I noticed the red velvet crumbs and marshmallow frosting emerging from below the layer of white fondant. We each picked up a piece of cake and gently fed it to each other—a beautiful bonding moment for a newly married couple. Our guests applauded and gushed with admiration as they watched us, and I could feel the love growing in the room. Neil and I returned to our table, my new husband taking his seat next to a blazing smile—anticipating the dessert being served by the friendly staff members.

After savoring Emma's delicious cake, we heard our DJ's voice again. "Okay, ladies and gentlemen. It's now time for our Best Man and Maid of Honor speeches."

Our guests applauded again as Archie and Sarah looked at each other. "Ladies first," he graciously offered.

Sarah stood up, and the DJ brought his microphone over and handed it to her. She smiled at Neil and me, then stepped a few feet over so she was standing next to our table.

"I was there the morning Neil and Abbie met," she began. "I will never forget the look on my sister's face as she got out of her car with coffee spilled on her pink scarf." She paused and smiled at me as our guests had a good chuckle. "When I asked her what happened, she told me she had spilled her coffee all over some poor guy wearing a very nice suit." She turned and looked at Neil. "You should have seen the way Abbie gushed over you in the parking lot—how handsome you looked and how nice you were to her."

I smiled at my husband and gave him an appreciative kiss. "You really were so sweet to me." He picked up my hand and kissed it; then we turned back toward Sarah.

"And I also remember the look on my sister's face when the door to a conference room opened. Abbie and I were making a big pitch that morning to decorate a resort in Milford, and while we were nervous, she had calmed down since her little coffee mishap. That is until the man who walked in was none other than the man she had spilled her coffee on."

She stopped talking as a gasp went around the room, followed by good-natured laughter. Neil kissed me on the cheek and smiled at me as we joined in the laughter.

"And I noticed the connection between them instantly," Sarah continued. Looking at two glowing faces, she said, "Grace and Madison were in the room with us, and the three of us looked at each other with amazement. These two lovebirds here"—she tilted her head in our direction—"were off in their own little world, and I think they forgot we were even in there."

She paused again as our loved ones gushed. "And after our presentation, Neil instantly gave us the job. And for the next two weeks, Grace, Madison, and I got to see the love blossoming between our happy couple." Sarah laughed as she said, "My sister reminded me of a lovestruck teenager, doodling 'Abbie Rutherford' on her math notebook." As our guests joined in Sarah's good-natured laughter, my sister suddenly stopped. A serious look came across her face as she looked at Grandpa and said, "But they were very appropriate, Mr. Rutherford."

He acknowledged her with a nod, then she continued, "And then, as soon as Abbie and I finished decorating the resort, I left the two of them alone in the conference room. I went to find Grace and Madison and thank them for being so wonderful to work with. When they asked me what my sister was doing, I said, 'With any luck, she's getting asked out by your hot boss right now!'"

The room erupted into laughter, and even Grandpa smiled a bit. The only person who didn't seem amused was my mom, who was glaring at Sarah.

Noticing my mom's expression, my sister said with a tone that stated the obvious, "Well, look at him, Mother." As my sister rolled her eyes, my mom put her face in her hands and shook her head. And I could just hear my mom's thoughts: *Where did I go wrong?* Helen reached over and patted her arm sympathetically, which seemed to ease her embarrassment.

"So, anyways," my sister continued, "that's when Madison said, 'And when they get married, make sure we get an invitation to their wedding.'"

My eyes brightened as I looked at Grace sitting with her husband and Madison next to them with her boyfriend. They had huge smiles on their faces and nodded in agreement as my sister commented, "We all saw it that first morning, Abs."

I smiled at my sweet husband. "I guess we were that obvious, huh?" I teased playfully. He leaned his forehead against mine as we shared a good-natured laugh. His laughter calmed to a loving smile as he kissed me, and then we turned back to my sister.

"And that night, Neil and Abbie went on their first official date. And as my sister told me more and more about him, I stopped seeing Neil as the hot guy who works out all the time." She turned and looked at my husband. "I started seeing you as the amazing man that my sister deserves. The way you treat my sister, Neil...it's unbelievable."

He acknowledged her with a grateful smile as she turned to face our guests. "That man right over there is the best thing that has ever happened to my sister. Abbie is so kind and so sweet, and she dreamed for years about finding a great man. And she found him in a coffee shop. And dumped her coffee all over him." As our guests had another good-natured laugh, my sister concluded, "And he was nice to my sister right from that very first moment."

She returned to the table and picked up her glass. Raising it, she said, "Please join me in toasting our happy couple. To Neil and Abbie."

"To Neil and Abbie," everyone echoed as they sipped their sparkling cider.

Even my mom was smiling as Sarah set down the microphone and took her seat next to me. I leaned over to hug her and said, "Thank you, Sarah. That was beautiful."

"You're welcome, Abbie," she replied, her smile glowing as she looked at me. "I'm so happy I got to witness the spark between the two of you that first morning."

Once the chatter about Sarah's sweet and funny toast died down, Archie got up and claimed the microphone. Returning to stand a few feet from his brother, he began, "I also remember the morning Neil and Abbie met. I was in my office, already buried under a mountain of paperwork, when my phone rang. It was my brother, wanting to know if Grandpa had left yet. I told him no, but he was about ready to. And that's when he asked me to do him the ultimate favor. He said he needed me to go into Grandpa's office and stall him. And a feeling of dread instantly came over me. Neil and I do not go into Grandpa's office alone, so I figured it must be important, and I asked him why." He turned and smiled at his brother. "That's when you said, 'I just met the girl I'm going to marry.'"

A gasp of surprise went around the room. I looked at my husband, my eyes brightening as I saw his handsome smile. "I knew right from the moment I first saw you, Abbie." I leaned forward and kissed him, loving his confidence right from the start.

We turned back to Archie as he continued, "And I was so happy for my brother. But after I thought about it for a moment, I asked him what this had to do with Grandpa. And that's when he said, 'She's Grandpa's eight-thirty appointment, and she just spilled her coffee all over me. You should have heard her voice as she talked about him, Archie. She hasn't even met Grandpa, and she's already terrified of him. And I can't make her stand in front of him, so I'm going to attend that meeting myself. But I need a few minutes to change my suit, and I need you to stall Grandpa until I can call him.'"

I looked at my husband again as a gush of sweet appreciation went around the room. He picked up my hands and said, "I knew you would be scared to see me walk through that door. But I also knew you would be more scared to face Grandpa. That's why I walked in smiling and held your hands like I did. I saw the way you calmed down in the coffee shop when I smiled at you. And it worked in the conference room, too."

I squeezed his hands in gratitude. "Thank you," I replied, remembering back to that morning.

"So," Archie continued, "I mustered up every bit of courage I could find, and I went next door to Grandpa's office. I walked in and smiled and said, 'What's up, Grandpa?' And he looked at me funny and barked, 'I'm shaving. What does it look like I'm up to? I missed a couple of hairs this morning, and I can't show up to a business meeting looking like a hobo.'"

He paused as we all laughed, loving his impression of his grandfather. Glancing in his direction, even Grandpa had a slight smile on his face, and I think he was enjoying this story just as much as the rest of us.

"Abbie and Sarah would have gotten lucky. Grandpa was in a pretty good mood that morning," Archie continued. "That is until I sat down. Two things Grandpa hates are small talk and wasting time, and I was doing both. So, while he finished shaving, I thought of ways to stall him. Luckily, as he put his jacket back on, I noticed some lint on the back. Knowing that Cornelius Rutherford hates it when his appearance is anything less than impeccable, I grabbed the lint roller out of his desk drawer. And that actually earned me a few brownie points."

Our guests laughed again, loving his speech. "So, as I took my time getting Grandpa's jacket looking perfect, I glanced around. There was one piece of paper on his desk, and I picked it up and asked him to explain the spreadsheet to me. And there went all my brownie points." As our guests laughed again, he said, "Explaining the spreadsheets is my job."

As much as I loved this story, my heart went out to Archie. I know that any time spent in Grandpa's office is difficult for him, so realizing how much he did to help Neil and me that morning makes me even more grateful for him.

"So, as Grandpa glared at me, I knew I had to take advantage of the one trick that works every time. I smiled brightly at him and said, 'Tell me about the first time you talked to Grammy.' If there's one thing Grandpa cannot resist talking about, it's my grandmother."

He paused again as a collective sigh of love went around the room. "Grandpa's face instantly softened, and he told me all about talking to a pretty waitress in a diner. And then his phone rang. That pulled him out of his memory, and he glared at the phone. When I asked him who it was, he barked at me, 'It's your brother.' So, I ran out of his office and back into mine, slamming both doors behind me, and I dove for cover under my desk."

A roar of laughter went around the room, and even Grandpa's face softened as he heard Archie's recollection. After the room quieted down, Archie looked at his brother. "And you looked completely different when I saw you at the gym that night. You didn't work out as hard as usual, and you seemed very unburdened." He turned back to face our guests. "And the way Neil talked about Abbie..." He shook his head and laughed. "I think we had two lovestruck teenagers doodling 'Neil and Abbie Rutherford' on their math notebooks."

I laughed as I turned to see the playful smile on my husband's face. "Why not start practicing?" Neil teased. "I already knew I was going to marry you."

I gave him another kiss, and then we turned back to Archie.

"And then, two weeks later, I had a horrible day at work. Neil got home, took my suit to his bedroom, and organized my paperwork. Then he smiled and said, 'I have something that will make you feel better, Archie.' He took out his phone, showed me a picture, and said, 'This is the ring I'm going to buy for Abbie.' And he was right. My smile instantly returned, and we spent the next hour talking about ways he could propose to her." He laughed and added, "We probably sounded like Abbie and Sarah giggling about Neil."

"We really did sound like the two of you that night," Neil agreed as we all laughed.

"And then, the next day, Neil returned to the office and told me he asked her out, and they had made dinner plans for that night. The two of us were hard at work in his office—" He stopped and corrected himself, "Well, I was hard at work. I looked over at my brother, and he had the biggest smile on his face. I said, 'Those spreadsheets can't possibly be that exciting, Neil.' And he turned his computer screen around, showed me a picture of this place, and said, 'This resort is where I want to marry Abbie. And I'm going to propose to her with a Christmas Eve scavenger hunt. I'll have her sister and two nice ladies at the grocery store help me.'"

"Abbie!" my sister exclaimed behind me. I turned around to see her bright smile. "He had it all planned out right from the start." Looking at Neil, she laughed and said, "You really are organized."

Turning to my husband, he smiled gently and praised me, "You deserved the perfect proposal and the wedding of your dreams. And I couldn't wait to see your face each time. And every time, you've gotten even more beautiful."

I kissed him again, my heart surging with love for my organized and thoughtful husband. Looking at my ring, I smiled and said, "So you knew for months this was the one you would buy me?"

He took my hand and kissed it. "As soon as I saw it, I imagined how beautiful it would look on your hand. And when I slipped it on your finger, it became even more beautiful." He placed his left hand next to mine, our matching platinum bands shining in the early-evening sunshine. "And when I saw these wedding bands in the store, I knew instantly that they were the perfect rings to symbolize our ultimate commitment."

"And I love them," I whispered, my smile glowing as I looked at him.

"Me too," he agreed, his brown eyes shining with love.

Our attention switched to Archie as he resumed speaking. "And then I met you, Abbie. And I immediately understood why Neil loves you so much. You are polite, kind, and genuinely grateful for my brother." He looked at our guests. "And what truly impressed all of us was when Abbie told us she was looking forward to meeting Grandpa. *Nobody* wants to meet Cornelius Rutherford, but she wanted to thank him for how nicely Neil treats her."

He paused again as all the ladies covered their hearts, looking at me with genuine fondness. Helen and my mom slid their arms around each other as Grandpa smiled at me.

"And I am honored to call Abbie my sister-in-law," Archie concluded his speech. "We're all honored to have you as part of our family, Abbie, knowing how much you love and appreciate Neil." He picked up his glass and held it out to us. "To Neil and Abbie."

"To Neil and Abbie," everyone echoed again, sipping their cider.

As he set the microphone down, I got up to hug him. "Thanks, Archie."

"You're welcome, Abbie," he replied with a bright smile.

"And not just for your wonderful speech," I continued, taking Neil's hand, who was now standing next to us. "But also, for helping your brother that first morning. I was absolutely terrified to meet your grandfather that first day." Turning to look at Grandpa, I marveled, "It's amazing how I went from being scared to meet him to looking forward to the day I got to thank him."

Neil pulled me in for a hug. "And that's another reason why I love you, Abbie. My family means a lot to me, and I love how much you care about them."

"Okay, thank you, Sarah and Archie," our DJ said as he retrieved his microphone from the table. "Can we get one more round of applause for our Best Man and Maid of Honor?" As our guests applauded our siblings, the DJ returned to his equipment. "Now, let's have the happy couple out on the dance floor for their first dance."

Neil intertwined our fingers and led me to the dance floor. I gazed into brown eyes so full of love as 'When a Man Loves a Woman' started to play. Neil held me close, and we swayed back and forth to the beautiful song, silently enjoying each other's embrace. All my dreams came true when I met this remarkable man, and just like those first few moments in the conference room, everyone else faded away. I indulged in my new husband stroking my back as we danced, feeling like the most cherished bride in the world.

Applause from our guests pulled me back to reality, and I looked up to see my handsome groom smiling at me. Our guests joined us on the dance floor, with Archie making sure to include Aunt Dottie in the fun. We had been having a good time, switching between slow, romantic ballads and upbeat, cheerful rhythms, when I felt someone tap me on the shoulder. I turned around to see my sister smiling at me.

She took my hand and smiled at my husband. "I'll bring her right back, I promise." Pulling me a few feet over, she said, "A lovely girl from housekeeping told me my room was ready, so I got all my stuff out of your room." She wiggled her eyebrows at me. "So now it's all set for you and your new husband."

I couldn't help but laugh. "Thanks, Sarah."

Her smile turned playful as she continued, "And I put your wedding night surprise from Aunt Dottie in the bathroom."

I hugged her and said, "Thanks, Sarah. You are the best Maid of Honor ever."

"Thanks, Abbie." She pulled back and looked at me. "You and Neil really are the sweetest couple. And I love that he included Archie in saving you from Darth Rutherford that first morning."

"Me too," I agreed as we shared a laugh. My heart flooded with love as the two of us turned to look at the brothers dancing with their favorite great-aunt.

As the upbeat tune of 'YMCA' started, my sister's eyes brightened with excitement. "I'll let you get back to your husband now, Abs. I have to go dance to this!" I laughed as I watched her excitedly scamper onto the dance floor and jump in on the action.

My smile grew brighter as I caught the eye of my handsome groom. Coming over to me, he slid his hands around my waist and smiled at me. "You are so beautiful, Abbie Rutherford."

"Ooh, Abbie Rutherford," I repeated, reaching up to give him a kiss. "I love the way that sounds."

"I've been waiting a year to call you that." He kissed me again, then stood behind me, and we watched our guests have fun with the Village People. When the song switched to 'Wonderful Tonight,' my handsome groom leaned down and asked me, "Would my beautiful wife like to dance with me?"

"In a minute," I answered, turning around with a playful smile. "Do you remember my little plan I mentioned at Aunt Dottie's birthday party?"

"I do," he answered, his smile matching mine. "So, is this when I finally get to see your mystery plan that I've been wondering about for months?"

"Yes, and you get to help me with it," I teased. Neil's expression became even more curious as I stepped aside to speak with the DJ. A moment later, I returned to my husband with a mischievous grin. "I'm going to ask your brother to dance, and I need you to ask my sister. When 'Unchained Melody' starts, cut in on us and casually slide Sarah into Archie's arms."

His brown eyes sparkled with delight. "Abbie Rutherford, I love this plan."

I gave Neil a smile of satisfaction, then walked up to his brother. "Can I dance with my husband's Best Man?"

"Of course, Abbie," he replied, his smile brightening. "I could never say no to the bride."

Archie took my hand, and I twirled around cheerfully, looking for my husband. Finding him a few yards away, I faced Archie and casually steered him in the direction I wanted to go. He happily took the hint, making sure the bride got her way.

"You're a good dancer, Abbie," he complimented me.

"Thanks, Archie," I replied with a smile. "You're not so bad yourself."

"And you look really pretty, too," he said. "I couldn't believe the look on my brother's face when he saw you walking down the aisle earlier. That was the happiest I've ever seen him."

"Thank you, Archie," I said again, my smile glowing even brighter at hearing him rave about how happy I make his brother. "And you look nice too. I'm glad Neil suggested you wear this suit."

"Thanks," he said, twirling me around again.

As Archie and I turned with the music, I caught my husband's eye with every rotation. He made sure to stay close to us with my sister, ready to help me carry out my master plan. Finally, the music switched, and I felt a tap on my shoulder.

Casually glancing behind me, I saw two smiling faces. "Can I have this dance, Abbie Rutherford?" the most handsome man in the room asked me.

"Why, yes, you may, Neil Rutherford," I answered playfully. In one smooth motion, I slid into my husband's arms as he effortlessly directed my sister into Archie's.

As we danced a few feet away from them, my husband's eyes sparkled with happiness. "It worked, Abbie." Glancing in their direction, he said, "They're still dancing. And they look like they're enjoying it too."

"Oh, just wait," I said, my voice full of mischief. "There's more to come."

Twenty seconds later, we heard the DJ's voice. "Okay, gentlemen. Dip the lady you're dancing with."

Following the DJ's orders, my husband grinned at me as he held me in his arms, level with the dance floor. "Oh, Abbie Rutherford, I love this plan more and more."

My expression matched his as I asked, "So what do they look like over there?"

Neil looked up, and his expression instantly changed to amazement. "Abbie," he said, standing me up, "you have to see this."

I turned around to see Archie holding my sister in his arms—their eyes locked on each other. Seeming to have tuned out everyone else in the room, she gazed into his blue eyes as he effortlessly held her level to the floor.

"Oh, wow!" I breathed, my eyes glued to them. "I told myself at Aunt Dottie's birthday party that I would give them until tonight to figure out they're in love with each other. And if they didn't figure it out on their own, I would help them figure it out. And the hopeless romantic in me secretly hoped they wouldn't because I wanted to have fun with my plan and see what they would look like together." I turned to Neil with raised eyebrows. "But I didn't realize they would look like that."

"They look perfect together, don't they?" he asked with a smile.

As my focus returned to Archie, still holding Sarah, a loving smile took over my face. "They do," I agreed.

"Even more perfect than I figured they would. It's like my sister belongs in your brother's arms."

"I wonder if anyone else notices?" he asked.

Looking around, everyone was now standing, dancing with their partners. There was one set of eyes, however, glued to our siblings. Blue eyes that matched Archie's were intently watching them. But instead of their usual sharpness, they were full of love and memories—no doubt of his own wedding day. There was a soft smile on Grandpa's face, his expression as happy as when he looks at his wife.

I playfully grinned at my husband. "Even Darth Rutherford can't resist two sweet people in love with each other." We laughed as I admitted, "And I had this whole thing planned out—right down to Archie's suit."

Neil raised his eyebrows at me.

"Why do you think I suggested he wear that suit to our wedding?"

He thought for a moment, and then his eyes brightened with realization. "It's the one Sarah saw hanging up in his car, and then she complimented him when he wore it at the office." He leaned in and kissed me. "Abbie Rutherford, you are a genius. You really did think of everything."

Looking back at our siblings, we watched as Archie gently raised Sarah to her feet—their eyes not leaving each other. When the song ended, they silently parted—both with different expressions. Archie seemed relieved—having silently communicated his feelings while he held Sarah in his arms. He told her exactly how much he loves her in just those few minutes.

My sister, on the other hand, looked...disappointed, maybe? As she walked across the dance floor, her eyes were unfocused, like she was still imagining herself in Archie's strong embrace. I knew they both enjoyed that dance—it was written all over their faces. And I also knew my sister never wanted that song to end. So maybe her expression was more of confusion than anything else. She's sure of her feelings for Archie—and his feelings for her—but she's unsure what to do next.

I hope she finds that answer soon, though, because seeing her and Archie dance like that tonight...that was the perfect way to end my perfect wedding.

Chapter 16

"ABIGAIL, YOU LOOKED POSITIVELY stunning today," Helen complimented me as she kissed me on both cheeks. Turning to her son, she said, "And Cornelius, your father and I have never been more proud of you."

"Thanks, Mom," he said with a smile as he kissed her on both cheeks.

"And thank you again, Helen, for letting me wear your mom's pearls and Laura's special bracelet," I said, reaching up and affectionately running my fingers along the strand that still decorated my neckline.

"You're welcome, Abigail," she replied with a soft smile. Then she looked at John, and her expression told him everything he needed to know. Stepping behind me, he unhooked the clasp on the pearls and returned them to his wife's neckline. She reached up and lovingly caressed the elegant beads, making tears come to her eyes again. John slid his arm around her shoulders and kissed the side of her head, his simple comfort bringing a smile to her face.

I turned toward Grandpa and held out my arm. "Why don't you do the honors?"

With a soft smile, he unhooked the bracelet and held it in his hand. Looking at it with eyes full of love, he quietly said, "Thank you, Abbie, for wearing this bracelet today." Pausing for a moment, he gently touched the dainty bracelet, his wedding ring shining under the light of the chandelier. Then he looked at me, his blue eyes full of emotion. "It means the world to Eleanor and me that you carried on our family tradition."

Helen gently touched her father-in-law's hand, looking first at the bracelet and then into his eyes. "I told Abigail that Mom loves her."

"Thank you, Helen," he replied quietly.

Neil slid his arm around my shoulders and smiled gently at his grandfather. "I felt Grammy here with us today."

"I did, too," Grandpa said, smiling as he looked at the two of us together. Then, handing the bracelet to Helen, he pulled an envelope from the interior pocket of his jacket. Giving it to Neil, he kindly offered, "And here is a gift from your grandmother and me."

"Oh, Grandpa," I breathed, looking from him to Neil. "Thank you."

"Yes, Grandpa, thank you," Neil graciously repeated.

"Open it," my sister said next to me with an excited grin.

"Do you know what this is?" I asked her.

She shook her head. "No, but I'm just as curious as you two."

"Actually, Sarah," Grandpa commented with a smile. "You had a hand in this gift too."

Her eyes lit up as she looked at Grandpa, and then her focus switched to Neil and me. "Now I have to see what this is!"

Neil and I smiled at each other as he opened the envelope. He pulled out two plane tickets and hotel reservations. "Bora Bora?" he asked, looking at his grandfather.

"During your Aunt Dottie's birthday party, Sarah asked me where your grandmother and I went on our honeymoon," Grandpa said, smiling at my sister.

"Oh, Sarah, that was so nice of you," my mom praised her.

"Thanks, Mom," she said with a bright smile. Looking at Grandpa, she raved, "I loved hearing your story about how the two of you went to a cute little bed and breakfast in the Poconos."

"And I loved sharing that story with you, Sarah," he replied. Turning to John, he recalled, "Your mother wanted to go somewhere romantic, and she told me to surprise her. So, one day, when I stopped by the diner to pick her up for a date, I browsed through the travel brochures just inside the door. And that's when I saw it." He paused for a moment, his eyes filling with love.

"There was a picture of a bed and breakfast, decorated for Christmas, and underneath 'Red Barn Inn' were the words, 'The coziest place on earth.' I picked up that brochure, tucked it in my pocket, and called the innkeeper the next morning. I told her I was getting married in three weeks and wanted to bring my beautiful bride there for our honeymoon."

His eyes brightened as he stared off into the distance. "I will never forget the look on Eleanor's face as we pulled into the driveway, and she saw the Christmas lights decorating the inn and the large pine trees outside. And then, stepping inside, her eyes brightened even more when she saw the beautiful Christmas tree in the parlor. The couple who owned the inn gave us the royal treatment that week. And their brochure was right. It was the coziest place on earth."

"And Eleanor came home raving about how romantic that bed and breakfast was, Junior," Aunt Dottie gushed, reaching out and taking his hand. "And she especially loved the way you cuddled with her in that parlor for hours. Mom and I were so proud of you."

He smiled at his sister. "Thank you, Dottie. Eleanor deserved the honeymoon of her dreams." He turned to us and said, "And so do the two of you. And while Sarah and I were chatting at the party, I asked her if she knew of anywhere special that Abbie always wanted to go. And she said Bora Bora."

"Oh, Sarah," I gushed, hugging her. "Thank you for remembering."

"Of course, Abbie," she replied with a smile as she let me go. "I remembered you talking about how romantic those over-the-water bungalows looked."

"And Sarah came by the house a few weeks ago to watch a picture with my sister," Grandpa continued. "As I was passing through the parlor on my way to the kitchen, Dottie asked Sarah how the wedding plans were coming along, and she said everything was finished. A few minutes later, as I passed through again, Sarah suddenly looked at my sister and said, 'Oh, wait, that's right. They still haven't planned a honeymoon.' So, I returned to my study and looked at the picture of your grandmother and me on the wall. I smiled at her and said, 'Let's surprise them with a honeymoon, Eleanor.'"

"Oh, Grandpa," I breathed. "That's so sweet."

"Yes, Grandpa," Neil agreed. "And knowing that it's from you and Grammy makes it even more special."

Grandpa smiled gently at us. "We booked your plane tickets for tomorrow evening. That way, you have enough time for breakfast with the family, and then you can go home and pack and make it to the airport on time." Then his focus switched to me. He was silent for a moment as he took my hands. Kissing me on the cheek, his blue eyes softened as he looked at me. "Eleanor loves you, Abbie. And I love you too. Welcome to the family."

"I love you too, Grandpa," I whispered as tears started to form in my eyes. "And your wife."

"Yes, Grandpa, we both love you and Grammy," Neil said, smiling at his grandfather.

After admiring the two of us for one final moment, Grandpa's focus switched to his sister. "Are we ready to go home?"

"Yes, Junior," she answered quietly, her voice full of emotion. After we all hugged Lydia and Aunt Dottie, Grandpa pushed his sister out the front door.

"Oh, John," Helen whispered tearfully.

"I know," he agreed, nothing more needing to be said. Then, they hugged and kissed us goodnight and went to their room.

"Yeah, Abbie," my dad said. "That was incredible."

I just nodded as tears escaped my eyes. My parents hugged us goodnight as Neil and Archie kissed my mom on both cheeks. Then, taking my mom's hand, my dad led her back to their room.

Archie's eyes were full of happiness as he looked at me. "Congratulations, Abbie. Grandpa rarely tells people he loves them." His focus switched to his brother. "Well, except for Grammy, of course. He was always telling her he loves her."

I smiled at my husband. "I love hearing the way your family talks about your grandparents."

"You should have seen them together," Neil reminisced as he smiled at Archie. "Grandpa definitely set the best example for how to be a great husband."

"And you're already off to an amazing start," I complimented him with a kiss. Then I looked at my sister, my eyes brightening. "Thanks again for remembering Bora Bora, Sarah. I can't wait to leave tomorrow."

"I'm so excited for you, Abbie!" she exclaimed with a huge smile. "You'll have to tell me all about it." After a pause, she clarified, "Well, you don't have to tell me *everything* about your honeymoon."

After the four of us shared a good laugh, my husband smiled at me lovingly. "Are we ready to go to our room now?"

My smile matched his as I answered, "Yes, we are."

We hugged and kissed our siblings goodnight, and then my husband took my hand, interlacing our fingers. Stopping in front of our room, he unlocked the door and propped it open. He lifted me in his arms, and we smiled at each other as he carried me over the threshold. After he set me down gently, I watched as he closed the door. Turning around, we marveled at the sweet surprise waiting for us.

Red rose petals scattered all over the white down comforter made the sleigh bed even more inviting. A cozy fire burning in the gas fireplace filled the room with intimacy. A stunning crystal vase with an assortment of our wedding flowers was a sweet reminder of my husband fulfilling my ultimate wish. The bottle of sparkling cider chilling in an ice bucket, accompanied by two crystal glasses, was the perfect companion to the plate of chocolate-covered strawberries. In front of the vase, there was a note folded in half. Neil smiled at me and took my hand, and we went over to read the message together.

"Neil and Abbie," I read out loud. *"Congratulations on your beautiful wedding. You two deserve all the happiness in the world. And may that happiness start tonight. Love, Sarah."*

Our smiles brightened as Neil and I looked at each other. "This was so thoughtful of your sister," he acknowledged fondly.

"Yes, it was," I agreed. As something she said earlier popped into my head, I kissed my sweet husband, my smile turning mischievous. "And if you will excuse me for a moment, I have one more surprise for you."

"Ooh, another surprise," he teased.

"And this one is all for you." I turned around and requested, "Can you please unzip my dress?"

"I am already loving this surprise," he raved, kissing my neck as he slowly pulled down the zipper.

I gave him one more smile and then disappeared into the bathroom. I chuckled to myself as I noticed a hanger on the sink and a note that read: *Hang your dress over the shower door, not the sprinklers!*

I stepped out of my dress and carefully hung it up, loving my sister's attention to every detail. Then I reached into the gift bag and pulled out the delicate nightie. Slipping it over my head, I took a moment to admire myself in the mirror. I felt elegant and sexy—the perfect combination for my wedding night. Eager to share this special gift with my husband, I opened the door to see him standing next to the table. Looking relaxed without his jacket, he was pouring sparkling cider into the glasses as soft music played in the background. Hearing the door open, he turned around, and his eyes instantly brightened.

"Abbie!" he breathed. His eyes delighted in the ivory lace and chiffon, gently swaying as I walked toward him. "You definitely saved the best surprise for last. You look absolutely stunning."

"Thank you," I replied with a smile, loving the kiss he rewarded me with.

Picking up the glasses, he handed one to me as he raised his and admired, "To the most exquisite wife a man could ask for."

My smile brightened as I raised mine and complimented, "To the most handsome and thoughtful husband a lady could ask for."

We clinked glasses and enjoyed a celebratory sip. Taking my drink, he returned them to the table and turned to face me. Pulling me into his arms, he smiled at me with so much love in his eyes, and my smile instantly matched his. Slowly, his face inched toward mine until, finally, our smiles met. We continued kissing as we swayed gently to the music, delighting in the romance and intimacy of our wedding night.

Then, sliding his hands slowly up my back, he slipped the delicate straps off my shoulders, and the nightgown fell to the floor...

Chapter 17

I, Sarah Perkins, have never been more confused in my entire life.

One minute, I was dancing with my new brother-in-law, and the next minute, I found myself in his brother's arms. And I loved it. As soon as I felt Archie's arms around me, I never wanted him to let me go. And then, when the DJ told every man to dip the lady he's dancing with? Oh, wow, was that amazing! Having Archie hold me in his strong arms like that was like nothing I've ever experienced before.

And it wasn't like any of my other encounters with Archie either. From the moment I first saw him, I was enamored with him—and that ripped body of his. And then every time he would smile at me...

But being held in his arms tonight? Everyone else in that ballroom instantly disappeared. I don't know if anyone even saw us. For those few minutes, the only person who existed was him. And the way he looked at me? I could not tear my eyes away from those blue eyes of his. They held me, mesmerized, just like how his strong arms held me effortlessly level to the dance floor. And as much as I loved feeling his arms around me, I especially loved what I saw in his eyes. It was as if he was telling me all of his feelings in just a few short minutes. At least, I think I understood his silent communication correctly.

But I have no clue where to go from here. I think Archie enjoyed that dance as much as I did, but then we just parted ways after the song ended.

And the hardest part of all was keeping a straight face in front of our families afterward. As Mr. Rutherford was giving Neil and Abbie that sweet gift of a honeymoon, I was so happy for my sister and brother-in-law. And I loved that Mr. Rutherford remembered our conversation at Aunt Dottie's birthday party. But the entire time I was chatting with our families, I was still thinking about that dance with Archie. And still feeling his arms around me.

Then, after everyone left, Archie and I said goodnight to each other, and I came back here to my room. Alone. But I don't want to be alone. And I'm still not sure what exactly he wants.

Looking in the mirror, I felt so pretty, with my hair softly curled and gathered over my left shoulder. And I felt beautiful and sexy in my dress. I even chose this dress because of Archie. As soon as I noticed how the side slit showed a teasing amount of skin, his blue eyes instantly popped into my head. I was hoping it would get his attention—and get him to make his move. And when he dipped me in his arms, the slit exposed my left leg—which I so badly wanted him to touch.

And when he stood me back up, his eyes never left mine. His face was only a few inches from mine for the rest of the song, and I wanted so badly to kiss him—more than I'd ever wanted to kiss him before. And I've been dying to kiss him for months—to feel his lips on mine and his hands all over me. And tonight, dancing with him was the first time we've actually touched. He always kisses my mom and sister on both cheeks, but he's never done it to me. Not once. So, feeling his arms around me tonight finally...

My mind was all over the place as I wandered aimlessly around my room. I smiled as I noticed my monogrammed *Maid of Honor* robe lying on my bed. I loved that my sister got these for us. We had so much fun getting ready for her wedding today. I'm thrilled that she and Neil found each other, and I loved being such a big part of their day. But as much as today was about them, my favorite part of today had nothing to do with them.

Or maybe it did. I paced faster as I remembered the moment Neil randomly asked me to dance. At the time, I thought nothing of it. But then, all of a sudden, he just cut in on my sister and Archie. And he very skillfully slid me into his brother's arms. Was he up to something? And if so, who was in on it? Did Archie put him up to it because he wanted to dance with me but was too afraid to ask me? Or was this my sister's doing? As I thought about my hopeless romantic of a sister, this does seem to have her ultra-princessy, fairy tale, I-love-everything-romantic mushy-gushy, lovey-doveyness written all over it.

And this time, I'm grateful for that hopeless romantic who loves everything lovey. If Neil hadn't slid me into Archie's arms tonight, I'm not sure if we ever would have gotten together. As we've been sharing little moments over the past several months, neither one of us has ever acted on our feelings. So maybe we needed the nudge.

But I'm still unbelievably confused about what to do next. My thoughts kept racing a mile a minute as I went through my suitcase. I fumbled through clothing as I tried to focus.

...pajamas...that's what I'm looking for...where are they?

I thought to myself.

...god he's hot...

"No!" I screamed at myself. "Think about something else!"

...did I take care of everything Abbie needed?

I started to worry. I'm sure I did, but I was so wrapped up in the moment I don't really remember what I did after that dip.

Finally, I found my pajamas at the bottom of my luggage. I pulled them out and raised my hands to unzip my dress.

—Knock! Knock! Knock!—

I jumped at the sound coming from the door.

"Just a second!" I shouted as I lowered my hands away from my zipper.

I walked to the door and pulled it open.

"Archie!" I exclaimed with noticeable excitement.

"Hi, Sarah," he said with a slight smile on his face...

About the Author

Sheri Abild never imagined she would become a writer. Then one day, she decided to write the story she wanted to read. She does most of her writing in one of two places: the pretty pink bedroom in her home that belongs to two cats (with her furry co-author cuddled up next to her snoring), or sitting and looking cutesy in her husband's woodworking shop while he makes a lot of noise. She is the girliest Air Force Veteran who was laughed at by aircrews because of her high-pitched voice. A Vermont native, she grew up an exit down the Interstate from her husband, and they met on a cold yet sunny day in winter.

To stay up to date with her stories and learn neat tidbits about what influences her writing, go to:

www.sheriabild.com

Made in the USA
Middletown, DE
03 October 2023

39881111R00191